The Unknown

More Handheld Classics

Ernest Bramah, *What Might Have Been. The Story of a Social War* (1907)
D K Broster, *From the Abyss. Weird Fiction, 1907–1940*
John Buchan, *The Runagates Club* (1928)
John Buchan, *The Gap in the Curtain* (1932)
Melissa Edmundson (ed.), *Women's Weird. Strange Stories by Women, 1890–1940*
Melissa Edmundson (ed.), *Women's Weird 2. More Strange Stories by Women, 1891–1937*
Zelda Fitzgerald, *Save Me The Waltz* (1932)
Marjorie Grant, *Latchkey Ladies* (1921)
Inez Holden, *Blitz Writing. Night Shift & It Was Different At The Time* (1941 & 1943)
Inez Holden, *There's No Story There. Wartime Writing, 1944–1945*
Margaret Kennedy, *Where Stands A Wingèd Sentry* (1941)
Rose Macaulay, *Non-Combatants and Others. Writings Against War, 1916–1945*
Rose Macaulay, *Personal Pleasures. Essays on Enjoying Life* (1935)
Rose Macaulay, *Potterism. A Tragi-Farcical Tract* (1920)
Rose Macaulay, *What Not. A Prophetic Comedy* (1918)
James Machin (ed.) *British Weird. Selected Short Fiction, 1893–1937*
Vonda N McIntyre, *The Exile Waiting* (1975)
Elinor Mordaunt, *The Villa and The Vortex. Supernatural Stories, 1916–1924*
John Llewelyn Rhys, *England Is My Village, and The World Owes Me A Living* (1939 & 1941)
John Llewelyn Rhys, *The Flying Shadow* (1936)
Malcolm Saville, *Jane's Country Year* (1946)
Helen de Guerry Simpson, *The Outcast and The Rite. Stories of Landscape and Fear, 1925–1938*
Jane Oliver and Ann Stafford, *Business as Usual* (1933)
J Slauerhoff, *Adrift in the Middle Kingdom*, translated by David McKay (1934)
Amara Thornton and Katy Soar (eds), *Strange Relics. Stories of Archaeology and the Supernatural, 1895–1954*
Elizabeth von Arnim, *The Caravaners* (1909)
Sylvia Townsend Warner, *Kingdoms of Elfin* (1977)
Sylvia Townsend Warner, *Of Cats and Elfins. Short Tales and Fantasies* (1927–1976)
Sylvia Townsend Warner, *T H White. A Biography* (1967)

The Unknown

Weird Writings, 1900–1937

by Algernon Blackwood

Edited by Henry Bartholomew

Handheld Classic 32

This edition published in 2023 by Handheld Press
72 Warminster Road, Bath BA2 6RU, United Kingdom.
www.handheldpress.co.uk

ISBN 978-1-912766-68-0

1 2 3 4 5 6 7 8 9 0

Series design by Nadja Guggi and typeset in Adobe Caslon Pro and Open Sans.

Printed and bound in Great Britain by Short Run Press, Exeter.

FSC
www.fsc.org
MIX
Paper from responsible sources
FSC® C014540

Contents

Acknowledgements

My thanks, firstly, to Kate Macdonald at Handheld Press for bringing this project to life. A debt of gratitude is owed also to David Punter, Nick Groom, and William Hughes, who all brought Blackwood into my life in one way or another. Special thanks must go also to Mike Ashley for his decades of Blackwood research and for clarifying a few biographical details for me. I would also like to express my gratitude to Irena Kossowska for sharing her expertise on the painter Wacław Borowski with me. Thanks are due, also, to my family, who, despite having almost no idea what I've been doing for the last year, never doubted that it was worth doing. Finally, to Elia, to whom I am joyously indebted – thank you.

Henry Bartholomew specialises in nineteenth- and early twentieth-century supernatural fiction and has taught at the University of Exeter and the University of Plymouth. He is the editor of *Dangerous Dimensions: Mind-bending Tales of the Mathematical Weird* (British Library Press, 2021) and has published work in *The Palgrave Handbook to the Vampire* and the journal *Open Philosophy*.

Introduction

HENRY BARTHOLOMEW

While Algernon Henry Blackwood (1869–1951) is a well-known figure to horror and weird fiction aficionados, outside this enclave of academics and enthusiasts his remarkable life and writings have been almost entirely forgotten. His public reputation today rests primarily on a handful of stories and on his two weird novellas – 'The Willows' (1907) and 'The Wendigo' (1908). Despite their merit, however, these represent a fraction of his prodigious output. While Blackwood is now considered to be a minor writer, he was, in his own lifetime, a celebrated author and media star, acquainted with many of the leading celebrities of the day, from the poet and mystic W B Yeats to the great English composer Edward Elgar – as well as the aristocratic circles to which he was connected by birth.

An author, occultist, and inveterate traveller, he never owned a house, preferring to stay in hotels or rented accommodation or, as was often the case, with friends and family. He never married and never had children, leading to some speculation about his sexuality. His biographer, Mike Ashley, proposes that Blackwood may have been asexual, though this is a difficult thesis to prove conclusively (Ashley 2019, 101). His early work was admired by many young writers including H P Lovecraft, C S Lewis, J R R Tolkien and Siegfried Sassoon while the success of his later radio and television work meant that, at the time of his death in 1951, he was one of the most famous media personalities in Britain.[1]

Blackwood produced a substantial body of work over his forty-year career. His published fiction includes some two hundred and thirty short stories, a dozen novels, several plays, and numerous children's tales – many of them still hard to find and out of print.

Blackwood began his writing career almost by accident at the unusually late age of thirty-seven. An old acquaintance, Angus Hamilton, bumped into him by chance in London and asked if he had manuscripts for any of the old stories he used to tell of an evening back when they were both newspaper men in New York. Upon receiving them, without asking Blackwood, Hamilton sent them to the publisher Eveleigh Nash. A surprised Blackwood received a letter from the publisher soon after. The resulting collection was published as *The Empty House and Other Ghost Stories* in November 1906; Blackwood's career as a writer of strange tales had begun. Sadly, Hamilton committed suicide some years later. Admirers of Blackwood's work, no less than Blackwood himself, owe him a great deal.

The success of Blackwood's third book, *John Silence: Physician Extraordinary* (1908), allowed him to write fiction full-time. Even so, he had been writing for newspapers and periodicals for over a decade and continued to write stories and articles for the periodical press for the rest of his life. Often these contributions were brand-new stories, some of which would not be printed in book form for many years. Much of this writing, however, was non-fiction. Like other luminaries of the weird, including Arthur Machen and Ambrose Bierce, Blackwood laboured for a number of years as a journalist, working as a reporter for the *Evening Sun* and the *New York Times* in America in the 1890s. This was just the beginning, however. His mature articles, dating from after his return to England in 1899 and appearing in a range of different publications, offer a fascinating insight into the life and mind of one of the twentieth century's most original and thought-provoking authors of the supernatural. These essays and articles cover a wide variety of topics, from accounts of his youthful adventures in Canada and America to sombre reflections on the ravages of war, evocative travel narratives through Egypt, the Alps, and the Caucasus to ponderous articles for occult magazines like *The Occult Review, Prediction, Lucifer,* and *The Aryan Path.*

Taken together, this body of work provides a rich context for understanding Blackwood's life and literature. Of the many early twentieth-century authors writing in the supernatural mode, Blackwood's fiction is by far the most autobiographical. Almost all of his stories were inspired by real people, places, or events, or worked up from tales he had heard or strange occurrences he had been made privy to. In a letter written only a few months before his death, he claimed that all of his novels were 'more or less autobiographical' (quoted in Ashley 2019, 10), and his protagonists are typically avatars of himself: middle-aged men who seem to stand in some sense outside society and the vicissitudes of modernity, often with Everyman names like Smith or Jones.

Yet, at the time of writing, there are no dedicated books placing Blackwood's fiction and nonfiction in relation to one another. This new anthology deliberately pairs his stories with relevant non-fiction pieces from across his career – not to force a prescriptive biographical reading of his fiction, but to demonstrate the richness of their interconnections. It is not exhaustive – other stories and articles might have been chosen – but it is representative, and covers a wide range of styles, themes, and periods, and will be of interest to both first-time readers and Blackwood acolytes alike. Blackwood's stories have a strange, bewitching quality to them. His tales attempt to inculcate their reader – to draw them into the ritual and, ultimately, transform their perception. If nothing else, it is hoped that the reader will not leave these pages quite as they came to them.

The Ghost Man

Blackwood left little behind. The few papers he had kept from his youth were destroyed during the Blitz when a bomb fell on the house where he was staying. Fortunately, Blackwood and his host (his nephew) were cooking sausages in their Anderson shelter in the garden at the time and so survived the blast. In any case, Blackwood lived as he travelled – light. As he stresses in a letter from 1937: 'I aim to get rid of things rather than to accumulate them!' (Blackwood, 8 October 1937). Thanks to decades of research by Mike Ashley, however, much is now known about Blackwood's life that would otherwise be obscure.

Born in Kent in 1869 to a wealthy family with aristocratic connections, Blackwood went on to live a nomadic life interspersed with extended periods of residency in England and Switzerland. His parents were nurturing and widely respected, but they were also vehement evangelical Christians. Blackwood and his siblings were thus brought up according to 'the narrowest imaginable evangelical path' and felt ostracized from wider society (Blackwood 1923, 22). At the age of seventeen, however, Blackwood discovered Bhagwan Shree Patanjali's *Yoga Aphorisms* – a book that he secretly read and re-read over the course of a single night – which set him on a very different path.

After an erratic education at various schools, including a German Moravian institution in the Black Forest, Blackwood toured Canada and parts of America in 1887 with his father. He returned to study agriculture and rural economy at the University of Edinburgh but did not complete his studies. At the age of twenty-one he moved to Toronto. In his autobiography, *Episodes Before Thirty* (1923), he notes that he took with him, 'in the order of their importance – a fiddle, the *Bhagavad Gita*, Shelley, *Sartor Resartus*, Berkeley's "Dialogues", Patanjali's *Yoga Aphorisms*, de Quincey's *Confessions* and – a unique ignorance of life' (Blackwood 1923, 6). Thus armed, he sought out work, companionship, and the wild beauty of the Canadian landscape. After the establishment and collapse of a dairy business, and the 'Hub' – a hotel and bar he co-owned with a friend – Blackwood escaped to New York where he eventually found work as a reporter for the *Evening Sun.* His autobiography marks this as a difficult time for him, one of poverty and desperation. When the throng of the city became overwhelming, and the strain of interviewing high-profile criminals (including Lizzie Borden) or the President of the Police Board (Theodore Roosevelt) became too much, he found solace in playing the violin and in visits to Bronx Park and the free library.

Things improved when Blackwood joined the *New York Times* in 1895, but his early life and career is a mesh of various trials and adventures, including a failed attempt at gold prospecting, a stint as a private secretary to a millionaire banker, and the arrest of a close friend and roommate for the theft of thirty-two dollars from his room – a crime reported by newspapers even in the UK. Blackwood returned to England in 1899 where, after a few years in the dried milk business, he finally began his career as a writer. In 1908, he moved to Switzerland which became a favourite haunt and, in time, a home of sorts.

Throughout this time Blackwood was developing a notably occult worldview. Determining the parameters of a belief system shaped over years of study, practice, and experience poses a significant challenge. Blackwood himself was not forthcoming about his occult beliefs. His autobiography, for example, ends with the disclaimer 'of mystical, psychic, or so-called "occult" experiences, I have purposefully said nothing' (Blackwood 1923, 304). What is clear is that his interest in occultism and esotericism started early. He notes that, as a boy, he was 'full of wild fancies and imagination and a great believer in ghosts, communings with spirits and dealings with charms and amulets, which latter I invented and consecrated myself by the dozen [...] long before I had read a single book' (Blackwood 1923, 33). His reading, once begun, was unusual, and included books like Gustav Fechner's panpsychist account of reality *Zend-Avesta* (1851), Richard Bucke's *Cosmic Consciousness* (1901), and William James's *A Pluralistic Universe* (1909). Blackwood read voraciously throughout his life and drew inspiration from a variety of sources, from the mathematician and proto-science fiction novelist Charles Howard Hinton and the Russian esotericist

P D Ouspensky to the utopian socialist Edward Carpenter and the Theosophist Mabel Collins.

His early interest in ghosts grew into a fascination with haunted houses and, by extension, 'psychical research'. Founded in 1882 by a group of respected scientists and philosophers, The Society for Psychical Research was engaged in 'proving' and, conversely, 'exposing' psychic or paranormal phenomena. Though Blackwood was never an official member, he did conduct research with their Haunted House Committee and several of these investigations were later re-worked as stories (Luckhurst 2012, 178). Blackwood's Eastern-inflected interests would find their natural expression in Theosophy, an occult society founded by the enigmatic Helena Blavatsky in 1875. Blackwood, by his own admission, swallowed its teachings whole and was a charter member of the Toronto branch, even writing a few articles for the society's official journal, *Lucifer*. From here, Blackwood advanced inexorably to the most beguiling institution of Western esotericism in the late Victorian and early Edwardian period, The Hermetic Order of the Golden Dawn – a secret society formed in London in 1887 for the express purpose of occult study and practice. In this iteration of the Order, Blackwood rose from Neophyte, the entrance grade, to Philosophus, the highest grade in the outer order (see Graf 2015, 8–10). In order to advance through the grades, he would have needed to have passed various tests and rituals requiring much learning and dedication. He was initiated into the Order on 30 October 1900 at the age of thirty-one.

Blackwood's prolonged membership of these occult societies coupled with the sincerity of the beliefs expressed in his fiction would suggest that he was a serious and committed practitioner of esotericism, and that his adult life was defined by his spiritual development and practices. However, there is very little evidence concerning Blackwood's occultism, and this aspect of his life remains aptly mysterious. In any case, as his autobiography intimates, these affiliations with organised occult groups seem to have been an exploration of a more foundational set of beliefs and experiences concerning Nature (often spelt with a capital 'N' by Blackwood):

> By far the strongest influence in my life, however, was Nature; it betrayed itself early, growing in intensity with every year. Bringing comfort, companionship, inspiration, joy, the spell of Nature has remained dominant, a truly magical spell. Always immense and potent, the years have strengthened it. The early feeling that everything was alive, a dim sense that some kind of consciousness struggled through every form, even that a sort of inarticulate communication with this 'other life' was possible, could I but discover the way – these moods coloured its opening wonder. (Blackwood 1923, 32–33)

Here, the natural verges on the super-natural. The nonhuman world is alive; indeed, perhaps more authentically alive than the human one. It can be dangerous, Blackwood's stories warn, even fatal, to forget this. In an age of climate catastrophe, Blackwood's repeated evocations of a weird, animistic ecology have become eerily resonant. His stories ask us to think and feel more deeply about our connections to, and separation from, the nonhuman, and rebuff, often with great flair, the vanity of human exceptionalism.

This love affair with the natural world made him an itinerant wanderer and he spent long periods travelling. During the First World War he served as an operative for the secret service in Switzerland where he was engaged in clandestine recruitment and the sending and receiving of information. He continued writing stories during and after the war. In 1915, his novel *A Prisoner in Fairyland* (1913) was adapted for the stage by Violet Pearn as *The Starlight Express* with a score by Sir Edward Elgar.

Other stories followed, including a number of children's books, as well as reprints and anthologies of his earlier writing. However, a new career and a new medium were on the horizon. On 7 April

1934, Blackwood gave his first radio performance – reading aloud a ghost story. This was the first of many appearances made over the next few years. On 2 November 1936 he progressed from radio, taking part in the first television broadcast in Britain. In his sixties, the 'ghost man', as he became known, was now more famous than he had ever been. Indeed, in the final years of his life Blackwood was a media star. As one commentator remarked in 1949, the entertainment end of television had so far produced only two stars: Milton Berle in America and Algernon Blackwood in Britain (Holt 1949, 276). Blackwood was awarded a CBE in 1949 and died on 10 December 1951. His ashes were scattered in the hills near his home in the Valais Alps.

Contents and Contexts

Canada

This anthology has been organised into four sections. Each section gives voice to a particular facet of Blackwood's work and consists of an essay or article followed by two short stories. The first section explores Blackwood's early experiences in Canada. His first visit was a tantalising one. In 1887, aged just eighteen, he toured the country with his father, Sir Stevenson Arthur Blackwood, hoping to find somewhere suitable to begin a career in farming. The trip also allowed Blackwood's father, then Secretary to the Post Office, to survey the recently completed Canadian Pacific Railway and, later in the journey, inspect a tract of land that had been given to his father by King William IV. Blackwood was enthralled, so much so that in 1890 he abandoned his agriculture course at the University of Edinburgh to return to Toronto. This proved a difficult time for him. His attempts to become a successful businessman failed, and, after two years, and with his father's funds exhausted, he fled to New York where new tribulations awaited.

It was not a complete disaster, however. Away from the stifling religiosity of the family home, he had been able to devote himself freely to his esoteric interests and, in 1891, had become a charter member of the Toronto branch of the Theosophical Society. Canada also introduced him to nature on a grander scale than he had yet encountered. Before the move to New York, he spent five months on a small, ten-acre island on Lake Muskoka in Northern Ontario with his friend and business partner Johann Kay Pauw. For Blackwood, it was paradise: 'the nearest approach to a dream come true I had yet known'; 'I had seen and known at last the primeval woods' (Blackwood 1923, 74, 78). When not exploring the lakes or mainland, or performing the day's chores, Blackwood would read or engage in 'intense Yoga experiments' (Blackwood 1923, 77). At night, beneath the stars, the two would watch the 'awful splendour' of the Northern Lights (Blackwood 1923, 74).

Several years later, in October 1898, Blackwood returned to Canada. This trip proved inspirational, supplying him with material for several stories and articles, including the three selected here. With him was John Prince, Professor of Semitic Languages at New York University, and Prince's wife, Adeline Loomis. Prince was interested in 'Indian' folklore and languages, including those of the Algonquin tribe. Blackwood was also drawn to them and would later write a two-part article 'Algonquin Songs and Legends' for *Country Life* magazine in 1912. He was there chiefly to hunt, however, and his account of this adventure, written soon after his return to England, is "Mid the Haunts of the Moose'. Published in *Blackwood's Magazine* in July 1900, the article recounts the fascinating details of the expedition, from descriptions of the terrain to notes on how to track game and set up camp. Often these practical considerations are combined with more intimate reflections on the forbidding beauty and isolation of the forests and lakes.

A number of stories might have been paired with this article including the early story 'A Haunted Island' (1899), the mystical tales 'Running Wolf' (1920) and 'The Valley of the Beasts' (1921), and 'The Wendigo'. In the end, the excruciatingly tense 'Skeleton Lake: An Episode in Camp' from Blackwood's first book, *The Empty House and Other Ghost Stories*, was chosen together with 'The Wolves of God' from his 1921 collection, *The Wolves of God and Other Fey Stories*. Though it features no supernatural elements, 'Skeleton Lake: An Episode in Camp' is a masterclass in creating and maintaining atmosphere. Three friends – a professor, his wife, and the narrator – are on a hunting expedition in the Quebec backwoods with their guides. Another pair of white hunters are in the area, relatively close at some fifty miles away. Suddenly, one of these men stumbles into the narrator's camp. He is alone and won't stop talking – something has happened to his guide and companion, Jake the Swede. As the tension mounts, the story he tells will make the camp (and the reader) increasingly uneasy. The story was inspired by real events and is an early example of Blackwood's keen insight into human psychology. He recounted the 'story behind the story' in the radio talk 'Minor Memories' almost half a century later, in 1949.

In many ways, 'The Wolves of God' is a spiritual sequel to 'Skeleton Lake'. Exchanging ancient Canadian forests for the exposed terrain of Orkney in the Scottish archipelago, an old crime receives a supernatural punishment. Jim Peace is returning home to his brother after thirty years' work in Canada for the Hudson Bay Company. But something is not quite as it should be, and his homecoming takes a dark and unsettling turn. Blackwood knew Scotland well. He was familiar with Edinburgh from his university days, but he had also visited Inverurie and the Isle of Skye on family holidays as a teenager and some of his descriptions of Sanday suggest he may have visited Orkney as well. What is most notable about the story, however, is that instead of drawing on Scotland's own myth, folklore, and superstition, Blackwood brings an Indigenous Peoples 'superstition' to Orkney. There is clearly a colonial subtext here. Another character, the grizzled 'old Rossiter', has also worked for the Company, while a third character has recently returned from a rubber plantation in Malay: threads of Britain's colonial past (and present) intertwine.

The Hudson's Bay Company, as it was originally called, was founded in the seventeenth century as an extension of English commercial and colonial interests in the 'New World' and its charter did not recognize the claims of First Nations or Indigenous Peoples to their own land. As with every colonial venture founded on conquest, its history is awash with violence and exploitation. In typical Blackwood fashion, however, this is not a simple colonial revenge narrative. The Wolves of God, as the reader finds out, are not aligned with racial groups or geographical boundaries. They are, rather, a more primordial and mysterious retributive power in the world.

It should also be noted that *The Wolves of God and Other Fey Stories* is Blackwood's only co-authored short story volume, though it is unclear to what extent his co-author, Wilfred Wilson, was involved in the writing of the tales. Not much is known about Wilson except that he was an old friend of Blackwood's from their Canada days and that they shared many an adventure, including the canoe trip down the Danube that inspired Blackwood's most famous story, 'The Willows' (included in Handheld's earlier anthology *British Weird*). There are no detectable stylistic differences between *The Wolves of God and Other Fey Stories* and any of Blackwood's other books. Ashley speculates that the co-author credit may have been a wedding present to Wilson, though there is no evidence for this, and it does not account for the fact that the last story in the volume is attributed solely to Blackwood (Ashley 2019, 317).

Mountains

The second section takes the reader to the majesty and mystery of the mountains. A passionate skier and hiker into his eighties, Blackwood set many of his stories in the mountains or their immediate surroundings. For Blackwood, their sublimity and gigantic proportions invested them with a degree of sentience and divinity. Often, as in stories like 'Perspective' (1910) and 'Initiation' (1916), they become fragments of God or the world-soul – titanic 'Countenances' with unfathomable wills of their own. Blackwood received his first taste of mountain life as a teenager in 1886 with a trip to Bôle in Switzerland, a small town near the shores of Lake Neuchâtel by the French border. He returned in 1908, this time for several years, taking rooms above the town post office where he could work peacefully on his writing. In 1913, he left Bôle for a hotel in Saanenmöser near the Valais Alps. The town would become a home of sorts for Blackwood, and he spent much of his life there.

The rhythms of the seasons together with the waxing and waning of the sporting and social calendar were a source of both ire and wonder for Blackwood, and he routinely worked up his thoughts into articles. Most of these, around sixteen or so, were published in *Country Life* magazine, often with accompanying photographs, between 1909 and 1913. A number of these articles focused on the increasingly popular sport of skiing, of which Blackwood was an early and skilful practitioner. A painting of Blackwood by the Polish artist Wacław Borowski, who was also living in Switzerland in the 1910s, shows a reclined Blackwood dipping his ski pole into a pot of ink, the manuscript of his mystical novel *The Centaur* (1911) lying open before him.

This section opens with the most brooding and evocative piece from his *Country Life* articles. 'The Winter Alps', published on Christmas Eve of 1910, drifts away from the mundanities of Alpine tourism to explore the darker sublimity of the mountains. It is only in the dark and the cold and the silence, Blackwood writes, that the Alps come terrifyingly into their own. It is a notably poetic piece, and the descriptions he gives of the slopes and peaks at night would sit comfortably in one of his short stories. Indeed, in 1914, when Blackwood found himself obliged to assemble a collection of his short tales for the publishing house John Murray, he included three of his *Country Life* articles, of which 'The Winter Alps' was the third.

Again, the list of stories that might have been paired with this piece is long. 'The Story of Karl Ott' (1896), 'The Lock of Grey Hair' (1909), 'The Occupant of the Room' (1909), 'The Man Who Played Upon the Leaf' (1909), 'Special Delivery' (1910), 'The Messenger' (1911), 'La Mauvaise Riche' (1912), 'H S H' (1913), 'The Regeneration of Lord Ernie' (1914), 'The Falling Glass' (1914), 'S O S' (1918), 'Lost!' (1922), and 'Revenge' (1930) were all excellent candidates. The two stories that were chosen, however, epitomize Blackwood's deep connection with, and reverence for, the mountain region he called home: they are 'The Glamour of the Snow' and 'The Sacrifice'.

'The Glamour of the Snow' first appeared in December 1911 in two journals, *The Forum* and the *Pall Mall Magazine*. In the following year it was reprinted in Blackwood's fifth story collection, *Pan's Garden: A Volume of Nature Stories* (1912). The story follows Hibbert as he slowly succumbs to the fatal allure of a person whom he meets one night while ice skating. The figure, however, is not quite who she seems; her touch is icy, and she is connected, in some strange way, with the winter snow. Here, the uncanny majesty of the nonhuman world makes contact with the human one through a kind of intuitive worship.

Hibbert, like Blackwood himself, is torn between dread and desire for this world, and his body and soul hang in the balance. Blackwood, influenced by Eastern and Theosophical texts, was enticed by the idea of 'Deva Evolution' or, as he put it, a 'non-human Evolutionary System that runs parallel to our Human Evolution, yet without intercourse between the two' (Blackwood 'The Little People', 45). The notion of a separate evolutionary tree, filled with inscrutable nonhuman intelligences and populated by a hierarchy of beings, ranging from flower fairies to cosmic spirits, informs a significant portion of Blackwood's weird fiction, and the stories in *Pan's Garden* in particular.

The second story, 'The Sacrifice', is a solemn, symbolic tale about faith – its denial and its return. Transcending the genre, it contains some of Blackwood's most powerful prose. Published in the thoughtful esoteric journal *The Quest* in April 1913 and collected the following year in *Incredible Adventures* (1914), it tells the story of John Limasson, a man who finds himself dealt a series of undisclosed personal and professional blows that leave his life, and his faith, in ruins. He is a seasoned climber and he processes these setbacks by hiking in the mountains. What follows is a profoundly mystical tale about spiritual rebirth. Pagan deities are passing through the mountains. Fragments of himself tussle with the ruin of his life. A sacrifice must be made. As the story progresses, it becomes clear that, for Limasson, hiking is its own kind of potent ritual. In the mountains, movement becomes a ceremonial language – a speech of the body. Ultimately, the story explores the tensions between the self and universe, the one and the whole, Gods and men. Blackwood believed that subjective, inner experiences could have a profound effect on 'external' reality, and often tried to dramatize this fragile idea in his fiction. 'The Sacrifice' is one of his most visionary and successful attempts to do so. It is unclear whether Blackwood himself received any ruinous 'blows' in 1913. In any case, the details of Limasson's ruin are less important than the spiritual resolution they effect – an important distinction for Blackwood.

Reincarnation

The third section explores one of Blackwood's lifelong philosophical interests: reincarnation. From adolescence onwards he grew increasingly dissatisfied with the moral teachings of Christianity. Of his parents' evangelical beliefs he writes that he was '*afraid* they were true, not glad' (Blackwood 1923, 23). However, he soon found through Buddhist and Hindu texts a more appealing framework for understanding the great suffering and injustice in the world. His education in reincarnation began with Patanjali's *Yoga Aphorisms* – a book he stole from one of his father's visitors who had left it on a table. Blackwood devoured the book in a single sitting and its effect was quick and profound: '[t]he entire paraphernalia of my evangelical teaching thenceforth began to withdraw' (Blackwood 1923, 29). This serendipitous discovery, quite by chance, of an alternate philosophy of the spirit, changed the course of Blackwood's life:

> Here was another outlook upon life, another explanation of the world; caprice was eliminated and justice entered; the present was the result of the past, the future determined by the present; I must reap what I had sown, but, also, I could sow what I wished to reap. Hope was born. (Blackwood 1923, 29)

Other books made their way into his hands – *Esoteric Buddhism* (1883) by A P Sinnett, *The Voice of the Silence* (1889) by Helena Blavatsky, and Blackwood's favourite of the world-scriptures, the *Bhagavad Gita* – an unusual reading list for an upper-class 'evangelical' adolescent in the 1880s. These books would ultimately steer Blackwood towards Theosophy, but he still had to attend university, and it was at Edinburgh that he came to understand karma, rebirth, and past lives more deeply. This was thanks to a fourth-year medical student and Hindu whom Blackwood befriended one day in a university dissecting room. This man explained Patanjali to the young Blackwood at length and turned theory into practice by showing him 'strange methods of breathing, of concentration, [and] of meditation' (Blackwood 1923, 53).

This early exposure to the concept of reincarnation would go on to inspire several articles on the topic. However, despite the significance of karma to his early life, Blackwood seems to have always maintained a degree of agnosticism about rebirth. How, for example, would such a phenomenon work in practice, and would it even be desirable? 'To recall the failures of a mere forty years is bad enough,' Blackwood once wrote, but 'to look back over a hundred lives would be disastrous: one could only sit down and cry' (Blackwood 1923, 157).

The article that opens this section, 'On Reincarnation', strikes a similarly agnostic note. Published in the esoteric journal *The Aryan Path* in March 1930, it is a notably circumspect piece. Blackwood, now sixty years old, recollects his youthful infatuation with reincarnation before proceeding – somewhat candidly, considering the nature of the journal and its audience – to discuss his doubts about its inner truth. Ever a seeker, however, he finishes on the same note that Patanjali's aphorisms had inspired in him so long ago – hope.

Whatever his personal beliefs may have been, it is clear that the topic was ripe for imaginative treatment and Blackwood engaged with the subject in a more sustained manner than any other writer of the period. Numerous short stories pivot on reincarnation, of which 'Old Clothes' (1910), 'Wayfarers' (1912), and 'Cain's Atonement' (1915) are among the best. Likewise, several of his novels, in particular *Julius LeVallon: An Episode* (1916), based in part on his friend at Edinburgh, and *The Wave: An Egyptian Aftermath* (1916), are meditations on reincarnation, as is the play, *Karma: A Re-incarnation Play* (1918), co-authored with Violet Pearn.

The first story in this section is one of Blackwood's great tales, 'The Insanity of Jones (A Study in Reincarnation)' – first published in his second collection, *The Listener* (1907). A brutal act of torture in the sixteenth century comes to haunt Jones, an unassuming twentieth-century office clerk. As the story progresses, it is revealed to him how lives and debts are laid on top of one another, and Jones must decide between revenge and forgiveness. The story grapples with some of the issues Blackwood was contending with – how might karma be meted out if one were to have access to their previous lives? Is justice a sword? At what point might spiritual insight become indistinguishable from psychosis? The story is one of Blackwood's most graphic and the climax still maintains the power to shock.

Excepting the odd word or phrase, Blackwood tended not to

revise stories between publications. Instead, he would rework the same idea into a fresh story, approaching the issue from another perspective, as it were. 'The Insanity of Jones', however, is notable for the fact that one of its central scenes reuses a story Blackwood had published three years earlier. This earlier story – 'The House of the Past', published in *The Theosophical Review* in April 1904 – is powerful but lacks narrative drive. Clearly, Blackwood was taken with the idea as it stuck with him over the ensuing years, awaiting a larger canvas into which it could be incorporated.

The second story in this section explores one of Blackwood's favourite themes, reincarnated lovers. 'The Tarn of Sacrifice' (1921), another story from *The Wolves of God and Other Fey Stories,* gives shape to Blackwood's interest in antiquity, a theme he touched on several times in later life in stories such as 'The Olive' (1921), 'Nephelé' (1921), and 'Roman Remains' (1948, also republished in the Handheld Classics anthology *Strange Relics*). While on a walking tour of the Lake District, John Holt comes under the spell of the barren landscape and its violent history. A local legend about the 'Blood Tarn' and ritual sacrifice starts to replay. Strong emotions, passion, and violence quickly bubble up to the surface of modern living, and the story can be read as a commentary on the barbarism of war. Holt is a veteran of the Battle of the Somme and struggles to shake off a strange bloodlust that grips him while he walks the ancient Roman roads. In the end, the story suggests that while violence is cyclical, love might act as a counterbalance to redeem the savagery of war. Blackwood never saw the front lines himself, though he did work as a 'searcher' for the Red Cross at a field camp in Rouen in 1918. As with 'The Insanity of Jones', the ending of 'The Tarn of Sacrifice' is ambiguous, and it is left to the reader to separate fact from fiction, sanity from madness.

While there is no direct evidence of Blackwood visiting the Lake District before 1924, he rarely wrote about places he had not visited himself. The remains of the Roman fort at Ambleside, referenced briefly in the story, had only recently been uncovered in a series of excavations between 1913 and 1920. It is likely, therefore, that Blackwood visited at some time during these eight years, though it cannot be ruled out that he had simply heard or read about the excavations elsewhere. In any case, he certainly visited in later years, both with his friends, the Ainley family, and for occasional stays with the author Hugh Walpole at his house near Lake Derwentwater.[2]

Imagination

For the fourth and final section, we turn inward to explore the nature of Blackwood's creative process. There are several extant articles, letters, and radio pieces that offer some insight into how and why Blackwood wrote his stories. In 1923, for example, he contributed to Arthur Sullivant Hoffman's book *Fiction Writers on Fiction Writing*. Blackwood's responses are brief but intriguing. Asked where his inspiration for a story comes from, he replies: 'The genesis of a story with me is invariably – an emotion, caused in my particular case by something in nature rather than in human nature: a scrap of colour in the sky, a flower, a sound of wind or water; briefly, an emotion produced by beauty' (quoted in Hoffman 1923, 12). Asked about the writing process itself, he returns, again, to emotion:

> An emotion produces its own setting, usually bringing with it a character who shall interpret it. The emotion dramatizes itself. The end alone is clearly in my mind. I never begin to write until this is so. Then I write fragments, scenes, fragments of the psychology, fitting them in later. Occasionally, however, when the emotion is strong, the story writes itself straightaway. Revision is endless. Often the story, when finished, is put aside and forgotten. The revision that comes weeks later, on reading over the whole tale as though it had been written by someone else, is the most helpful of all. (quoted in Hoffman 1923, 48–49)

Finally, asked whether he ever has an audience in mind while writing, he gives the following brusque response:

> I never give the reader a single thought. To some imaginary reader, sitting at a desk inside my own mind, I tell my story. It is written to express – to relieve – an emotion in my own being. It is never written to please other readers or any imaginable public. (quoted in Hoffman 1923, 216)

Emotion, it is clear, was key for Blackwood; strong or unusual emotions both justified and produced his fiction. But how? He did not publish on the subject again until February 1937. This essay, titled 'The Genesis of Ideas' and first published in *The Writer*, is structured as a series of anecdotes as opposed to theories, lending the piece an enjoyable story-like quality in its own right. Ideas have their genesis, Blackwood argues, in strong emotions. If this emotion cannot be expressed immediately it is stored in the 'Subconscious', awaiting future release. Blackwood's twist to this model is that the subconscious invariably dramatizes these emotions, moulding them into scenes, characters, or ideas that flash up into the author's mind when the time is ripe. Only once this dramatized emotion has made itself clear can the author begin the writing process proper. There is a strong psychoanalytical flavour to this model; Blackwood was an early and informed reader of Sigmund Freud and Carl Jung. Psychoanalysis, which assigned unprecedented power and significance to the unconscious portions of the mind, appealed to Blackwood, and provided a more legitimate explanation for supernatural extensions of consciousness than the esoteric tradition did.

The ideas expressed in the piece were clearly important to Blackwood as he adapted the article for a radio broadcast given over a decade later, in 1948. A version of the essay appeared again two years later, this time as 'The Birth of an Idea', in the *London Mystery Magazine*. However, while the basic content is similar to the original, this latter piece, published after the Second World War, is bogged down by Jungian interpretations of Hitler and the German unconscious, and suffers as a result.

The stories paired with 'The Genesis of Ideas' are directly related to its content. 'By Water' (1914) is the unnamed story that Blackwood deconstructs in the essay. Written while Blackwood was in Egypt and first published in *The Westminster Gazette,* it is a *conte cruel* about a man who finds himself lost in the desert. There are hints of nonhuman powers in the story as the protagonist battles with the rippling menace of the desert. However, these moments are brief. A deeper treatment of this theme can be found in the novellas 'Sand' (1912), 'A Descent into Egypt' (1914), and 'The Wings of Horus' (1914). 'By Water' was read on one of Blackwood's first radio performances, broadcast on 30 October 1934 in a series titled, appropriately, *Nightmare*.

The second half of 'The Genesis of Ideas' shifts focus to Blackwood's powerful 1911 novel, *The Centaur.* Considered by Blackwood to be his magnum opus, this story of one man's profoundly spiritual encounter with the 'Soul of the Caucasus' has been read by some as providing a better, perhaps even 'truer', autobiography of Blackwood than his nonfiction writings (Joshi 2003, 94). 'Imagination', a short story published in *The Westminster Gazette* in December 1910 and reprinted in *Ten Minute Stories* four years later, shines a light on both *The Centaur* and Blackwood's creative process. William Jones is working on his novel but cannot figure out how to depict the mythological being at the centre of the story. Suddenly he receives a strange and wonderous visitor, and imagination is rekindled. The story is Blackwood at his most self-reflexive, dramatizing how the subconscious mind dramatizes with his signature blend of beauty, imagination, and terrific wonder.

The Lure of the Unknown

Given the popularity and success of Blackwood's writings, and his involvement with the new media of his lifetime, it is curious that his cultural presence today should be so peripheral. Twenty-nine of his stories were even adapted for television as *Tales of Mystery,* which ran for three seasons between 1961 and 1963 on the British independent television channel ITV. Not one episode is believed to have survived, and no further television adaptations of his work have been made as yet. One explanation may be that Blackwood's work is difficult to categorize. His fiction inhabits several genres and markets – supernatural fiction, weird fiction, children's fiction, detective fiction, fantasy, New Age, even romance – but cannot be contained by any one of them. Consequently, his writing has been categorised, not unjustly, as weird or horror fiction. But fear is rarely the goal in Blackwood's work. In his writing, fear is simply a by-product of encounters with that which is outside or beyond human understanding. His stories are more concerned with thresholds, with choices or tensions between the self and the whole, the individual and the collective, the material and the spiritual. Both fear and ecstasy are found here; to gain the whole one must sacrifice the self, or, as the narrator of *The Centaur* puts it:

> If he yielded entirely, something he dreaded without being able to define, would happen; the structure of his being would suffer a nameless violence, so that he would have to break with the world [...] complete surrender would involve somehow a disintegration, a dissociation of his personality that carried with it the loss of personal identity. (Blackwood 1911, 6)

Another reason for Blackwood's gradual disappearance from wider literary awareness in the latter half of the twentieth century may be the strange intimacy his fiction requires from the reader. Running throughout his *oeuvre* is a sincerity of belief that contemporary readers may find jarring. This sincerity can certainly be overworked. His longer fiction in particular often succumbs to a saccharine spirituality at odds with contemporary sensibilities and the void-circling cosmicism that underpins much of the weird fiction published in his day. But this is also what distinguishes Blackwood's work from the perfunctory terror fiction of his contemporaries and what makes his work ripe for a comeback. While Blackwood was adept at writing traditional tales of terror, the guiding principle of his fiction concerns the re-enchantment of a world that global war and the rush of modernity had effaced. For Blackwood there were still deep reserves of magic in the wild places of the world, including in the subconscious mind. Writing in 1948, just a few years before he died, he reaffirmed his position: 'I am called the "ghost man"; editors want "ghost stories" from me. Yet my chief interest I should describe as an interest in the Extension of Human Faculty: in other words, latent powers that suggest we are all potentially much greater and more wonderful than we suspect' (Blackwood 'Looking Back', 8). Fear and wonder intersect.

Ultimately, one can perhaps say this of Blackwood's writings: his stories concern the communion or encounter – whether major or minor, catastrophic or successful, forced or desired – between people and forces from the other-side or Outside, including their own 'higher selves'. If his characters survive such an encounter, they are fundamentally changed or, as he liked to put it, they 'become otherwise' (Blackwood 1912, 505). Unlike, for example, H P Lovecraft's 'cosmic indifferentism', Blackwood's writings are more often than not reconciliatory. They ask what would happen were one to be in closer communion with the world, if – by accident, ritual, sensitivity, or proximity – one could reach the indescribable 'life' that churns behind the visible appearances of things. What glories and dangers attend an encounter with the unknown? There is only one way to find out.

> The moment the doorposts are left behind – of a railway carriage, your dentist's house, an afternoon call even! – the adventure has begun. It is the moment of birth, of life, thrill, excitement. The pre*limen*aries are over; you have entered the Unknown. (Blackwood 'Psychology', 124)[3]

Notes

1: Blackwood was laureled as one of Lovecraft's 'modern masters' of the supernatural in his essay on the topic from 1927. C S Lewis discusses his enjoyment of Blackwood's stories repeatedly in his letters to Arthur Greeves: 'Oh, Arthur, aren't they priceless? Particularly the "Ancient Sorceries" one, which I think I shall remember all my life.' (Lewis 1979, 123). Siegfried Sassoon wrote to Blackwood in 1912 to express his admiration (Ashley 2019, 228), while Tolkien once noted that his use of the word 'crack' in the 'Crack of Doom' was inspired directly by one of Blackwood's novels (Ordway 2021, 234–236).

2: From correspondence with Mike Ashley, May 2022.

3: This passage comes from a discussion of doors and thresholds, hence the italicization of 'limen' (Latin for 'threshold') in 'pre*limen*aries'.

Works Cited

Ashley, Mike *Starlight Man: The Extraordinary Life of Algernon Blackwood* (Stark House Press, 2019).

Blackwood, Algernon, *Episodes Before Thirty* (Cassell and Company, 1923).

—, Letter to Vera Wainwright, 8 October 1937, Vera Wainwright Archive, letter 33, The British Library, London.

—, 'Looking Back at Christmas', *The Lure of the Unknown: Essays on the Strange* (Swan River Press, 2022, 3-10).

—, *Pan's Garden: A Volume of Nature Stories* (Macmillan, 1912).

—, *The Centaur,* (Macmillan, 1911).

—, 'The Little People & Co', *The Lure of the Unknown: Essays on the Strange* (Swan River Press, 2022, 39–49).

—, 'The Psychology of Places', *The Lure of the Unknown: Essays on the Strange* (Swan River Press, 2022, 121–125).

Graf, Susan Johnston, *Talking to the Gods: Occultism in the Work of W B Yeats, Arthur Machen, Algernon Blackwood, and Dion Fortune* (State University of New York Press, 2015).

Hoffman, Arthur Sullivant, *Fiction Writers on Fiction Writing* (The Bobbs-Merrill Company, 1923).

Holt, Paul, 'Friends Tell Me ...', *The Tatler*, 9 November 1949, 276.

Joshi, S T, *The Weird Tale* (Wildside Press, 2003).

Lewis, C S, 'Letter 39; July 1916', *They Stand Together: The Letters of C S Lewis to Arthur Greeves (1914–1963),* ed. Walter Hooper (Macmillan, 1979, 122–125).

Luckhurst, Roger, *The Mummy's Curse: The True History of a Dark Fantasy* (Oxford University Press, 2012).

Ordway, Holly, *Tolkien's Modern Reading: Middle-Earth Beyond the Middle Ages* (Word on Fire Academic, 2021).

Sources

Blackwood's stories were often published in magazines and periodicals before their later collection in volume format. For this anthology, however, the texts were sourced from their first volume appearances. Not only were these the more influential, but, unlike his periodical submissions which, once sold, could not be altered, Blackwood saw proofs for his books and was able to make slight revisions, making these later texts the more authoritative. Where applicable, however, earlier publication details have been provided in square brackets. The four non-fiction pieces have been transcribed from their original periodical appearances. In a few instances, punctuation and formatting have been silently corrected for uniformity.

''Mid the Haunts of the Moose', *Blackwood's Magazine*, July 1900, 58–72.

'Skeleton Lake: An Episode in Camp', *The Empty House and Other Ghost Stories* (Eveleigh Nash, 1906).

'The Wolves of God', *The Wolves of God and Other Fey Stories* (Cassell, 1921).

'The Winter Alps', *Country Life*, 24 December 1910, 930–933.

'The Glamour of the Snow', *Pan's Garden: A Volume of Nature Stories* (Macmillan, 1912). [Originally published in *Pall Mall Magazine*, December 1911, 911–923, and in *The Forum*, December 1911, 641–661.]

'The Sacrifice', *Incredible Adventures* (Macmillan, 1914). [Originally published in *The Quest,* April 1913, 540–563.]

'On Reincarnation', *The Aryan Path,* March 1930, 155–158.

'The Insanity of Jones (A Study in Reincarnation)', *The Listener and Other Stories* (Eveleigh Nash, 1907).

'The Tarn of Sacrifice', *The Wolves of God and Other Fey Stories* (Cassell, 1921).

'The Genesis of Ideas', *The Writer,* February 1937, 35–37; 63.

'By Water', *Day and Night Stories* (Cassell, 1917). [Originally published in *The Westminster Gazette,* 18 April 1914, 3.]

'Imagination', *Ten Minute Stories* (John Murray, 1914). [Originally published in *The Westminster Gazette,* 17 December 1910, 15.]

The Unknown

Canada

‘Mid the Haunts of the Moose (1900)

Deux Rivières is a stopping-place – it can hardly be called a station – on the Canadian Pacific Railway before you come to Port Arthur and Winnipeg, and the few wooden shanties of which it consists stand on the border-line between Quebec and Ontario. It stands, moreover, on the edge of that vast wilderness that stretches unbroken to James Bay, the southern loop of Hudson’s Bay itself. Just below this little ‘lumber village’ runs the Ottawa river, icy cold, swift, and narrow. It has not here attained the width and power that many miles farther on render it of paramount importance to the lumber trade; and, last year in October, when our little party went up into this wilderness to hunt moose, we found that the Ottawa river here formed the dividing-line between danger and safety. In Ontario *l’orignal* (moose) was still protected by Government, and had been for three years; but in Quebec, across the river, any one who could get within range of a moose after October 1 was allowed to shoot it. The moose seemed to know where they were well off, for Ontario was reported ‘thunderin’ full of ‘em,’ whereas Quebec was comparatively deserted.

‘It’s easy huntin’,’ an indiscreet fellow in Deux Rivières observed to us as we made ready to start; ‘you can shoot yer moose on one side of the river and bring ower his horns and pelt on the other. The game-warden ain’t agoin’ to hunt for that carcass, you bet. And even if he do, he ain’t agoin’ to find it before the wolves and meat-hawks and ants have had their go at it.’ The licence for each gun is £5; and the fine for shooting out of season is exceedingly heavy. It is divided between the warden and the man who reports the discovery.

No camera can ever reproduce the still beauty of that morning scene when we left the train at 5 am and made ready to leave the little outpost of civilisation. The cool autumn air, fragrant with a hundred scents from the surrounding woods, was still hazy with the smoke of forest-fires that had been smouldering all the summer. Through this gauze-like veil the maples and birches, already turned to gold and crimson beneath the touch of early frosts, shone with a strange luminous beauty that for miles in every direction lit up the ocean of trees with flaming patches of glory. And all was still and silent. There was no wind astir, and the air only trembled very faintly to the musical roar of the waterfalls and tumbling rapids of the Ottawa below. A few human figures moved here and there among the little wooden shanties.

The river swept swiftly round a sharp bend, and rushed on to a dangerous fall two hundred yards farther down. Along either bank there was a vigorous back-water. To cross this water with our packs, tents, &c, we embarked in a clumsy lumber barge propelled by immense oars. The first back-water carried us a considerable distance up-stream, the men heading the boat straight across all the time, and rowing as hard as they could. Then we suddenly entered the main current, and were swiftly borne down the centre of the stream, the boat turning round like a huge top all the way. The banks seemed to fly past. The roar of the fall, and the horrible edge where the river dropped abruptly out of sight, seemed to us unpleasantly close, when the prow of the boat caught the other back-water and our direction was instantly reversed. With a shudder and a splash the unwieldy boat spun round and shot up-stream again, finally landing us in safety at a spot exactly opposite our original point of embarkation. During this brief but exciting journey the French-Canadian oarsmen regaled us with pleasant stories of boats swept over the falls and lives lost in the spring when the river was high and the strength of the two back-waters was easily miscalculated by a few seconds.

Then, for two days and two nights we travelled by canoe and 'portages' inland to the lake of Cogawanna, whose lonely beaches were said to be haunted by 'the biggest moose yer ever seen'. The scenery these two days was in a sense monotonous. Miles upon miles of undulating forest and low hills – no open spaces, except black patches of desolation, where fires had consumed the underbrush and licked the branches off the giant trees till they had died. The second growth on the scene of a fire is never the same as the trees that were destroyed, but usually silver birch or scrub-oak and maple. Everywhere we passed these lighter greens among the sombre shades of the hemlocks, cedars, and pines. Lakes of all sizes and shapes came suddenly into view, blue as the Mediterranean, or green and black as the ocean itself. The constant repetition produced the sense of monotony; but the real charm of it all lay in the utter loneliness and remoteness from the scenes of men's labours. Wild-duck of all descriptions we saw; cranes, huge fish-hawks, divers, laughing loons, eagles, tracks of otter, mink, bear, deer, and occasionally of wolves along the shores – and moose-tracks, where the great beasts had blundered through the dense scrub to find a drinking-place. But no men, not even Indians; no farms, no shanties. We had the great woods to ourselves. Chipmunks, chattering on the crests of lofty pines, dropped cones upon us as we glided silently by, close to shore. Loons dived in front of us, and popped up again, many hundreds of yards away, with fish in their beaks. More than once, as we turned a sharp corner, a startled buck looked up and stared in amazement at us before it turned and crashed away into the forest, 'whistling' as it went. There were no mosquitoes. The cold nights had mercifully destroyed them. No singing-birds, nor any of brighter plumage than the rich blue of the blue jay and the light greys of the meat-hawks or carrion-birds. No wild-flowers, or hardly any. The merciless winter does not encourage their growth. Better still, no flies, no snakes, no poisonous insects of any kind. There is a decided note of grimness in these northern woods of Canada – almost as if the shadow of the cruel winter hung somewhere in the air, even in summer, and held up a warning finger: 'This is sacred to the life of the forest. You may venture here in the warm months, but never let yourselves be caught here when the frost comes, and the snow on the wings of the north wind.'

Meanwhile, we had reached the old haunts of the lumber companies. On all sides we saw their traces. In days gone by there had been lumber-camps at remote points. In the deep snows the men cut the trees and 'skid' them over the slippery surface to the edge of the nearest water. The logs are piled up 20 feet high on the shores, and when the ice melts they are tumbled down into the water, and in huge 'booms', acres in extent, are floated for weeks down streams and across lakes till they reach the Ottawa river and eventually the great saw-mills. In the spring these booms choke up many a good fishing-stream. Perhaps the first big fellow gets caught by a projection on the bank. Instantly the others pile up on his back, till in a few hours a towering heap of logs dams the river and forms a 'jam'. To break a jam is to lead a forlorn hope, and it is not uncommon in these solitudes to come across a plain wooden cross, close to some tumbling stream, with the inscription roughly hewn with a knife, 'Jean Garnier', or 'Jim Smith, killed by jam' – with the date. And these lonely graves beneath the 'murmuring pines and the hemlocks' have their poetry and their lesson of duty nobly done without hope of reward.

The apology for this digression is that the lumber companies proved of great value to us. In order to skid the logs they have to cut roads, so that the horses may have a tolerably clear path. These roads are on the surface of the snow, lying perhaps four feet deep, and in the springs are only recognisable as faint vistas in the forest. They always lead to water. Following these woodland vistas, canoeing down winding lakes shut in by lofty cliffs and dotted with picturesque islands, we covered the fifty miles that lay between us and our destination. About sunset on the second day our 'birch-barks' grated in a sandy bay of Cogawanna's northern shore, and we pitched a permanent camp on a promontory covered with silver birches and maples.

Water-fowl of various descriptions scattered with whirring wings as we landed, and more than one porcupine ambled leisurely away into the woods when we began to chop the tent-poles and get the stones for the fireplace. When the sun finally disappeared, the shadows of the night fell over a camp as cosy as any hunter could desire, and perhaps a little more comfortable, because one of the party happened to be a young lady. The stillness was almost unearthly when the moon rose over the lake, silvering untold distances, and throwing impenetrable shadows under the trees. I sat over the little fire at the mouth of my tent long after the others were asleep. It seemed unnatural that the whole country should be so silent when the woods were full of life – moving life too. Everything alive in the forest moves at night and rests by day. The woods travel in the darkness. At that very moment, as I sat in the cold moonlight looking out upon immense stretches of forest, there was not a hundred yards anywhere in which some living creature was not moving. Yet there was no sound – not the breaking of a twig or the crackling of a dry leaf beneath the lightest paw. Nothing but silence, and moonlight, and the stars, and distance. As I imagined the moose prowling and feeding not very far from us, they almost seemed to me a survival of the antediluvian monsters, a species all by themselves, having no part or portion with the degenerate animals of modern days.

With the earliest morning came the sound of fish jumping in the lake and the chipmunks scampering through the trees overhead. But the excitement began at breakfast (trout and buckwheat cakes), when one of the men announced the discovery of fresh deer-tracks not half a mile behind our tents. Deer are not plentiful in these regions. The wolves keep their ranks thin. No wolf can catch a deer in the woods; but in the winter, ferocious with long fasts, they chase them on to the ice, and soon get their teeth into their tender flanks. They double more easily than deer on the slippery surface, and, being lighter, do not sink so deep in the soft patches of snow. The barking of a few wolves in pursuit of a deer sounds like the fighting and snarling of a lot of angry dogs. It must be an unpleasant sound to have at your heels at any time, and the poor deer makes the most frantic efforts, but only slips from side to side, growing momentarily weaker, till it is at length overhauled and torn to pieces. The discovery of deer so close to us was only exciting because it meant we should not lack fresh meat; but moose was the magic word in our camp, and the first thing to do was to find out where the moose were in relation to ourselves. These creatures, it may be said, move generally in groups of four or five, or less. Several groups of this size travel in the same direction, and cover practically the same country at the same time. In this sense they may be described as moving in widely scattered herds. They get over vast distances, moving with great rapidity, and the enormous territory at their disposal of course makes difficult hunting. You must have iron muscles and be tireless. A fresh moose-track – that is, one with no water or cobwebs in it – may be followed fifty miles, the creature always keeping half-a-dozen miles ahead of the hunter. If, meanwhile, it chooses to take to the water, the tracks of course are lost, and so much time has been wasted, that's all! The utmost caution has to be observed. Their ears are sharper than those of a deer. If a twig snaps beneath your mocassin, or your coat brushes noisily against a low branch of some maple-tree, they will put another mile to their credit before you have gone a hundred yards.

It is upon their unrivalled powers of scent, however, that they chiefly depend for their safety. Nature, or evolution, has endowed them with a proboscis of rare proportion, and their title of 'Hebrew of the Woods' is thoroughly deserved. In the wide nostrils gaping at the end of that expansive muzzle, the least scent, the faintest odour, is faithfully registered, and the owners are off at top speed in less than a second. With their heads lowered, and in spite of the bull's spreading horns, they charge through the woods at full tilt, crashing through the densest underbrush as if it were standing hay, and smashing young tree-stems as if they were the stalks of sunflowers. Everywhere, in these northern woods, can be seen the traces of their passage – trunks with the bark scraped off, broken saplings, tufts of hair caught on pointed branches, and on the ground the imprint of their hoofs and tremendous stride.

Accustomed to the dim twilight of the great woods, the eyeballs of these creatures are oblique, as with deer, and do not seem to be specially sensitive. They never turn their heads at shadows. Provided the wind is right, you can approach a moose to within a few feet, if you go straight in front of him, and he will never see you. If he does raise his head, it will mean that his *ears* have warned him of your approach. If you can fool his ears and his nose, you can put salt on his tail, say the hunters. But wind and rain are the best aids. Noisy weather is good hunting weather. The roar of the branches, the rattle of the rain, and the constant dripping from the trees upon the leaves on the ground, combine to drown the inevitable sounds of your approach. Then there is good chance of success. The front legs of the moose are longer than the hind ones. To drink (if the bank be steep) he has to kneel;

to crop the sweet shoots of the wild rice they must assume the humble attitude of prayer. Their food consists chiefly of the ground hemlock, whose low bushes cover the ground in the neighbourhood of big hemlock-trees, and can be easily got at in winter by scraping away the surface snow; but they are also fond of the topmost leaves of the young maples, which their great height enables them to pull down with ease. On all sides, where moose have been travelling in the autumn, the maple saplings can be seen bent double to the ground. When the earth is too hard to hold a track, the experienced hunter can follow the path of a moose for miles, by observing where he has cropped the hemlock and the sweet maple leaves on both sides as he sauntered slowly along, enjoying his vegetarian meal.

In the great heats of July and August these animals suffer terribly from the sun, owing to the thickness of a hairy skin that also keeps them warm when the thermometer is 40° below zero. In these months they commonly wade into the lakes and stand up to their necks in the cool water, where the Indians, to their shame, slaughter them without mercy. They offer a large target, as may be imagined, and, though strong swimmers, cannot get away from the bullet in time. These same Indians affirm that the bear is the shyest animal of the woods. Bruin certainly is a very wary beast; but the moose, in my humble opinion, comes in an uncommonly close second. On all sides you can see the rotten logs the bears have torn open in their search for ants and honey, and the deep trail leading up to, and away from, them; but the bear itself is probably miles away, covering the ground in that rolling, tumbling gait of his that carries him along at incredible speed. It is no uncommon sight to surprise a bear among the low fruit-bushes, no matter what way the wind is. When berries are thick you may stumble frequently enough upon them in the midst of the blueberries, with both front paws round a particularly rich clump, and gluttonously devouring the ripe purple fruit. Yet who ever came upon a moose in the middle of his dinner, unless wind and weather and everything else were against him?

The first two days we spent reconnoitring. It was necessary to find out in what special portion of their great park the moose were enjoying the splendid 'fall' weather. In three parties of two each, with compasses and canoes, we separated, after a very early breakfast, and spent the day following the freshest trails we could come across. At night we met again round the blazing logs of the open camp-fire, and compared notes. All of us had come across very recent trails of deer, bear, beaver, otter, fox, skunk, even wolves – but the moose-tracks were all old. There was nothing worth following, nothing fresher than a week. They had moved.

'They're travellin' fast, and we've got to shunt along purty fast to get up with 'em.'

'Unless they're movin' in a circle, which they often do – darn 'em!'

Then followed the usual consultation of maps, which we laid over a flat stone beside the fire, and studied intently while the owls hooted in the woods behind us, and more than one pair of glowing eyes watched our proceedings from a safe distance.

Ten miles to the north of us Garden Lake stretched its lonely bays and arms over an immense surface, dotted with wooded islands, on one of which the Indians had built their annual crop of birch-bark canoes. I found the thin strips of cedar, and the root they use for strings, still lying among the long grass. Garden river, the exit of this lake, was trampled and pounded for hundreds of yards along the banks, but the owners of the monstrous hoofs had gone. Blue Lake, to the west of us, with its cold blue waters; Sand Lake, with its yellow stretches of shore; Green Lake, with its deep green waves and precipitous cliffs, Roscoe Lake, Round Pond, Lindsay Lake, and a dozen more besides, all bore traces of the giants' thirst along their quiet shores. Maple leaves had been cropped and ground hemlock devoured; tree stems scraped; projecting twigs left with a tuft of coarse hair streaming in the wind, and the ground manured in patches. But the moose themselves, shy mammoths, were hiding somewhere out of our way, and the second day's search brought us to the trails of their sentries, that were by no means too old for hope. The hoarse croaking of the ravens, always a sign of their neighbourhood, was heard at intervals; and the carrion-birds, that follow them in the air, feeding temporarily on a parasite of their thick hair, and hoping eventually for a whole carcass, were seen flitting about in all directions. This reconnoitring is pleasant work. The air is dry and cool, wonderfully invigorating, and laden with the hundred scents of a primeval forest that stretches unbroken to the icy shores of James Bay. You tread all the time on a carpet of deep moss or crimson and golden leaves. On all sides the partridges are 'drumming', or flying quietly into the lower branches of the trees, where half-a-dozen will stand and let you shoot them one by one. Squirrels dart everywhere, chattering and squeaking, with tails erect, and a rare nest of nuts hidden somewhere for the coming winter. The quiet bays of the lakes shelter wild-fowl of all descriptions, and the springs fill your flasks with the best brand of champagne you have ever tasted.

So we peeled the crackling bark from the silver birch-trees and fashioned calling-horns, and prepared in other ways for night-watches and vigorous hunting measures generally. The cry of the cow moose is admirably imitated by means of this rude horn. While an amateur exaggerates it into something between a fog-horn and a cornet, the practised hunter produces the long deep 'moo' that carries an incredible distance, and rarely fails to bring the bull, if within hearing length, crashing headlong down to his death.

The third day my guide and I loaded our pack with a few provisions, and with tent and canoe started for a series of little ponds beyond the northern shores of Garden Lake. We journeyed all day down 'lumber roads' that were simply vistas of glowing colour. I was always in front, with a 50lb pack strapped across the shoulders and a loaded rifle, while behind me the man, with the canoe over his head like a gigantic pantomime hat, followed awkwardly. Frequent rests were necessary; but who could wish to go fast in such woods on a fine day in October, with the blue sky overhead, and the slanting sunlight putting the match to autumn bonfires on every side. We moved as quietly as possible in mocassins.

'Hunt *all* the time; you never kin guess when your chance'll come.'

Once the man stopped suddenly and sniffed the air like a dog. He made a sign to me, and I helped the canoe off his shoulders. He went a few feet ahead of me and pointed to the ground. I looked and saw a heap of gorgeous leaves left by an eddy of wind. It was indeed a patch of beauty; but I thought it strange for this rough woodsman to take so much trouble to show it to me.

'Beautiful, indeed,' I whispered.

'Ain't it, though?' he whispered back. 'It's a young cow. Guess she ain't been away long either!'

It was not the poetry of autumn that had moved him, but the smell of a moose, and the deep imprint of her body where she had recently rested upon the leaves. I saw it plainly enough when his finger outlined it for me. He kept sniffing the air as he gazed.

'There's a moose within ...' He hesitated. I gasped. 'A couple of miles, maybe,' he concluded.

He showed me the faint hoof-marks on the thick carpet of leaves where it entered the wood.

'That thar cow was lyin' thar not ten minutes ago. But the wind's wrong, and I guess she smelt us pretty strong.'

Speaking for himself, I have no doubt she did!

We followed the trail some distance into the woods. The underbrush was very thick, and we had to scramble on all-fours. The cow had doubled a good deal on her tracks. We presently came to a spot where she had evidently waited a moment.

'She stopped to listen here,' he explained, sitting down on a huge fallen tree and gazing sadly at the hoof-marks. 'When one of them animals is startled it runs 200 yards, maybe, into the woods, and then stops to listen. This is whar that cow stopped to listen, or I'm a – Injin.'

'She didn't stop long,' I ventured.

He looked at me without speaking, and then motioned me to follow. For half a mile through the woods we followed the tracks. Soon they began to get longer and wider apart.

'She was scared here. She's runnin'.'

The tracks got wider and wider apart, till finally they reached a big tree lying on the ground, with its branches sticking out like the spokes of a wheel in the air. There they seemed to come to a full stop. But the woodsman soon found their continuation – on the other side of the tree.

'That's whar she jumped – see!' he explained. And, measuring it as accurately as we could, it came to 18 feet. A very fair jump, I thought, for a cow moose. To clear the branches she must have crossed the tree at an elevation of nearly 4 feet.

It was just sunset when we reached the shores of Garden Lake and saw the expanse of still water, with dark patches in all directions showing the islands. There was no wind, and not a cloud in the sky; so we launched our canoe in silence, and for the next two hours paddled across the deserted waters, skirting points and islands, and occasionally long reefs of black rocks. Like Hiawatha, we

> Sailed into the fiery sunset,
> Sailed into the purple vapours,
> Sailed into the dusk of evening, –

and before we were half-way across this arm of Garden Lake the moon rose over the ridge of forest and silvered a picture of fairy-like enchantment such as I have never seen equalled. It was peace beyond all telling, and the only sound was the water splashing musically against the sides of the frail canoe and the monotonous dripping of the paddles. It didn't matter where we landed to camp. All was ours – islands, points, bays, and mainland. No one could interfere. The loneliness was real.

By the light of the moon, then high in the heavens, we pitched our tent upon the farther shore on the edge of the mighty woods, and after devouring the two partridges shot *en route*, and drinking a quart each of black tea, we crawled into the narrow tent and were soon fast asleep – I in a sleeping-bag with a red woollen nightcap on my head, and my companion in his clothes with his ordinary slouch-hat drawn down over his eyes.

The day following was clear and still. In the afternoon we portaged into a narrow little pond, unhonoured by a name, that lay several miles in the forest, and at a much higher level than the main lake.

'It ain't fur from the ridge, and if they're travellin' in this country they're bound to come within callin' distance.' He never deigned to use the word moose. It was always 'they' or 'them beasts', 'cow', 'bull', or 'calf'.

It was late in the afternoon, and very little wind was stirring. Stealthily we lowered the canoe from our shoulders and pushed it into the lake, and then with the utmost care got in ourselves and paddled cautiously down the near shore. The canoe moved on the quiet water like a spirit, silently, almost without ripple, as if it knew what was expected of it. I sat in the bows, the rifle across my knees, and the man propelled us with a slight movement of his wrist, never taking the paddle out of the water. In such still weather the dripping of the drops carries dangerous distances, and the sun shining on its wet blade flashes signals that can be seen literally for miles. Neither of us spoke a word, and, in spite of occasional spasms of 'canoe cramp' that shot up my legs and back, I sat motionless. The least movement, and a birch-bark canoe crackles like a pop-gun. The opposite shore, about a quarter of a mile across, lay in front of the sun, and therefore in shadow. The sun was fast nearing the edge of the ridge above. Nothing seemed more likely than that a moose should come down to drink, and nothing less likely than that it should distinguish us from one of the many logs that line the shore beside us. It could never make us out across 400 yards of water. The lake was perhaps two miles long. About half-way down the man stopped paddling, and, with very slow even movements, raised the horn to his lips and blew a long sad 'moo', that echoed numberless times before it finally died away in the sea of silent woods round us. Twice he did this, with due intervals, and there was no answer; but just as the third 'moo' was losing itself in the distance, a new sound rose after the echoes. We paused and listened intently. It was the breaking of branches a long way off … The guide's keen brown eyes flashed a message to me as I turned my head towards him.

'There he comes … but a long way off.'

A tremor ran through me, and I strained my ears so much to listen that I heard the blood singing under the skin. The sound of breaking branches continued to reach us at intervals, each time a little closer than before. Some great animal was moving through the long stretch of forest on the opposite shores. He seemed to be at a spot half-way between the lake and the ridge. It was getting dusk, and drinking-time was close at hand. Every now and then came a louder report, as some young tree was snapped off short, and then followed a period of silence again. The shadows were settling down over the trees. Already the sun was below the ridge, and probably within a short hour of the horizon itself.

'He's feedin',' whispered the man; 'he ain't travellin' fast.'

'Is he coming this way?'

'Guess so, if we don't scare him any. The wind's right.'

A puff of air came against our faces at that very moment as if to verify his words. It came from across the water. For another half-hour we waited in cramps and silence. The beast never deigned to answer our cry, nor to hasten his step, yet he was certainly coming nearer and nearer. It was just about drinking-time; but the poor brute did not bargain for a piece of lead in his cup.

'It may be a b'ar,' whispered the man.

Scarcely were the words out of his mouth when a roar that made the air shake issued from the shadows directly opposite.

'There he is,' whispered the man excitedly, pointing.

It was some seconds before I could distinguish anything at all save the dense growth of bushes that lined the shore. My rifle was raised and ready, but I could see nothing to aim at. Then suddenly the bushes parted and I saw a form, dim and immense, rise up out of the very ground it seemed. The width of the horns was lost in the shadows; but there was no mistaking those broad shoulders and that big brown bulk. Instantly the canoe shot round, and began to move swiftly towards him across the lake. I pointed ready to fire, and the light bark trembled beneath us like a thing of life as we moved steadily forwards. There was a touch of buck-fever; but the steel-tipped bullet sped true, and the monster fell with a crash to its knees.

'Steady – now another one,' said the man behind me, urging on the canoe as fast as he could.

A second shot, and the moose rolled sideways into the lake and lay motionless. Next day the other men went over to skin it, and the horns and pelt were just about all they could manage. The horns measured 52 inches across, and there were 28 points.

The night we watched for moose I shall never forget. Sleeping for several hours in the afternoon, we took an early supper, and just as the shadows were falling started out for our adventure. The lake had to be crossed and a mile 'portaged'; then a second lake came, and after it a second portage. It was nine o'clock when we cautiously slipped the canoe into the still waters of a secluded pond far from camp. A frosty night without wind seemed in our favour. A host of stars in a sky as clear as winter was the only light we dared use. Wrapping ourselves up in blankets, we crawled in the canoe to a suitable spot twenty yards from shore, and there prepared to wait till the dawn. No tobacco was permissible. No fire could, of course, be made, nor anything cooked. A nip of whisky about two am was all that warmed.

How still the night was. Our breathing seemed the only sound. The pond was barely three-quarters of a mile long, and very narrow. It seemed, so far as we could judge, to be in the direct route the moose had been taking of late. Surely some one of them would deign to drink of its sweet waters at sunrise. Everything alive in the woods travels at night. Everything is awake and moving. Yet, how silently. The shores of the lake rose up into the sky by gentle slopes, and from the shadows of the remoter shore came occasionally the splash of an otter or the wet patter of a mink running along over the stones. Once or twice we distinctly heard a deer drinking; but the noises of our heavier game were not yet audible. Men hunt moose often for days and days in this country without getting even a 'smell of one'. A New York man, who for years has sought his favourite game in these regions, told me that one season he spent seven weeks here – 'hard huntin', you bet, it was, too!' – without seeing a single animal. As I sat cold and shivering in the cramped canoe, I passed some of the time working out mathematically the chances that a moose would, or would not, come our way. Millions of square acres, thousands of lakes to drink at, miles of forest – and, then how many moose? My companion interrupted my calculations by pointing to the other shore. Had he heard something, and could so huge a beast move so stealthily? No! it was not a moose. The moon was rising, that was all; and we should soon have to change our position and shift into the shadow. A single motion of the paddle accomplished this, and we glided under the lee of the other shore, with no sound but the rustle of the man's coat-sleeve and the drip-drip of the paddle, as he drew it shining and wet in the moonlight from the water.

As the moon rose over the hill, the shadows deepened along the shores, though retreating a little, and the air seemed to grow colder. A flood of silver light shone on the flat surface of that sea of trees opposite; but behind us we could see nothing at all. It was too dark to distinguish even one tree-trunk from another. Now and then a wave of cooler, richer air seemed to breathe out upon us from the deep recesses at our backs, bringing scents of moss and bark and pine-needles and all that is sweet and good in the heart of the woods. Distant sounds, too, faint and muffled, reached our ears, and kept the blood tingling. I was too excited to feel sleepy. Every minute I thought the hum of indistinct murmurs would grow louder and differentiate itself into the tread of hoofs, the breaking of boughs, the crashing of saplings. Every instant I thought those immense shadows, that foregathered and waxed and waned on the farther shore, would suddenly step forth into the moonlight and assume the shape of a great animal with spreading horns. But the hours passed, and the moon crossed over to the other side, and the stars began to fade. Already the eastern sky was beginning to ... Hark! What was that? A sound like the cracking of distant branches trembled on the air and died away. Presently it was repeated, again, and again. Something was coming at last. It is needless to say what our emotions were, after the long cold night, when we distinctly heard the animals – for there were several – breaking through the underbrush at the far end of the lake and coming out to drink.

A confused mass, a big moving shadow, was all we saw. It was too far away, and the light was too uncertain. Crack, crack, went the rifles, and when the echoes had subsided, we heard the whole hillside crashing to a mighty tread as the moose thundered away at full speed ... And that was our last chance. Soon the sun was up, and after visiting the drinking-place and inspecting the deep hoof-marks, we dragged wearily home the twelve miles to hot coffee and fried trout.

It was a pleasant camp we had there beneath the slender silver birches on the point of a sandy little promontory. On one side was the sandy bay sacred to the men, and in a little cove on the other side the solitary lady-hunter of the party was supposed to disport herself matutinally in the cold waters. As a matter of fact, it was generally believed that she preferred a basin of hot water in the tent; and towards the end of our stay, when it grew really cold, her husband was brought round without difficulty to her view of the situation. The point of the promontory was kept for the guides, though it must be recorded to their honour that they made no ablutionary use of it, and that the deep pools seemed to them better fitted for cleaning the fish and partridges in. From our tent-doors we looked straight down seven miles of blue Cogawanna water. Soon the surface would be a solid sheet of ice, over two feet thick, and covered with snow; but then it was dancing and alive, full of fish, and warm enough even in October to make an occasional swim enjoyable. Cogawanna was a Chippewa Indian who died about 1860, and was buried on a little pine-clad island at the far end of the lake, and in the centre of his favourite fishing-grounds. A grave marks the spot. At its head stands a rude wooden slab in which some one (I never could ascertain who) annually cuts a little deeper the wooden cross. The island just appears in the centre of my tent, and fills its narrow opening as I lie in bed. Cogawanna's grave, too, has its mystery and pathos.

Our guides were thorough woodsmen, hunters by instinct as well as experience, and skilled in all branches of wood-craft. They could build a canoe, carve a yoke for the shoulders to carry it on, or fashion a 'dug-out' boat from a log with equal facility. They never get lost as long as they are provided with a compass; and a small axe hanging from the belt, which also holds a hunting-knife, is their chief tool and weapon. They profess contempt for the French-Canadian guides as well as for the Indians. The former are lazy and too often dishonest. Moreover, they have indifferent lasting powers. The Indians, on the other hand, as guides, are untrustworthy in another sense. They are paid by the day, and the longer the trip lasts the more money they make. The consequence is, they keep their hunting-party a safe distance from the game as long as possible. It is always the next day or the day after that they promise to discover it. In this way the inexperienced hunter who relies upon their tender mercies often goes home with a poor bag – just enough to keep up the Indian's reputation (and therefore income) as a game-finder – when he might have had twice the sport. The Indians then report as quickly as possible to the nearest station of the Hudson's Bay Company where the game are lying, and receive orders to go out again and bring back the hides and furs, for which they of course are paid commissions. As guides they generally are paid, with the French Canucks, six shillings a day. Our men, who came from the Adirondack Mountains (New York State), received twice as much; and they enjoyed the hunting as much as we did!

They are rarely willing, however, to go on an expedition into the woods without plenty of whisky. Our chief guide, as soon as we got into camp, made a 'cache' of the bottles somewhere in the dense brush behind the tents, and thus controlled the quantity consumed. The other fellows never knew where it was. When more was wanted he would only get it at night. Taking a lantern, he would pretend to search among the trees for ten minutes or more, and though the others watched him carefully from a distance, they never could tell when or where he picked it up. Yet he always returned with a bottle.

There was a spawning-bed just opposite our camp, and the speckled and salmon trout fairly swarmed over it. The water was shallow and covered a nice sandy bottom. At night, when the moon was on the water, it was a sight worth observing to see the hundreds of scaly backs sliding and slithering over one another just beneath the surface. A sudden spurt in the canoe often brought the fish knocking and tumbling against its thin sides. The paddles struck them at every stroke.

There were wolves in the neighbourhood, and the lady of the party, an unerring shot and enthusiastic hunter, held these creatures in special abhorrence. She hated to hear them bark. Several nights running some animal had been heard sniffing and snuffing round their tent. The ground was too bare and hard to leave any tracks, and the opinion was divided between a wolf, a bear, and a porcupine. 'It seems to be a largish animal,' she said.

Just as I was dozing off one night, after a hard day's hunting, I heard voices in the tent next to me.

'There's that thing again,' in the lady's voice. 'You *must* get up and see what it is.'

'Oh! It's nothing but a silly porcupine,' growled the husband. It was a cold night, and those camp-beds are warm and cosy, besides being hard to remake.

'But it's trying to get in.'

'That's no reason why I should get out, though.'

However, the lady thought it was, so after a few more growls he got out of bed, and peeped through the opening of the tent. The moon shone brightly, but only served to make the shadows beneath the trees the darker.

'Take the gun.'

'I've got it. Give me the lantern. I hope the beast won't go for my legs, whatever it is.'

'Put on your top-boots, then.'

A sound of laughter came from the guides' tent beyond. Evidently they were listening as attentively as I was. There were manifold sounds of preparation, and in due course the brave husband, in pyjamas, top-boots, red woollen nightcap, and pea-jacket, issued forth into the cold night. The lantern swung over his arm, and the loaded rifle was pointed. His footsteps were soon lost in the silence, and I lay and listened in my sleeping-bag, praying devoutly that he would not aim hastily and send a bullet whizzing through my canvas or my skin. Suddenly there was a shout, 'I see it!' and the next instant the rifle cracked. 'It's a skunk!' he cried with a roar of laughter. And that's all it was. But the guides thought a good deal of that skunk. The wind was blowing in their direction, and the whole benefit of the penetrating and offensive odour of that otherwise harmless little animal was wafted into their tent. They got up and burned the body – but you cannot burn the stink of a skunk. The language of the guides at intervals during the night was fully as picturesque as the other surroundings of our camp.

Skeleton Lake: An Episode in Camp (1906)

The utter loneliness of our moose-camp on Skeleton Lake had impressed us from the beginning – in the Quebec backwoods, five days by trail and canoe from civilisation – and perhaps the singular name contributed a little to the sensation of eeriness that made itself felt in the camp circle when once the sun was down and the late October mists began rising from the lake and winding their way in among the tree trunks.

For, in these regions, all names of lakes and hills and islands have their origin in some actual event, taking either the name of a chief participant, such as Smith's Ridge, or claiming a place in the map by perpetuating some special feature of the journey or the scenery, such as Long Island, Deep Rapids, or Rainy Lake.

All names thus have their meaning and are usually pretty recently acquired, while the majority are self-explanatory and suggest human and pioneer relations. Skeleton Lake, therefore, was a name full of suggestion, and though none of us knew the origin or the story of its birth, we all were conscious of a certain lugubrious atmosphere that haunted its shores and islands, and but for the evidences of recent moose tracks in its neighbourhood we should probably have pitched our tents elsewhere.

For several hundred miles in any direction we knew of only one other party of whites. They had journeyed up on the train with us, getting in at North Bay, and hailing from Boston way. A common goal and object had served by way of introduction. But the acquaintance had made little progress. This noisy, aggressive Yankee did not suit our fancy much as a possible neighbour, and it was only a slight intimacy between his chief guide, Jake the Swede, and one of our men that kept the thing going at all. They went into camp on Beaver Creek, fifty miles and more to the west of us.

But that was six weeks ago, and seemed as many months, for days and nights pass slowly in these solitudes and the scale of time changes wonderfully. Our men always seemed to know by instinct pretty well 'whar them other fellows was movin',' but in the interval no one had come across their trails, or once so much as heard their rifle shots.

Our little camp consisted of the professor, his wife, a splendid shot and keen woods-woman, and myself. We had a guide apiece, and hunted daily in pairs from before sunrise till dark.

It was our last evening in the woods, and the professor was lying in my little wedge tent, discussing the dangers of hunting alone in couples in this way. The flap of the tent hung back and let in fragrant odours of cooking over an open wood fire; everywhere there were bustle and preparation, and one canoe already lay packed with moose horns, her nose pointing southwards.

'If an accident happened to one of them,' he was saying, 'the survivor's story when he returned to camp would be entirely unsupported evidence, wouldn't it? Because, you see —'

And he went on laying down the law after the manner of professors, until I became so bored that my attention began to wander to pictures and memories of the scenes we were just about to leave: Garden Lake, with its hundred islands; the rapids out of Round Pond; the countless vistas of forest, crimson and gold in the autumn sunshine; and the starlit nights we had spent watching in cold, cramped positions for the wary moose on lonely lakes among the hills. The hum of the professor's voice in time grew more soothing. A nod or a grunt was all the reply he looked for. Fortunately, he loathed interruptions. I think I could almost have gone to sleep under his very nose; perhaps I did sleep for a brief interval.

Then it all came about so quickly, and the tragedy of it was so unexpected and painful, throwing our peaceful camp into momentary confusion, that now it all seems to have happened with the uncanny swiftness of a dream.

First, there was the abrupt ceasing of the droning voice, and then the running of quick little steps over the pine needles, and the confusion of men's voices; and the next instant the professor's wife was at the tent door, hatless, her face white, her hunting bloomers bagging at the wrong places, a rifle in her hand, and her words running into one another anyhow.

'Quick, Harry! It's Rushton. I was asleep and it woke me. Something's happened. You must deal with it!'

In a second we were outside the tent with our rifles.

'My God!' I heard the professor exclaim, as if he had first made the discovery. 'It *is* Rushton!'

I saw the guides helping – dragging – a man out of a canoe. A brief space of deep silence followed in which I heard only the waves from the canoe washing up on the sand; and then, immediately after, came the voice of a man talking with amazing rapidity and with odd gaps between his words. It was Rushton telling his story, and the tones of his voice, now whispering, now almost shouting, mixed with sobs and solemn oaths and frequent appeals to the Deity, somehow or other struck the false note at the very start, and before any of us guessed or knew anything at all. Something moved secretly between his words, a shadow veiling the stars, destroying the peace of our little camp, and touching us all personally with an undefinable sense of horror and distrust.

I can see that group to this day, with all the detail of a good photograph: standing half-way between the firelight and the darkness, a slight mist rising from the lake, the frosty stars, and our men, in silence that was all sympathy, dragging Rushton across the rocks towards the camp fire. Their moccasins crunched on the sand and slipped several times on the stones beneath the weight of the limp, exhausted body, and I can still see every inch of the pared cedar branch he had used for a paddle on that lonely and dreadful journey.

But what struck me most, as it struck us all, was the limp exhaustion of his body compared to the strength of his utterance and the tearing rush of his words. A vigorous driving-power was there at work, forcing out the tale, red-hot and throbbing, full of discrepancies and the strangest contradictions; and the nature of this driving-power I first began to appreciate when they had lifted him into the circle of firelight and I saw his face, grey under the tan, terror in the eyes, tears too, hair and beard awry, and listened to the wild stream of words pouring forth without ceasing.

I think we all understood then, but it was only after many years that anyone dared to confess what he thought.

There was Matt Morris, my guide; Silver Fizz, whose real name was unknown, and who bore the title of his favourite drink; and huge Hank Milligan – all ears and kind intention; and there was Rushton, pouring out his ready-made tale, with ever-shifting eyes, turning from face to face, seeking confirmation of details none had witnessed but himself – and *one other.*

Silver Fizz was the first to recover from the shock of the thing, and to realise, with the natural sense of chivalry common to most genuine back-woodsmen, that the man was at a terrible disadvantage. At any rate, he was the first to start putting the matter to rights.

'Never mind telling it just now,' he said in a gruff voice, but with real gentleness; 'get a bite t'eat first and then let her go afterwards. Better have a horn of whisky too. It ain't all packed yet, I guess.'

'Couldn't eat or drink a thing,' cried the other. 'Good Lord, don't you see, man, I want to *talk* to someone first? I want to get it out of me to someone who can answer – answer. I've had nothing but trees to talk with for three days, and I can't carry it alone any longer. Those cursed, silent trees – I've told it 'em a thousand times. Now, just see here, it was this way. When we started out from camp —'

He looked fearfully about him, and we realised it was useless to stop him. The story was bound to come, and come it did.

Now, the story itself was nothing out of the way; such tales are told by the dozen round any camp fire where men who have knocked about in the woods are in the circle. It was the way he told it that made our flesh creep. He was near the truth all along, but he was skimming it, and the skimming took off the cream that might have saved his soul.

Of course, he smothered it in words – odd words, too – melodramatic, poetic, out-of-the-way words that lie just on the edge of frenzy. Of course, too, he kept asking us each in turn, scanning our faces with those restless, frightened eyes of his, 'What would *you* have done?' 'What else could I do?' and 'Was that *my* fault?' But that was nothing, for he was no milk-and-water fellow who dealt in hints and suggestions; he told his story boldly, forcing his conclusions upon us as if we had been so many wax cylinders of a phonograph that would repeat accurately what had been told us, and these questions I have mentioned he used to emphasise any special point that he seemed to think required such emphasis.

The fact was, however, the picture of what had actually happened was so vivid still in his own mind that it reached ours by a process of telepathy which he could not control or prevent. All through his true-false words this picture stood forth in fearful detail against the shadows behind him. He could not veil, much less obliterate, it. We knew; and, I always thought, *he knew that we knew*.

The story itself, as I have said, was sufficiently ordinary. Jake and himself, in a nine-foot canoe, had upset in the middle of a lake, and had held hands across the upturned craft for several hours, eventually cutting holes in her ribs to stick their arms through and grasp hands lest the numbness of the cold water should overcome them. They were miles from shore, and the wind was drifting them down upon a little island. But when they got within a few hundred yards of the island, they realised to their horror that they would after all drift past it.

It was then the quarrel began. Jake was for leaving the canoe and swimming. Rushton believed in waiting till they actually had passed the island and were sheltered from the wind. Then they could make the island easily by swimming, canoe and all. But Jake refused to give in, and after a short struggle – Rushton admitted there was a struggle – got free from the canoe – and disappeared *without a single cry*.

Rushton held on and proved the correctness of his theory, and finally made the island, canoe and all, after being in the water over five hours. He described to us how he crawled up on to the shore, and fainted at once, with his feet lying half in the water; how lost and terrified he felt upon regaining consciousness in the dark; how the canoe had drifted away and his extraordinary luck in finding it caught again at the end of the island by a projecting cedar branch. He told us that the little axe – another bit of real luck – had caught in the thwart when the canoe turned over, and how the little bottle in his pocket holding the emergency matches was whole and dry. He made a blazing fire and searched the island from end to end, calling upon Jake in the darkness, but getting no answer; till, finally, so many half-drowned men seemed to come crawling out of the water on to the rocks, and vanish among the shadows when he came up with them, that he lost his nerve completely and returned to lie down by the fire till the daylight came.

He then cut a bough to replace the lost paddles, and after one more useless search for his lost companion, he got into the canoe, fearing every moment he would upset again, and crossed over to the mainland. He knew roughly the position of our camping place, and after paddling day and night, and making many weary portages, without food or covering, he reached us two days later.

This, more or less, was the story, and we, knowing whereof he spoke, knew that every word was literally true, and at the same time went to the building up of a hideous and prodigious lie.

Once the recital was over, he collapsed, and Silver Fizz, after a general expression of sympathy from the rest of us, came again to the rescue.

'But now, Mister, you just *got* to eat and drink whether you've a mind to, or no.'

And Matt Morris, cook that night, soon had the fried trout and bacon, and the wheat cakes and hot coffee passing round a rather silent and oppressed circle. So we ate round the fire, ravenously, as we had eaten every night for the past six weeks, but with this difference: that there was one among us who was more than ravenous – and he gorged.

In spite of all our devices he somehow kept himself the centre of observation. When his tin mug was empty, Morris instantly passed the tea-pail; when he began to mop up the bacon grease with the dough on his fork, Hank reached out for the frying pan; and the can of steaming boiled potatoes was always by his side. And there was another difference as well: he was sick, terribly sick before the meal was over, and this sudden nausea after food was more eloquent than words of what the man had passed through on his dreadful, foodless, ghost-haunted journey of forty miles to our camp. In the darkness he thought he would go crazy, he said. There were voices in the trees, and figures were always lifting themselves out of the water, or from behind boulders, to look at him and make awful signs. Jake constantly peered at him through the underbrush, and everywhere the shadows were moving, with eyes, footsteps, and following shapes.

We tried hard to talk of other things, but it was no use, for he was bursting with the rehearsal of his story and refused to allow himself the chances we were so willing and anxious to grant him. After a good night's rest he might have had more self-control and better judgment, and would probably have acted differently. But, as it was, we found it impossible to help him.

Once the pipes were lit, and the dishes cleared away, it was useless to pretend any longer. The sparks from the burning logs zigzagged upwards into a sky brilliant with stars. It was all wonderfully still and peaceful, and the forest odours floated to us on the sharp autumn air. The cedar fire smelt sweet and we could just hear the gentle wash of tiny waves along the shore. All was calm, beautiful, and remote from the world of men and passion. It was, indeed, a night to touch the soul, and yet, I think, none of us heeded these things. A bull-moose might almost have thrust his great head over our shoulders and have escaped unnoticed. The death of Jake the Swede, with its sinister setting, was the real presence that held the centre of the stage and compelled attention.

'You won't p'raps care to come along, Mister,' said Morris, by way of a beginning; 'but I guess I'll go with one of the boys here and have a hunt for it.'

'Sure,' said Hank. 'Jake an' I done some biggish trips together in the old days, and I'll do that much for'm.'

'It's deep water, they tell me, round them islands,' added Silver Fizz; 'but we'll find it, sure pop – if it's thar.'

They all spoke of the body as 'it.'

There was a minute or two of heavy silence, and then Rushton again burst out with his story in almost the identical words he had used before. It was almost as if he had learned it by heart. He wholly failed to appreciate the efforts of the others to let him off.

Silver Fizz rushed in, hoping to stop him, Morris and Hank closely following his lead.

'I once knew another travellin' partner of his,' he began quickly; 'used to live down Moosejaw Rapids way —'

'Is that so?' said Hank.

'Kind o' useful sort of feller,' chimed in Morris.

All the idea the men had was to stop the tongue wagging before the discrepancies became so glaring that we should be forced to take notice of them, and ask questions. But, just as well try to stop an angry bull-moose on the run, or prevent Beaver Creek freezing in mid-winter by throwing in pebbles near the shore. Out it came! And, though the discrepancy this time was insignificant, it somehow brought us all in a second face to face with the inevitable and dreaded climax.

'And so I tramped all over that little bit of an island, hoping he might somehow have gotten in without my knowing it, and always thinking I *heard that awful last cry of his* in the darkness – and then the night dropped down impenetrably, like a damn thick blanket out of the sky, and —'

All eyes fell away from his face. Hank poked up the logs with his boot, and Morris seized an ember in his bare fingers to light his pipe, although it was already emitting clouds of smoke. But the professor caught the ball flying.

'I thought you said he sank without a cry,' he remarked quietly, looking straight up into the frightened face opposite, and then riddling mercilessly the confused explanation that followed.

The cumulative effect of all these forces, hitherto so rigorously repressed, now made itself felt, and the circle spontaneously broke up, everybody moving at once by a common instinct. The professor's wife left the party abruptly, with excuses about an early start next morning. She first shook hands with Rushton, mumbling something about his comfort in the night.

The question of his comfort, however, devolved by force of circumstances upon myself, and he shared my tent. Just before wrapping up in my double blankets – for the night was bitterly cold – he turned and began to explain that he had a habit of talking in his sleep and hoped I would wake him if he disturbed me by doing so.

Well, he did talk in his sleep – and it disturbed me very much indeed. The anger and violence of his words remain with me to this day, and it was clear in a minute that he was living over again some portion of the scene upon the lake. I listened, horror-struck, for a moment or two, and then understood that I was face to face with one of two alternatives: I must continue an unwilling eavesdropper, or I must waken him. The former was impossible for me, yet I shrank from the latter with the greatest repugnance; and in my dilemma I saw the only way out of the difficulty and at once accepted it.

Cold though it was, I crawled stealthily out of my warm sleeping-bag and left the tent, intending to keep the old fire alight under the stars and spend the remaining hours till daylight in the open.

As soon as I was out I noticed at once another figure moving silently along the shore. It was Hank Milligan, and it was plain enough what he was doing: he was examining the holes that had been cut in the upper ribs of the canoe. He looked half ashamed when I came up with him, and mumbled something about not being able to sleep for the cold. But, there, standing together beside the over-turned canoe, we both saw that the holes were far too small for a man's hand and arm and could not possibly have been cut by two men hanging on for their lives in deep water. Those holes had been made afterwards.

Hank said nothing to me and I said nothing to Hank, and presently he moved off to collect logs for the fire, which needed replenishing, for it was a piercingly cold night and there were many degrees of frost.

Three days later Hank and Silver Fizz followed with stumbling footsteps the old Indian trail that leads from Beaver Creek to the southwards. A hammock was slung between them, and it weighed heavily. Yet neither of the men complained; and, indeed, speech between them was almost nothing. Their thoughts, however, were exceedingly busy, and the terrible secret of the woods which formed their burden weighed far more heavily than the uncouth, shifting mass that lay in the swinging hammock and tugged so severely at their shoulders.

They had found 'it' in four feet of water not more than a couple of yards from the lee shore of the island. And in the back of the head was a long, terrible wound which no man could possibly have inflicted upon himself.

The Wolves of God (1921)

1

As the little steamer entered the bay of Kettletoft in the Orkneys the beach at Sanday appeared so low that the houses almost seemed to be standing in the water; and to the big, dark man leaning over the rail of the upper deck the sight of them came with a pang of mingled pain and pleasure. The scene, to his eyes, had not changed. The houses, the low shore, the flat treeless country beyond, the vast open sky, all looked exactly the same as when he left the island thirty years ago to work for the Hudson Bay Company in distant N W Canada. A lad of eighteen then, he was now a man of forty-eight, old for his years, and this was the home-coming he had so often dreamed about in the lonely wilderness of trees where he had spent his life. Yet his grim face wore an anxious rather than a tender expression. The return was perhaps not quite as he had pictured it.

Jim Peace had not done too badly, however, in the Company's service. For an islander, he would be a rich man now; he had not married, he had saved the greater part of his salary, and even in the far-away Post where he had spent so many years there had been occasional opportunities of the kind common to new, wild countries where life and law are in the making. He had not hesitated to take them. None of the big Company Posts, it was true, had come his way, nor had he risen very high in the service; in another two years his turn would have come, yet he had left of his own accord before those two years were up. His decision, judging by the strength in the features, was not due to impulse; the move had been deliberately weighed and calculated; he had renounced his opportunity after full reflection. A man with those steady eyes, with that square jaw and determined mouth, certainly did not act without good reason.

A curious expression now flickered over his weather-hardened face as he saw again his childhood's home, and the return, so often dreamed about, actually took place at last. An uneasy light flashed for a moment in the deep-set grey eyes, but was quickly gone again, and the tanned visage recovered its accustomed look of stern composure. His keen sight took in a dark knot of figures on the landing-pier – his brother, he knew, among them. A wave of home-sickness swept over him. He longed to see his brother again, the old farm, the sweep of open country, the sand-dunes, and the breaking seas. The smell of long-forgotten days came to his nostrils with its sweet, painful pang of youthful memories.

How fine, he thought, to be back there in the old familiar fields of childhood, with sea and sand about him instead of the smother of endless woods that ran a thousand miles without a break. He was glad in particular that no trees were visible, and that rabbits scampering among the dunes were the only wild animals he need ever meet …

Those thirty years in the woods, it seemed, oppressed his mind; the forests, the countless multitudes of trees, had wearied him. His nerves, perhaps, had suffered finally. Snow, frost and sun, stars, and the wind had been his companions during the long days and endless nights in his lonely Post, but chiefly – trees. Trees, trees, trees! On the whole, he had preferred them in stormy weather, though, in another way, their rigid hosts, 'mid the deep silence of still days, had been equally oppressive. In the clear sunlight of a windless day they assumed a waiting, listening, watching aspect that had something spectral in it, but when in motion – well, he preferred a moving animal to one that stood stock-still and stared. Wind, moreover, in a million trees, even the lightest breeze, drowned all other sounds – the howling of the wolves, for instance, in winter, or the ceaseless harsh barking of the husky dogs he so disliked.

Even on this warm September afternoon a slight shiver ran over him as the background of dead years loomed up behind the present scene. He thrust the picture back, deep down inside himself. The self-control, the strong, even violent will that the face betrayed, came into operation instantly. The background was background; it belonged to what was past, and the past was over and done with. It was dead. Jim meant it to stay dead.

The figure waving to him from the pier was his brother. He knew Tom instantly; the years had dealt easily with him in this quiet island; there was no startling, no unkindly change, and a deep emotion, though unexpressed, rose in his heart. It was good to be home again, he realized, as he sat presently in the cart, Tom holding the reins, driving slowly back to the farm at the north end of the island. Everything he found familiar, yet at the same time strange. They passed the school where he used to go as a little bare-legged boy; other boys were now learning their lessons exactly as he used to do. Through the open window he could hear the droning voice of the schoolmaster, who, though invisible, wore the face of Mr Lovibond, his own teacher.

'Lovibond?' said Tom, in reply to his question. 'Oh, he's been dead these twenty years. He went south, you know – Glasgow, I think it was, or Edinburgh. He got typhoid.'

Stands of golden plover were to be seen as of old in the fields, or flashing overhead in swift flight with a whir of wings, wheeling and turning together like one huge bird. Down on the empty shore a curlew cried. Its piercing note rose clear above the noisy clamour of the gulls. The sun played softly on the quiet sea, the air was keen but pleasant, the tang of salt mixed sweetly with the clean smells of open country that he knew so well. Nothing of essentials had changed, even the low clouds beyond the heaving uplands were the clouds of childhood.

They came presently to the sand-dunes, where rabbits sat at their burrow-mouths, or ran helter-skelter across the road in front of the slow cart.

'They're safe till the colder weather comes and trapping begins,' he mentioned. It all came back to him in detail.

'And they know it, too – the canny little beggars,' replied Tom. 'Any rabbits out where you've been?' he asked casually.

'Not to hurt you,' returned his brother shortly.

Nothing seemed changed, although everything seemed different. He looked upon the old, familiar things, but with other eyes. There were, of course, changes, alterations, yet so slight, in a way so odd and curious, that they evaded him; not being of the physical order, they reported to his soul, not to his mind. But his soul, being troubled, sought to deny the changes; to admit them meant to admit a change in himself he had determined to conceal even if he could not entirely deny it.

'Same old place, Tom,' came one of his rare remarks. 'The years ain't done much to it.' He looked into his brother's face a moment squarely. 'Nor to you, either, Tom,' he added, affection and tenderness just touching his voice and breaking through a natural reserve that was almost taciturnity.

His brother returned the look; and something in that instant passed between the two men, something of understanding that no words had hinted at, much less expressed. The tie was real, they loved each other, they were loyal, true, steadfast fellows. In youth they had known no secrets. The shadow that now passed and vanished left a vague trouble in both hearts.

'The forests,' said Tom slowly, 'have made a silent man of you, Jim. You'll miss them here, I'm thinking.'

'Maybe,' was the curt reply, 'but I guess not.'

His lips snapped to as though they were of steel and could never open again, while the tone he used made Tom realize that the subject was not one his brother cared to talk about particularly. He was surprised, therefore, when, after a pause, Jim returned to it of his own accord. He was sitting a little sideways as he spoke, taking in the scene with hungry eyes. 'It's a queer thing,' he observed, 'to look round and see nothing but clean empty land, and not a single tree in sight. You see, it don't look natural quite.'

Again his brother was struck by the tone of voice, but this time by something else as well he could not name. Jim was excusing himself, explaining. The manner, too, arrested him. And thirty years disappeared as though they had not been, for it was thus Jim acted as a boy when there was something unpleasant he had to say and wished to get it over. The tone, the gesture, the manner, all were there. He was edging up to something he wished to say, yet dared not utter.

'You've had enough of trees then?' Tom said sympathetically, trying to help, 'and things?'

The instant the last two words were out he realized that they had been drawn from him instinctively, and that it was the anxiety of deep affection which had prompted them. He had guessed without knowing he had guessed, or rather, without intention or attempt to guess. Jim had a secret. Love's clairvoyance had discovered it, though not yet its hidden terms.

'I have —' began the other, then paused, evidently to choose his words with care. 'I've had enough of trees.' He was about to speak of something that his brother had unwittingly touched upon in his chance phrase, but instead of finding the words he sought, he gave a sudden start, his breath caught sharply. 'What's that?' he exclaimed, jerking his body round so abruptly that Tom automatically pulled the reins. 'What is it?'

'A dog barking,' Tom answered, much surprised. 'A farm dog barking. Why? What did you think it was?' he asked, as he flicked the horse to go on again. 'You made me jump,' he added, with a laugh. 'You're used to huskies, ain't you?'

'It sounded so – not like a dog, I mean,' came the slow explanation. 'It's long since I heard a sheep-dog bark, I suppose it startled me.'

'Oh, it's a dog all right,' Tom assured him comfortingly, for his heart told him infallibly the kind of tone to use. And presently, too, he changed the subject in his blunt, honest fashion, knowing that, also, was the right and kindly thing to do. He pointed out the old farms as they drove along, his brother silent again, sitting stiff and rigid at his side. 'And it's good to have you back, Jim, from those outlandish places. There are not too many of the family left now – just you and I, as a matter of fact.'

'Just you and I,' the other repeated gruffly, but in a sweetened tone that proved he appreciated the ready sympathy and tact. 'We'll stick together, Tom, eh? Blood's thicker than water, ain't it? I've learnt that much, anyhow.'

The voice had something gentle and appealing in it, something his brother heard now for the first time. An elbow nudged into his side, and Tom knew the gesture was not solely a sign of affection, but grew partly also from the comfort born of physical contact when the heart is anxious. The touch, like the last words, conveyed an appeal for help. Tom was so surprised he couldn't believe it quite.

Scared! Jim scared! The thought puzzled and afflicted him who knew his brother's character inside out, his courage, his presence of mind in danger, his resolution. Jim frightened seemed an impossibility, a contradiction in terms; he was the kind of man who did not know the meaning of fear, who shrank from nothing, whose spirits rose highest when things appeared most hopeless. It must, indeed, be an uncommon, even a terrible danger that could shake such nerves; yet Tom saw the signs and read them clearly. Explain them he could not, nor did he try. All he knew with certainty was that his brother, sitting now beside him in the cart, hid a secret terror in his heart. Sooner or later, in his own good time, he would share it with him.

He ascribed it, this simple Orkney farmer, to those thirty years of loneliness and exile in wild desolate places, without companionship, without the society of women, with only Indians, husky dogs, a few trappers or fur-dealers like himself, but none of the wholesome, natural influences that sweeten life within reach. Thirty years was a long, long time. He began planning schemes to help. Jim must see people as much as possible, and his mind ran quickly over the men and women available. In women the neighbourhood was not rich, but there were several men of the right sort who might be useful, good fellows all. There was John Rossiter, another old Hudson Bay man, who had been factor at Cartwright, Labrador, for many years, and had returned long ago to spend his last days in civilization. There was Sandy McKay, also back from a long spell of rubber-planting in Malay … Tom was still busy making plans when they reached the old farm and presently sat down to their first meal together since that early breakfast thirty years ago before Jim caught the steamer that bore him off to exile – an exile that now returned him with nerves unstrung and a secret terror hidden in his heart.

'I'll ask no questions,' he decided. 'Jim will tell me in his own good time. And, meanwhile, I'll get him to see as many folks as possible.' He meant it too; yet not only for his brother's sake. Jim's terror was so vivid it had touched his own heart too.

'Ah, a man can open his lungs here and breathe!' exclaimed Jim, as the two came out after supper and stood before the house, gazing across the open country. He drew a deep breath as though to prove his assertion, exhaling with slow satisfaction again. 'It's good to see a clear horizon and to know there's all that water between – between me and where I've been.' He turned his face to watch the plover in the sky, then looked towards the distant shore-line where the sea was just visible in the long evening light. 'There can't be too much water for me,' he added, half to himself. 'I guess they can't cross water – not that much water at any rate.'

Tom stared, wondering uneasily what to make of it.

'At the trees again, Jim?' he said laughingly. He had overheard the last words, though spoken low, and thought it best not to ignore them altogether. To be natural was the right way, he believed, natural and cheery. To make a joke of anything unpleasant, he felt, was to make it less serious. 'I've never seen a tree come across the Atlantic yet, except as a mast – dead,' he added.

'I wasn't thinking of the trees just then,' was the blunt reply, 'but of – something else. The damned trees are nothing, though I hate the sight of 'em. Not of much account, anyway' – as though he compared them mentally with another thing. He puffed at his pipe a moment.

'They certainly can't move,' put in his brother, 'nor swim either.'

'Nor another thing,' said Jim, his voice thick suddenly, but not with smoke, and his speech confused, though the idea in his mind was certainly clear as daylight. 'Things can't hide behind 'em – can they?'

'Not much cover hereabouts, I admit,' laughed Tom, though the look in his brother's eyes made his laughter as short as it sounded unnatural.

'That's so,' agreed the other. 'But what I meant was' – he threw out his chest, looked about him with an air of intense relief, drew in another deep breath, and again exhaled with satisfaction – 'if there are no trees, there's no hiding.'

It was the expression on the rugged, weathered face that sent the blood in a sudden gulping rush from his brother's heart. He had seen men frightened, seen men afraid before they were actually frightened; he had also seen men stiff with terror in the face both of natural and so-called supernatural things; but never in his life before had he seen the look of unearthly dread that now turned his brother's face as white as chalk and yet put the glow of fire in two haunted burning eyes.

Across the darkening landscape the sound of distant barking had floated to them on the evening wind.

'It's only a farm-dog barking.' Yet it was Jim's deep, quiet voice that said it, one hand upon his brother's arm.

'That's all,' replied Tom, ashamed that he had betrayed himself, and realizing with a shock of surprise that it was Jim who now played the rôle of comforter – a startling change in their relations. 'Why, what did you think it was?'

He tried hard to speak naturally and easily, but his voice shook. So deep was the brothers' love and intimacy that they could not help but share.

Jim lowered his great head. 'I thought,' he whispered, his grey beard touching the other's cheek, 'maybe it was the wolves' – an agony of terror made both voice and body tremble – 'the Wolves of God!'

2

The interval of thirty years had been bridged easily enough; it was the secret that left the open gap neither of them cared or dared to cross. Jim's reason for hesitation lay within reach of guesswork, but Tom's silence was more complicated.

With strong, simple men, strangers to affectation or pretence, reserve is a real, almost a sacred thing. Jim offered nothing more; Tom asked no single question. In the latter's mind lay, for one thing, a singular intuitive certainty: that if he knew the truth he would lose his brother. How, why, wherefore, he had no notion; whether by death, or because, having told an awful thing, Jim would hide – physically or mentally – he knew not, nor even asked himself. No subtlety lay in Tom, the Orkney farmer. He merely felt that a knowledge of the truth involved separation which was death.

Day and night, however, that extraordinary phrase which, at its first hearing, had frozen his blood, ran on beating in his mind. With it came always the original, nameless horror that had held him motionless where he stood, his brother's bearded lips against his ear: *The Wolves of God.* In some dim way, he sometimes felt – tried to persuade himself, rather – the horror did not belong to the phrase alone, but was a sympathetic echo of what Jim felt himself. It had entered his own mind and heart. They had always shared in this same strange, intimate way. The deep brotherly tie accounted for it. Of the possible transference of thought and emotion he knew nothing, but this was what he meant perhaps.

At the same time he fought and strove to keep it out, not because it brought uneasy and distressing feelings to him, but because he did not wish to pry, to ascertain, to discover his brother's secret as by some kind of subterfuge that seemed too near to eavesdropping almost. Also, he wished most earnestly to protect him. Meanwhile, in spite of himself, or perhaps because of himself, he watched his brother as a wild animal watches its young. Jim was the only tie he had on earth. He loved him with a brother's love, and Jim, similarly, he knew, loved him. His job was difficult. Love alone could guide him.

He gave openings, but he never questioned:

'Your letter did surprise me, Jim. I was never so delighted in my life. You had still two years to run.'

'I'd had enough,' was the short reply. 'God, man, it was good to get home again!'

This, and the blunt talk that followed their first meeting, was all Tom had to go upon, while those eyes that refused to shut watched ceaselessly always. There was improvement, unless, which never occurred to Tom, it was self-control; there was no more talk of trees and water, the barking of the dogs passed unnoticed, no reference to the loneliness of the backwoods life passed his lips; he spent his days fishing, shooting, helping with the work of the farm, his evenings smoking over a glass – he was more than temperate – and talking over the days of long ago.

The signs of uneasiness still were there, but they were negative, far more suggestive, therefore, than if open and direct. He desired no company, for instance – an unnatural thing, thought Tom, after so many years of loneliness.

It was this and the awkward fact that he had given up two years before his time was finished, renouncing, therefore, a comfortable pension – it was these two big details that stuck with such unkind persistence in his brother's thoughts. Behind both, moreover, ran ever the strange whispered phrase. What the words meant, or whence they were derived, Tom had no possible inkling. Like the wicked refrain of some forbidden song, they haunted him day and night, even his sleep not free from them entirely. All of which, to the simple Orkney farmer, was so new an experience that he knew not how to deal with it at all. Too strong to be flustered, he was at any rate bewildered. And it was for Jim, his brother, he suffered most.

What perplexed him chiefly, however, was the attitude his brother showed towards old John Rossiter. He could almost have imagined that the two men had met and known each other out in Canada, though Rossiter showed him how impossible that was, both in point of time and of geography as well. He had brought them together within the first few days, and Jim, silent, gloomy, morose, even surly, had eyed him like an enemy. Old Rossiter, the milk of human kindness as thick in his veins as cream, had taken no offence. Grizzled veteran of the wilds, he had served his full term with the Company and now enjoyed his well-earned pension. He was full of stories, reminiscences, adventures of every sort and kind; he knew men and values, had seen strange things that only the true wilderness delivers, and he loved nothing better than to tell them over a glass. He talked with Jim so genially and affably that little response was called for luckily, for Jim was glum and unresponsive almost to rudeness. Old Rossiter noticed nothing. What Tom noticed was, chiefly perhaps, his brother's acute uneasiness. Between his desire to help, his attachment to Rossiter, and his keen personal distress, he knew not what to do or say. The situation was becoming too much for him.

The two families, besides – Peace and Rossiter – had been neighbours for generations, had intermarried freely, and were related in various degrees. He was too fond of his brother to feel ashamed, but he was glad when the visit was over and they were out of their host's house. Jim had even declined to drink with him.

'They're good fellows on the island,' said Tom on their way home, 'but not specially entertaining, perhaps. We all stick together though. You can trust 'em mostly.'

'I never was a talker, Tom,' came the gruff reply. 'You know that.' And Tom, understanding more than he understood, accepted the apology and made generous allowances.

'John likes to talk,' he helped him. 'He appreciates a good listener.'

'It's the kind of talk I'm finished with,' was the rejoinder. 'The Company and their goings-on don't interest me any more. I've had enough.'

Tom noticed other things as well with those affectionate eyes of his that did not want to see yet would not close. As the days drew in, for instance, Jim seemed reluctant to leave the house towards evening. Once the full light of day had passed, he kept indoors. He was eager and ready enough to shoot in the early morning, no matter at what hour he had to get up, but he refused point blank to go with his brother to the lake for an evening flight. No excuse was offered; he simply declined to go.

The gap between them thus widened and deepened, while yet in another sense it grew less formidable. Both knew, that is, that a secret lay between them for the first time in their lives, yet both knew also that at the right and proper moment it would be revealed. Jim only waited till the proper moment came. And Tom understood. His deep, simple love was equal to all emergencies. He respected his brother's reserve. The obvious desire of John Rossiter to talk and ask questions, for instance, he resisted staunchly as far as he was able. Only when he could help and protect his brother did he yield a little. The talk was brief, even monosyllabic; neither the old Hudson Bay fellow nor the Orkney farmer ran to many words:

'He ain't right with himself,' offered John, taking his pipe out of his mouth and leaning forward. 'That's what I don't like to see.' He put a skinny hand on Tom's knee, and looked earnestly into his face as he said it.

'Jim!' replied the other. 'Jim ill, you mean!' It sounded ridiculous.

'His mind is sick.'

'I don't understand,' Tom said, though the truth bit like

rough-edged steel into the brother's heart.

'His soul, then, if you like that better.'

Tom fought with himself a moment, then asked him to be more explicit.

'More'n I can say,' rejoined the laconic old back-woodsman. 'I don't know myself. The woods heal some men and make others sick.'

'Maybe, John, maybe.' Tom fought back his resentment. 'You've lived, like him, in lonely places. You ought to know.' His mouth shut with a snap, as though he had said too much. Loyalty to his suffering brother caught him strongly. Already his heart ached for Jim. He felt angry with Rossiter for his divination, but perceived, too, that the old fellow meant well and was trying to help him. If he lost Jim, he lost the world – his all.

A considerable pause followed, during which both men puffed their pipes with reckless energy. Both, that is, were a bit excited. Yet both had their code, a code they would not exceed for worlds.

'Jim,' added Tom presently, making an effort to meet the sympathy half way, 'ain't quite up to the mark, I'll admit that.'

There was another long pause, while Rossiter kept his eyes on his companion steadily, though without a trace of expression in them – a habit that the woods had taught him.

'Jim,' he said at length, with an obvious effort, 'is skeered. And it's the soul in him that's skeered.'

Tom wavered dreadfully then. He saw that old Rossiter, experienced back-woodsman and taught by the Company as he was, knew where the secret lay, if he did not yet know its exact terms. It was easy enough to put the question, yet he hesitated, because loyalty forbade.

'It's a dirty outfit somewheres,' the old man mumbled to himself.

Tom sprang to his feet. 'If you talk that way,' he exclaimed angrily, 'you're no friend of mine – or his.' His anger gained upon him as he said it. 'Say that again,' he cried, 'and I'll knock your teeth —'

He sat back, stunned a moment.

'Forgive me, John,' he faltered, shamed yet still angry. 'It's pain to me, it's pain. Jim,' he went on, after a long breath and a pull at his glass, 'Jim *is* scared, I know it.' He waited a moment, hunting for the words that he could use without disloyalty. 'But it's nothing he's done himself,' he said, 'nothing to his discredit. I know *that*.'

Old Rossiter looked up, a strange light in his eyes.

'No offence,' he said quietly.

'Tell me what you know,' cried Tom suddenly, standing up again.

The old factor met his eye squarely, steadfastly. He laid his pipe aside.

'D'ye really want to hear?' he asked in a lowered voice. 'Because, if you don't – why, say so right now. I'm all for justice,' he added, 'and always was.'

'Tell me,' said Tom, his heart in his mouth. 'Maybe, if I knew – I might help him.' The old man's words woke fear in him. He well knew his passionate, remorseless sense of justice.

'Help him,' repeated the other. 'For a man skeered in his soul there ain't no help. But – if you want to hear – I'll tell you.'

'Tell me,' cried Tom. 'I *will* help him,' while rising anger fought back rising fear.

John took another pull at his glass.

'Jest between you and me like.'

'Between you and me,' said Tom. 'Get on with it.'

There was a deep silence in the little room. Only the sound of the sea came in, the wind behind it.

'The Wolves,' whispered old Rossiter. 'The Wolves of God.'

Tom sat still in his chair, as though struck in the face. He shivered. He kept silent and the silence seemed to him long and curious. His heart was throbbing, the blood in his veins played strange tricks. All he remembered was that old Rossiter had gone on talking. The voice, however, sounded far away and distant. It was all unreal, he felt, as he went homewards across the bleak, wind-swept upland, the sound of the sea for ever in his ears …

Yes, old John Rossiter, damned be his soul, had gone on talking. He had said wild, incredible things. Damned be his soul! His teeth should be smashed for that. It was outrageous, it was cowardly, it was not true.

'Jim,' he thought, 'my brother, Jim!' as he ploughed his way wearily against the wind. 'I'll teach him. I'll teach him to spread such wicked tales!' He referred to Rossiter. 'God blast these fellows! They come home from their outlandish places and think they can say anything! I'll knock his yellow dog's teeth …!'

While, inside, his heart went quailing, crying for help, afraid.

He tried hard to remember exactly what old John had said. Round Garden Lake – that's where Jim was located in his lonely Post – there was a tribe of Redskins. They were of unusual type. Malefactors among them – thieves, criminals, murderers – were not punished. They were merely turned out by the Tribe to die.

But how?

The Wolves of God took care of them. What were the Wolves of God?

A pack of wolves the Redskins held in awe, a sacred pack, a spirit pack – God curse the man! Absurd, outlandish nonsense! Superstitious humbug! A pack of wolves that punished malefactors, killing but never eating them. 'Torn but not eaten,' the words came back to him, 'white men as well as red. They could even cross the sea ...'

'He ought to be strung up for telling such wild yarns. By God – I'll teach him!'

'Jim! My brother, Jim! It's monstrous!'

But the old man, in his passionate cold justice, had said a yet more terrible thing, a thing that Tom would never forget, as he never could forgive it: 'You mustn't keep him here; you must send him away. We cannot have him on the island.' And for that, though he could scarcely believe his ears, wondering afterwards whether he heard aright, for that, the proper answer to which was a blow in the mouth, Tom knew that his old friendship and affection had turned to bitter hatred.

'If I don't kill him, for that cursed lie, may God – and Jim – forgive me!'

3

It was a few days later that the storm caught the islands, making them tremble in their sea-born bed. The wind tearing over the treeless expanse was terrible, the lightning lit the skies. No such rain had ever been known. The building shook and trembled. It almost seemed the sea had burst her limits, and the waves poured in. Its fury and the noises that the wind made affected both the brothers, but Jim disliked the uproar most. It made him gloomy, silent, morose. It made him – Tom perceived it at once – uneasy. 'Scared in his soul' – the ugly phrase came back to him.

'God save anyone who's out to-night,' said Jim anxiously, as the old farm rattled about his head. Where-upon the door opened as of itself. There was no knock. It flew wide, as if the wind had burst it. Two drenched and beaten figures showed in the gap against the lurid sky – old John Rossiter and Sandy.

They laid their fowling pieces down and took off their capes; they had been up at the lake for the evening flight and six birds were in the game bag. So suddenly had the storm come up that they had been caught before they could get home.

And, while Tom welcomed them, looked after their creature wants, and made them feel at home as in duty bound, no visit, he felt at the same time, could have been less opportune. Sandy did not matter – Sandy never did matter anywhere, his personality being negligible – but John Rossiter was the last man Tom wished to see just then. He hated the man; hated that sense of implacable justice that he knew was in him; with the slightest excuse he would have turned him out and sent him on to his own home, storm or no storm. But Rossiter provided no excuse; he was all gratitude and easy politeness, more pleasant and friendly to Jim even than to his brother. Tom set out the whisky and sugar, sliced the lemon, put the kettle on, and furnished dry coats while the soaked garments hung up before the roaring fire that Orkney makes customary even when days are warm.

'It might be the equinoctials,' observed Sandy, 'if it wasn't late October.' He shivered, for the tropics had thinned his blood.

'This ain't no ordinary storm,' put in Rossiter, drying his drenched boots. 'It reminds me a bit' – he jerked his head to the window that gave seawards, the rush of rain against the panes half drowning his voice – 'reminds me a bit of yonder.' He looked up, as though to find someone to agree with him, only one such person being in the room.

'Sure, it ain't,' agreed Jim at once, but speaking slowly, 'no ordinary storm.' His voice was quiet as a child's. Tom, stooping over the kettle, felt something cold go trickling down his back. 'It's from acrost the Atlantic too.'

'All our big storms come from the sea,' offered Sandy, saying just what Sandy was expected to say. His lank red hair lay matted on his forehead, making him look like an unhappy collie dog.

'There's no hospitality,' Rossiter changed the talk, 'like an islander's,' as Tom mixed and filled the glasses. 'He don't even ask "Say when?"' He chuckled in his beard and turned to Sandy, well pleased with the compliment to his host. 'Now, in Malay,' he added dryly, 'it's probably different, I guess.' And the two men, one from Labrador, the other from the tropics, fell to bantering one another with heavy humour, while Tom made things comfortable and Jim stood silent with his back to the fire. At each blow of the wind that shook the building, a suitable remark was made, generally by Sandy: 'Did you hear that now?' 'Ninety miles an hour at least!' 'Good thing you build solid in this country!' while Rossiter occasionally repeated that it was an 'uncommon storm' and that 'it reminded' him of the northern tempests he had known 'out yonder'.

Tom said little, one thought and one thought only in his heart – the wish that the storm would abate and his guests depart. He felt uneasy about Jim. He hated Rossiter. In the kitchen he had steadied himself already with a good stiff drink, and was now half-way through a second; the feeling was in him that he would need their help before the evening was out. Jim, he noticed, had left his glass untouched. His attention, clearly, went to the wind and the outer night; he added little to the conversation.

'Hark!' cried Sandy's shrill voice. 'Did you hear that? That wasn't wind, I'll swear.' He sat up, looking for all the world like a dog pricking its ears to something no one else could hear.

'The sea coming over the dunes,' said Rossiter. 'There'll be an awful tide to-night and a terrible sea off the Swarf. Moon at the full, too.' He cocked his head sideways to listen. The roaring was tremendous, waves and wind combining with a result that almost shook the ground. Rain hit the glass with incessant volleys like duck shot.

It was then that Jim spoke, having said no word for a long time.

'It's good there's no trees,' he mentioned quietly. 'I'm glad of that.'

'There'd be fearful damage, wouldn't there?' remarked Sandy. 'They might fall on the house too.'

But it was the tone Jim used that made Rossiter turn stiffly in his chair, looking first at the speaker, then at his brother. Tom caught both glances and saw the hard keen glitter in the eyes. This kind of talk, he decided, had got to stop, yet how to stop it he hardly knew, for his were not subtle methods, and rudeness to his guests ran too strong against the island customs. He refilled the glasses, thinking in his blunt fashion how best to achieve his object, when Sandy helped the situation without knowing it.

'That's my first,' he observed, and all burst out laughing. For Sandy's tenth glass was equally his 'first', and he absorbed his liquor like a sponge, yet showed no effects of it until the moment when he would suddenly collapse and sink helpless to the ground. The glass in question, however, was only his third, the final moment still far away.

'Three in one and one in three,' said Rossiter, amid the general laughter, while Sandy, grave as a judge, half emptied it at a single gulp. Good-natured, obtuse as a cart-horse, the tropics, it seemed, had first worn out his nerves, then removed them entirely from his body. 'That's Malay theology, I guess,' finished Rossiter. And the laugh broke out again. Whereupon, setting his glass down, Sandy offered his usual explanation that the hot lands had thinned his blood, that he felt the cold in these 'arctic islands', and that alcohol was a necessity of life with him. Tom, grateful for the unexpected help, encouraged him to talk, and Sandy, accustomed to neglect as a rule, responded readily. Having saved the situation, however, he now unwittingly led it back into the danger zone.

'A night for tales, eh?' he remarked, as the wind came howling with a burst of strangest noises against the house. 'Down there in the States,' he went on, 'they'd say the evil spirits were out. They're a superstitious crowd, the natives. I remember once —' And he told a tale, half foolish, half interesting, of a mysterious track he had seen when following buffalo in the jungle. It ran close to the spoor of a wounded buffalo for miles, a track unlike that of any known animal, and the natives, though unable to name it, regarded it with awe. It was a good sign, a kill was certain. They said it was a spirit track.

'You got your buffalo?' asked Tom.

'Found him two miles away, lying dead. The mysterious spoor came to an end close beside the carcass. It didn't continue.'

'And that reminds me —' began old Rossiter, ignoring Tom's attempt to introduce another subject. He told them of the haunted island at Eagle River, and a tale of the man who would not stay buried on another island off the coast. From that he went on to describe the strange man-beast that hides in the deep forests of Labrador, manifesting but rarely, and dangerous to men who stray too far from camp, men with a passion for wild life overstrong in their blood – the great mythical Wendigo. And while he talked, Tom noticed that Sandy used each pause as a good moment for a drink, but that Jim's glass still remained untouched.

The atmosphere of incredible things, thus, grew in the little room, much as it gathers among the shadows round a forest camp-fire when men who have seen strange places of the world give tongue about them, knowing they will not be laughed at – an atmosphere, once established, it is vain to fight against. The ingrained superstition that hides in every mother's son comes up at such times to breathe. It came up now. Sandy, closer by several glasses to the moment, Tom saw, when he would be suddenly drunk, gave birth again, a tale this time of a Scottish planter who had brutally dismissed a native servant for no other reason than that he disliked him. The man disappeared completely, but the villagers hinted that he would – soon indeed that he had – come back, though 'not quite as he went'. The planter armed, knowing that vengeance might be violent. A black panther, meanwhile, was seen prowling about the bungalow. One night a noise outside his door on the veranda roused him. Just in time to see the black brute leaping over the railings into the compound, he fired, and the beast fell with a savage growl of pain. Help arrived and more shots were fired into the animal, as it lay, mortally wounded already, lashing its tail upon the grass. The lanterns, however, showed that instead of a panther, it was the servant they had shot to shreds.

Sandy told the story well, a certain odd conviction in his tone and manner, neither of them at all to the liking of his host. Uneasiness and annoyance had been growing in Tom for some time already, his inability to control the situation adding to his anger. Emotion was accumulating in him dangerously; it was directed chiefly against Rossiter, who, though saying nothing definite, somehow deliberately encouraged both talk and atmosphere. Given the conditions, it was natural enough the talk should take the turn it did take, but what made Tom more and more angry was that, if Rossiter had not been present, he could have stopped it easily enough. It was the presence of the old Hudson Bay man that prevented his taking decided action. He was afraid of Rossiter, afraid of putting his back up. That was the truth. His recognition of it made him furious.

'Tell us another, Sandy McKay,' said the veteran. 'There's a lot in such tales. They're found the world over – men turning into animals and the like.'

And Sandy, yet nearer to his moment of collapse, but still showing no effects, obeyed willingly. He noticed nothing; the whisky was good, his tales were appreciated, and that sufficed him. He thanked Tom, who just then refilled his glass, and went on with his tale. But Tom, hatred and fury in his heart, had reached the point where he could no longer contain himself, and Rossiter's last words inflamed him. He went over, under cover of a tremendous clap of wind, to fill the old man's glass. The latter refused, covering the tumbler with his big, lean hand. Tom stood over him a moment, lowering his face. 'You keep still,' he whispered ferociously, but so that no one else heard it. He glared into his eyes with an intensity that held danger, and Rossiter, without answering, flung back that glare with equal, but with a calmer, anger.

The wind, meanwhile, had a trick of veering, and each time it shifted, Jim shifted his seat too. Apparently, he preferred to face the sound, rather than have his back to it.

'Your turn now for a tale,' said Rossiter with purpose, when Sandy finished. He looked across at him, just as Jim, hearing the burst of wind at the walls behind him, was in the act of moving his chair again. The same moment the attack rattled the door and windows facing him. Jim, without answering, stood for a moment still as death, not knowing which way to turn.

'It's beatin' up from all sides,' remarked Rossiter, 'like it was goin' round the building.'

There was a moment's pause, the four men listening with awe to the roar and power of the terrific wind. Tom listened too, but at the same time watched, wondering vaguely why he didn't cross the room and crash his fist into the old man's chattering mouth. Jim put out his hand and took his glass, but did not raise it to his lips. And a lull came abruptly in the storm, the wind sinking into a moment's dreadful silence. Tom and Rossiter turned their heads in the same instant and stared into each other's eyes. For Tom the instant seemed enormously prolonged. He realized the challenge in the other and that his rudeness had roused it into action. It had become a contest of wills – Justice battling against Love.

Jim's glass had now reached his lips, and the chattering of his teeth against its rim was audible.

But the lull passed quickly and the wind began again, though so gently at first, it had the sound of innumerable swift footsteps treading lightly, of countless hands fingering the doors and windows, but then suddenly with a mighty shout as it swept against the walls, rushed across the roof and descended like a battering-ram against the farther side.

'God, did you hear that?' cried Sandy. 'It's trying to get in!' and having said it, he sank in a heap beside his chair, all of a sudden completely drunk. 'It's wolves or panthersh,' he mumbled in his stupor on the floor, 'but whatsh's happened to Malay?' It was the last thing he said before unconsciousness took him, and apparently he was insensible to the kick on the head from a heavy farmer's boot. For Jim's glass had fallen with a crash and the second kick was stopped midway. Tom stood spellbound, unable to move or speak, as he watched his brother suddenly cross the room and open a window into the very teeth of the gale.

'Let be! Let be!' came the voice of Rossiter, an authority in it, a curious gentleness too, both of them new. He had risen, his lips were still moving, but the words that issued from them were inaudible, as the wind and rain leaped with a galloping violence into the room, smashing the glass to atoms and dashing a dozen loose objects helter-skelter on to the floor.

'I saw it!' cried Jim, in a voice that rose above the din and clamour of the elements. He turned and faced the others, but it was at Rossiter he looked. 'I saw the leader.' He shouted to make himself heard, although the tone was quiet. 'A splash of white on his great chest. I saw them all!'

At the words, and at the expression in Jim's eyes, old Rossiter, white to the lips, dropped back into his chair as if a blow had struck him. Tom, petrified, felt his own heart stop. For through the broken window, above yet within the wind, came the sound of a wolf-pack running, howling in deep, full-throated chorus, mad for blood. It passed like a whirlwind and was gone. And, of the three men so close together, one sitting and two standing, Jim alone was in that terrible moment wholly master of himself.

Before the others could move or speak, he turned and looked full into the eyes of each in succession. His speech went back to his wilderness days:

'I done it,' he said calmly. 'I killed him – and I got ter go.'

With a look of mystical horror on his face, he took one stride, flung the door wide, and vanished into the darkness.

So quick were both words and action, that Tom's paralysis passed only as the draught from the broken window banged the door behind him. He seemed to leap across the room, old Rossiter, tears on his cheeks and his lips mumbling foolish words, so close upon his heels that the backward blow of fury Tom aimed at his face caught him only in the neck and sent him reeling sideways to the floor instead of flat upon his back.

'Murderer! My brother's death upon you!' he shouted as he tore the door open again and plunged out into the night.

And the odd thing that happened then, the thing that touched old John Rossiter's reason, leaving him from that moment till his death a foolish man of uncertain mind and memory, happened when he and the unconscious, drink-sodden Sandy lay alone together on the stone floor of that farm-house room.

Rossiter, dazed by the blow and his fall, but in full possession of his senses, and the anger gone out of him owing to what he had brought about, this same John Rossiter sat up and saw Sandy also sitting up and staring at him hard. And Sandy was sober as a judge, his eyes and speech both clear, even his face unflushed.

'John Rossiter,' he said, 'it was not God who appointed you executioner. It was the devil.' And his eyes, thought Rossiter, were like the eyes of an angel.

'Sandy McKay,' he stammered, his teeth chattering and breath failing him. 'Sandy McKay!' It was all the words that he could find. But Sandy, already sunk back into his stupor again, was stretched drunk and incapable upon the farm-house floor, and remained in that condition till the dawn.

Jim's body lay hidden among the dunes for many months and in spite of the most careful and prolonged searching it was another storm that laid it bare. The sand had covered it. The clothes were gone, and the flesh, torn but not eaten, was naked to the December sun and wind.

Mountain

The Winter Alps (1910)

With an audacity of outline denied to them in the softer seasons, the Winter Alps rear themselves aloft more grandly self-revealed than at any other time – still with their brave and ancient pretence of being unconquerable. The black and white becomes them best; and they know it: the savage iron black that seems pitiless, and that shining, silvery white that dazzles so piercingly. They are really not summer things at all, but creatures of the winter – the short, brilliant day of icy keenness, and the long night of tempest, wind and drifting snows. Then, at least, clothed so simply in their robes of jet and ermine, they stand in something of their old true majesty, solemn, terrible and great. Summer, as it were, over-dresses them almost, with its skirts of emerald-bright meadows and fringe of purple forests, and all its flying scarves of painted air and mist. The colours are so brilliant, the skies so soft, the flowers climb so high. Then winter comes, undressing them slowly, from the head and shoulders downwards, till they emerge, austere in black and white, naked and unashamed to the skies.

The associations of summer, of course, help very largely to emphasise the contrast. Those stubborn peaks that lie in January beneath forty feet of packed and driven snow, on many a morning in July and August carried twenty tourists prattling to one another of the sunrise, sucking thermos flasks, giggling of the hotel dances to come, not a few having been bodily dragged up, probably, by guides and porters overburdened with the latest appliances for comfort and ease. And the mere thought of them all somehow makes the Alps – dwindle a little. But in winter they become free again, and hold uninterrupted converse with the winds and stars. Their greatest characteristic becomes manifest – their *silence*. For the silence of the Winter Alps is genuinely overwhelming. One feels that the whole world of strife and clamour and bustle, and with it all the clash of vulgar ambitions among men, has fallen away into some void whence resurrection is impossible. Stand upon one of the upper slopes in midwinter and listen: all sound whatsoever has fled away into the remotest corners of the universe. It seems as though such a thing had never existed even, the silence is so enormous, yet at the same time more stimulating than any possible music, more suggestive than the sweetest instrument ever heard. It encompasses the sky and the earth like an immense vacuum.

In summer, there would be bells, bells of goats and cows; voices, voices of climbers, tourists, shepherds; people singing, pipes playing, an occasional horn, and even the puffing and whistling of at least several funiculaires in the valley. But now all these are hushed and gone away – dead. Only silence reigns. Even above, among the precipices and ridges, there is no crack and thunder of falling stones, for the sun has hardly time to melt their fastenings and send them down; no hiss of sliding snow, no roar of avalanches. The very wind, too, whirring over this upper world too softly cushioned with thick snow to permit 'noise' – even the wind is muted and afraid to cry aloud. I know nothing more impressive than the silence that overwhelms the world of these high slopes. The faint 'sishing' of the ski as one flies over the powdery snow becomes almost loud in the ears by comparison. And with this silence that holds true awe comes that other characteristic of the winter alps – their *immobility*; that is, I mean, of course, the immobility of the various items that crowd their surface in summer with movement. All the engines that produce movement have withdrawn deep within their frozen selves, and lie smothered and asleep. The waving grasses are still, beneath three meters of snow; the shelves that in July so busily discharge their weights of snow into the depths stand rigid and fastened to the cliffs by nails of giant ice. Nothing moves, slides, stirs or bends; all is inflexible and fixed. The very trees, loaded with piled-up masses of snow, stand like things of steel pinned motionless against the background of running slope, or blue-black sky. Above all, the tumbling waters that fill the hollows of all these upper valleys with their dance of foam and spray, and with their echoing sweet thunder, are silent and invisible. One cannot even guess the place where they have been. Here sit Silence and Immobility, terrifically enthroned and close to heaven.

The Alps, tinged and tainted in summer with vulgarity, in winter are set free; for the hordes of human beings that scuttle about the fields at their base are ignored by the upper regions. Those few who dare the big peaks are perforce worthy and the bold ski-runners who challenge the hazards of the long, high courses are themselves, like the birds, almost a part of the mountain life. The Alps, as a whole, retire into their ancient splendour.

Yet their winter moods hold moments of tenderness as well, aye, and of colour, too, that at first the strong black and white might seem to deny. The monotony of the snow-world comes to reveal itself as a monotony of surface only, thinly hiding an exquisite variety. The shading is so delicate, however, that it eludes capture by words almost. Half unearthly seem to me sometimes the spread veils of tinted blues, greys and silvers that lie caught upon those leagues of upper snow; half hidden in the cup-like hollows, nestling just beneath the curved lip of some giant drift, or sifted like transparent coloured powder over half a hill when the sun is getting low. Under boulders, often, they lie so deep and thick that one might pick them up with the hands – rich, dark blues that seem almost to hold substance. And the purple troops of them that cloak the snow to the eastward of the pine forests surpass anything that summer can ever dream of, much less give. The long icicles that hang from branch or edge of stones, sparkling in the sun while they drip with sounds like the ticking of a clock, flash with crowded colours of a fairy world. And at the centre of the woods there are blacks that might paint all London, yet suffer no loss.

At dawn, or towards sunset, the magic is bewildering – *saisissant*. The wizardry of dreams lies over the world. Even the village street becomes transfigured. These winter mountains then breathe forth for a brief moment something of the glory the world knew of old in her youth before the coming of men. The ancient gods come close. One feels the awful potentialities of this wonderful white and silent landscape. Into the terms of modern life, however, it is with difficulty, if at all, translatable. Before the task were half completed, someone would come along with weights and scales in either hand and mention casually the exact mass and size and composition of it all – and rob the wondrous scene of half its awe and *all its wonder*.

The gathering of the enormous drifts that begins in November and continues until March is another winter fact that touches the imagination. The sight of these vast curled waves of snow is undeniably impressive – accumulating with every fresh fall for delivery in the spring. The stored power along those huge steep slopes is prodigious, for when it breaks loose with the first *Föhn* wind of April, the trees snap before it like little wooden matches, and the advance wind that heralds its coming can blow a solid châlet flat as a playing-card. One finds these mighty drifts everywhere along the ridges, smooth as a billiard-table along the surface, their projecting cornices running out into extensions that alter the entire shape of the ridge which supports them. They are delicately carved by the wind, curved and lined into beautiful sweeping contours that suggest suddenly arrested movement. Chamois tracks may be seen sometimes up to the very edge – the thin, pointed edge that hangs over the abyss. One thinks of an Atlantic suddenly changed into a solid frozen white, and as one whips by on ski it often seems as though these gigantic waves ran flying after, just about to break and overwhelm the valley. Outlined on a cloudless day against the skies of deep wintry blue – seen thus from below – they present a spectacle of weird beauty indeed. And the silence, this thick, white-coated silence that surrounds them, adds to their singular forms an element of desolate terror that is close to sublimity.

The whole point of the Winter Alps, indeed, seems to me that they then show themselves with immensities of splendour and terror that familiarity of summer days conceals. The more gaunt and sombre peaks, perhaps, change little from one season to another – like the sinister tooth of the old Matterhorn, for instance, that is too steep for snow to gather and change its aspect. But the general run of summits stand aloof in winter with an air of inaccessibility that adds vastly to their essential majesty. The five peaks of the Dent du Midi, to take a well-known group, that smile a welcome to men and women by the score in August, retreat with the advent of the short dark days into a remoter heaven, whence they frown down, genuinely terrific, with an aspect that excites worship rather than attack. In their winter seclusion, dressed in black and white, they belong to the clouds and tempests, rather than to the fields and woods out of which they grow. Watch them, for instance, on a January morning in the dawn, when the wild winds toss the frozen powdery snow hundreds of feet into the air from all their summits, and upon this exaggerated outline of the many-toothed ridge the sunrise strikes in red and gold – and you may see a sight that is not included in the very finest of the summer's repertoire. But it is at night, beneath the moon, that the Winter Alps become really supreme. The shadows are pitch black, the snow dazzling as with a radiance of its own, the 'battlements that on their front bear stars' loom awfully out of the sky. In close-shuttered châlets the peasants sleep. In the brilliant over-heated salons of hotels hundreds of little human beings dance and make music and play bridge. But out there, in this silent world of ice and stars, the enormous mountains dream solemnly upon their ancient thrones, unassailable, alone in the heavens, forgotten. The Alps, in these hours of the long winter night, come magnificently into their own.

The Glamour of the Snow (1911)

1

Hibbert, always conscious of two worlds, was in this mountain village conscious of three. It lay on the slopes of the Valais Alps, and he had taken a room in the little post office, where he could be at peace to write his book, yet at the same time enjoy the winter sports and find companionship in the hotels when he wanted it.

The three worlds that met and mingled here seemed to his imaginative temperament very obvious, though it is doubtful if another mind less intuitively equipped would have seen them so well-defined. There was the world of tourist English, civilised, quasi-educated, to which he belonged by birth, at any rate; there was the world of peasants to which he felt himself drawn by sympathy – for he loved and admired their toiling, simple life; and there was this other – which he could only call the world of Nature. To this last, however, in virtue of a vehement poetic imagination, and a tumultuous pagan instinct fed by his very blood, he felt that most of him belonged. The others borrowed from it, as it were, for visits. Here, with the soul of Nature, hid his central life.

Between all three was conflict – potential conflict. On the skating-rink each Sunday the tourists regarded the natives as intruders; in the church the peasants plainly questioned: 'Why do you come? We are here to worship; you to stare and whisper!' For neither of these two worlds accepted the other. And neither did Nature accept the tourists, for it took advantage of their least mistakes, and indeed, even of the peasant-world 'accepted' only those who were strong and bold enough to invade her savage domain with sufficient skill to protect themselves from several forms of – death.

Now Hibbert was keenly aware of this potential conflict and want of harmony; he felt outside, yet caught by it – torn in the three directions because he was partly of each world, but wholly in only one. There grew in him a constant, subtle effort – or, at least, desire – to unify them and decide positively to which he should belong and live in. The attempt, of course, was largely subconscious. It was the natural instinct of a richly imaginative nature seeking the point of equilibrium, so that the mind could feel at peace and his brain be free to do good work.

Among the guests no one especially claimed his interest. The men were nice but undistinguished – athletic schoolmasters, doctors snatching a holiday, good fellows all; the women, equally various – the clever, the would-be-fast, the dare-to-be-dull, the women 'who understood', and the usual pack of jolly dancing girls and 'flappers'. And Hibbert, with his forty odd years of thick experience behind him, got on well with the lot; he understood them all; they belonged to definite, predigested types that are the same the world over, and that he had met the world over long ago.

But to none of them did he belong. His nature was too 'multiple' to subscribe to the set of shibboleths of any one class. And, since all liked him, and felt that somehow he seemed outside of them – spectator, looker-on – all sought to claim him.

In a sense, therefore, the three worlds fought for him: natives, tourists, Nature ...

It was thus began the singular conflict for the soul of Hibbert. *In* his own soul, however, it took place. Neither the peasants nor the tourists were conscious that they fought for anything. And Nature, they say, is merely blind and automatic.

The assault upon him of the peasants may be left out of account, for it is obvious that they stood no chance of success.

The tourist world, however, made a gallant effort to subdue him to themselves. But the evenings in the hotel, when dancing was not in order, were – English. The provincial imagination was set upon a throne and worshipped heavily through incense of the stupidest conventions possible. Hibbert used to go back early to his room in the post office to work.

'It is a mistake on my part to have *realised* that there is any conflict at all,' he thought, as he crunched home over the snow at midnight after one of the dances. 'It would have been better to have kept outside it all and done my work. Better,' he added, looking back down the silent village street to the church tower, 'and – safer.'

The adjective slipped from his mind before he was aware of it. He turned with an involuntary start and looked about him. He knew perfectly well what it meant – this thought that had thrust its head up from the instinctive region. He understood, without being able to express it fully, the meaning that betrayed itself in the choice of the adjective. For if he had ignored the existence of this conflict he would at the same time have remained outside the arena. Whereas now he had entered the lists. Now this battle for his soul must have issue. And he knew that the spell of Nature was greater for him than all other spells in the world combined – greater than love, revelry, pleasure, greater even than study. He had always been afraid to let himself go. His pagan soul dreaded her terrific powers of witchery even while he worshipped.

The little village already slept. The world lay smothered in snow. The châlet roofs shone white beneath the moon, and pitch-black shadows gathered against the walls of the church. His eye rested a moment on the square stone tower with its frosted cross that pointed to the sky: then travelled with a leap of many thousand feet to the enormous mountains that brushed the brilliant stars. Like a forest rose the huge peaks above the slumbering village, measuring the night and heavens. They beckoned him. And something born of the snowy desolation, born of the midnight and the silent grandeur, born of the great listening hollows of the night, something that lay 'twixt terror and wonder, dropped from the vast wintry spaces down into his heart – and called him. Very softly, unrecorded in any word or thought his brain could compass, it laid its spell upon him. Fingers of snow brushed the surface of his heart. The power and quiet majesty of the winter's night appalled him …

Fumbling a moment with the big unwieldy key, he let himself in and went upstairs to bed. Two thoughts went with him – apparently quite ordinary and sensible ones:

'What fools these peasants are to sleep through such a night!' And the other:

'Those dances tire me. I'll never go again. My work only suffers in the morning.' The claims of peasants and tourists upon him seemed thus in a single instant weakened.

The clash of battle troubled half his dreams. Nature had sent her Beauty of the Night and won the first assault. The others, routed and dismayed, fled far away.

2

'Don't go back to your dreary old post office. We're going to have supper in my room – something hot. Come and join us. Hurry up!'

There had been an ice carnival, and the last party, tailing up the snow-slope to the hotel, called him. The Chinese lanterns smoked and sputtered on the wires; the band had long since gone. The cold was bitter and the moon came only momentarily between high, driving clouds. From the shed where the people changed from skates to snow-boots he shouted something to the effect that he was 'following'; but no answer came; the moving shadows of those who had called were already merged high up against the village darkness. The voices died away. Doors slammed. Hibbert found himself alone on the deserted rink.

And it was then, quite suddenly, the impulse came to – stay and skate alone. The thought of the stuffy hotel room, and of those noisy people with their obvious jokes and laughter, oppressed him. He felt a longing to be alone with the night, to taste her wonder all by himself there beneath the stars, gliding over the ice. It was not yet midnight, and he could skate for half an hour. That supper party, if they noticed his absence at all, would merely think he had changed his mind and gone to bed.

It was an impulse, yes, and not an unnatural one; yet even at the time it struck him that something more than impulse lay concealed behind it. More than invitation, yet certainly less than command, there was a vague queer feeling that he stayed because he had to, almost as though there was something he had forgotten, overlooked, left undone. Imaginative temperaments are often thus; and impulse is ever weakness. For with such ill-considered opening of the doors to hasty action may come an invasion of other forces at the same time – forces merely waiting their opportunity perhaps!

He caught the fugitive warning even while he dismissed it as absurd, and the next minute he was whirling over the smooth ice in delightful curves and loops beneath the moon. There was no fear of collision. He could take his own speed and space as he willed. The shadows of the towering mountains fell across the rink, and a wind of ice came from the forests, where the snow lay ten feet deep. The hotel lights winked and went out. The village slept. The high wire netting could not keep out the wonder of the winter night that grew about him like a presence. He skated on and on, keen exhilarating pleasure in his tingling blood, and weariness all forgotten.

And then, midway in the delight of rushing movement, he saw a figure gliding behind the wire netting, watching him. With a start that almost made him lose his balance – for the abruptness of the new arrival was so unlooked for – he paused and stared. Although the light was dim he made out that it was the figure of a woman and that she was feeling her way along the netting, trying to get in. Against the white background of the snow-field he watched her rather stealthy efforts as she passed with a silent step over the banked-up snow. She was tall and slim and graceful; he could see that even in the dark. And then, of course, he understood. It was another adventurous skater like himself, stolen down unawares from hotel or châlet, and searching for the opening. At once, making a sign and pointing with one hand, he turned swiftly and skated over to the little entrance on the other side.

But, even before he got there, there was a sound on the ice behind him and, with an exclamation of amazement he could not suppress, he turned to see her swerving up to his side across the width of the rink. She had somehow found another way in.

Hibbert, as a rule, was punctilious, and in these free-and-easy places, perhaps, especially so. If only for his own protection he did not seek to make advances unless some kind of introduction paved the way. But for these two to skate together in the semi-darkness without speech, often of necessity brushing shoulders almost, was too absurd to think of. Accordingly he raised his cap and spoke. His actual words he seems unable to recall, nor what the girl said in reply, except that she answered him in accented English with some commonplace about doing figures at midnight on an empty rink. Quite natural it was, and right. She wore grey clothes of some kind, though not the customary long gloves or sweater, for indeed her hands were bare, and presently when he skated with her, he wondered with something like astonishment at their dry and icy coldness.

And she was delicious to skate with – supple, sure, and light, fast as a man yet with the freedom of a child, sinuous and steady at the same time. Her flexibility made him wonder, and when he asked where she had learned she murmured – he caught the breath against his ear and recalled later that it was singularly cold –– that she could hardly tell, for she had been accustomed to the ice ever since she could remember.

But her face he never properly saw. A muffler of white fur buried her neck to the ears, and her cap came over the eyes. He only saw that she was young. Nor could he gather her hotel or châlet, for she pointed vaguely, when he asked her, up the slopes. 'Just over there –' she said, quickly taking his hand again. He did not press her; no doubt she wished to hide her escapade. And the touch of her hand thrilled him more than anything he could remember; even through his thick glove he felt the softness of that cold and delicate touch.

The clouds thickened over the mountains. It grew darker. They talked very little, and did not always skate together. Often they separated, curving about in corners by themselves, but always coming together again in the centre of the rink; and when she left him thus Hibbert was conscious of – yes, of missing her. He found a peculiar satisfaction, almost a fascination, in skating by her side. It was quite an adventure – these two strangers with the ice and snow and night!

Midnight had long since sounded from the old church tower before they parted. She gave the sign, and he skated quickly to the shed, meaning to find a seat and help her take her skates off. Yet when he turned – she had already gone. He saw her slim figure gliding away across the snow . . . and hurrying for the last time round the rink alone he searched in vain for the opening she had twice used in this curious way.

'How very queer!' he thought, referring to the wire netting. 'She must have lifted it and wriggled under . . .!'

Wondering how in the world she managed it, what in the world had possessed him to be so free with her, and who in the world she was, he went up the steep slope to the post office and so to bed, her promise to come again another night still ringing delightfully in his ears. And curious were the thoughts and sensations that accompanied him. Most of all, perhaps, was the half suggestion of some dim memory that he had known this girl before, had met her somewhere, more – that she knew him. For in her voice – a low, soft, windy little voice it was, tender and soothing for all its quiet coldness – there lay some faint reminder of two others he had known, both long since gone: the voice of the woman he had loved, and – the voice of his mother.

But this time through his dreams there ran no clash of battle. He was conscious, rather, of something cold and clinging that made him think of sifting snowflakes climbing slowly with entangling touch and thickness round his feet. The snow, coming without noise, each flake so light and tiny none can mark the spot whereon it settles, yet the mass of it able to smother whole villages, wove through the very texture of his mind – cold, bewildering, deadening effort with its clinging network of ten million feathery touches.

3

In the morning Hibbert realised he had done, perhaps, a foolish thing. The brilliant sunshine that drenched the valley made him see this, and the sight of his work-table with its typewriter, books, papers, and the rest, brought additional conviction. To have skated with a girl alone at midnight, no matter how innocently the thing had come about, was unwise – unfair, especially to her. Gossip in these little winter resorts was worse than in a provincial town. He hoped no one had seen them. Luckily the night had been dark. Most likely none had heard the ring of skates.

Deciding that in future he would be more careful, he plunged into work, and sought to dismiss the matter from his mind.

But in his times of leisure the memory returned persistently to haunt him. When he 'ski-d', 'luged', or danced in the evenings, and especially when he skated on the little rink, he was aware that the eyes of his mind forever sought this strange companion of the night. A hundred times he fancied that he saw her, but always sight deceived him. Her face he might not know, but he could hardly fail to recognise her figure. Yet nowhere among the others did he catch a glimpse of that slim young creature he had skated with alone beneath the clouded stars. He searched in vain. Even his inquiries as to the occupants of the private châlets brought no results. He had lost her. But the queer thing was that he felt as though she were somewhere close; he *knew* she had not really gone. While people came and left with every day, it never once occurred to him that she had left. On the contrary, he felt assured that they would meet again.

This thought he never quite acknowledged. Perhaps it was the wish that fathered it only. And, even when he did meet her, it was a question how he would speak and claim acquaintance, or whether *she* would recognise himself. It might be awkward. He almost came to dread a meeting, though 'dread', of course, was far too strong a word to describe an emotion that was half delight, half wondering anticipation.

Meanwhile the season was in full swing. Hibbert felt in perfect health, worked hard, ski-d, skated, luged, and at night danced fairly often – in spite of his decision. This dancing was, however, an act of subconscious surrender; it really meant he hoped to find her among the whirling couples. He was searching for her without quite acknowledging it to himself; and the hotel-world, meanwhile, thinking it had won him over, teased and chaffed him. He made excuses in a similar vein; but all the time he watched and searched and – waited.

For several days the sky held clear and bright and frosty, bitterly cold, everything crisp and sparkling in the sun; but there was no sign of fresh snow, and the ski-ers began to grumble. On the mountains was an icy crust that made 'running' dangerous; they wanted the frozen, dry, and powdery snow that makes for speed, renders steering easier and falling less severe. But the keen east wind showed no signs of changing for a whole ten days. Then, suddenly, there came a touch of softer air and the weather-wise began to prophesy.

Hibbert, who was delicately sensitive to the least change in earth or sky, was perhaps the first to feel it. Only he did not prophesy. He knew through every nerve in his body that moisture had crept into the air, was accumulating, and that presently a fall would come. For he responded to the moods of Nature like a fine barometer.

And the knowledge, this time, brought into his heart a strange little wayward emotion that was hard to account for – a feeling of unexplained uneasiness and disquieting joy. For behind it, woven through it rather, ran a faint exhilaration that connected remotely somewhere with that touch of delicious alarm, that tiny anticipating 'dread', that so puzzled him when he thought of his next meeting with his skating companion of the night. It lay beyond all words, all telling, this queer relationship between the two; but somehow the girl and snow ran in a pair across his mind.

Perhaps for imaginative writing-men, more than for other workers, the smallest change of mood betrays itself at once. His work at any rate revealed this slight shifting of emotional values in his soul. Not that his writing suffered, but that it altered, subtly as those changes of sky or sea or landscape that come with the passing of afternoon into evening – imperceptibly. A subconscious excitement sought to push outwards and express itself … and, knowing the uneven effect such moods produced in his work, he laid his pen aside and took instead to reading that he had to do.

Meanwhile the brilliance passed from the sunshine, the sky grew slowly overcast; by dusk the mountain tops came singularly close and sharp; the distant valley rose into absurdly near perspective. The moisture increased, rapidly approaching saturation point, when it must fall in snow. Hibbert watched and waited.

And in the morning the world lay smothered beneath its fresh white carpet. It snowed heavily till noon, thickly, incessantly, chokingly, a foot or more; then the sky cleared, the sun came out in splendour, the wind shifted back to the east, and frost came down upon the mountains with its keenest and most biting tooth. The drop in the temperature was tremendous, but the ski-ers were jubilant. Next day the 'running' would be fast and perfect. Already the mass was settling, and the surface freezing into those moss-like, powdery crystals that make the ski run almost of their own accord with the faint 'sishing' as of a bird's wings through the air.

4

That night there was excitement in the little hotel-world, first because there was a *bal costumé*, but chiefly because the new snow had come. And Hibbert went – felt drawn to go; he did not go in costume, but he wanted to talk about the slopes and ski-ing with the other men, and at the same time …

Ah, there was the truth, the deeper necessity that called. For the singular connection between the stranger and the snow again betrayed itself, utterly beyond explanation as before, but vital and insistent. Some hidden instinct in his pagan soul – heaven knows how he phrased it even to himself, if he phrased it at all – whispered that with the snow the girl would be somewhere about, would emerge from her hiding place, would even look for him.

Absolutely unwarranted it was. He laughed while he stood before the little glass and trimmed his moustache, tried to make his black tie sit straight, and shook down his dinner jacket so that it should lie upon the shoulders without a crease. His brown eyes were very bright. 'I look younger than I usually do,' he thought. It was unusual, even significant, in a man who had no vanity about his appearance and certainly never questioned his age or tried to look younger than he was. Affairs of the heart, with one tumultuous exception that left no fuel for lesser subsequent fires, had never troubled him. The forces of his soul and mind not called upon for 'work' and obvious duties, all went to Nature. The desolate, wild places of the earth were what he loved; night, and the beauty of the stars and snow. And this evening he felt their claims upon him mightily stirring. A rising wildness caught his blood, quickened his pulse, woke longing and passion too. But chiefly snow. The snow whirred softly through his thoughts like white, seductive dreams … For the snow had come; and She, it seemed, had somehow come with it – into his mind.

And yet he stood before that twisted mirror and pulled his tie and coat askew a dozen times, as though it mattered. 'What in the world is up with me?' he thought. Then, laughing a little, he turned before leaving the room to put his private papers in order. The green morocco desk that held them he took down from the shelf and laid upon the table. Tied to the lid was the visiting card with his brother's London address 'in case of accident'. On the way down to the hotel he wondered why he had done this, for though imaginative, he was not the kind of man who dealt in presentiments. Moods with him were strong, but ever held in leash.

'It's almost like a warning,' he thought, smiling. He drew his thick coat tightly round the throat as the freezing air bit at him. 'Those warnings one reads of in stories sometimes ...!'

A delicious happiness was in his blood. Over the edge of the hills across the valley rose the moon. He saw her silver sheet the world of snow. Snow covered all. It smothered sound and distance. It smothered houses, streets, and human beings. It smothered – life.

5

In the hall there was light and bustle; people were already arriving from the other hotels and châlets, their costumes hidden beneath many wraps. Groups of men in evening dress stood about smoking, talking 'snow' and 'ski-ing'. The band was tuning up. The claims of the hotel-world clashed about him faintly as of old. At the big glass windows of the verandah, peasants stopped a moment on their way home from the *café* to peer. Hibbert thought laughingly of that conflict he used to imagine. He laughed because it suddenly seemed so unreal. He belonged so utterly to Nature and the mountains, and especially to those desolate slopes where now the snow lay thick and fresh and sweet, that there was no question of a conflict at all. The power of the newly fallen snow had caught him, proving it without effort. Out there, upon those lonely reaches of the moonlit ridges, the snow lay ready – masses and masses of it – cool, soft, inviting. He longed for it. It awaited him. He thought of the intoxicating delight of ski-ing in the moonlight …

Thus, somehow, in vivid flashing vision, he thought of it while he stood there smoking with the other men and talking all the 'shop' of ski-ing.

And, ever mysteriously blended with this power of the snow, poured also through his inner being the power of the girl. He could not disabuse his mind of the insinuating presence of the two together. He remembered that queer skating-impulse of ten days ago, the impulse that had let her in. That any mind, even an imaginative one, could pass beneath the sway of such a fancy was strange enough; and Hibbert, while fully aware of the disorder, yet found a curious joy in yielding to it. This insubordinate centre that drew him towards old pagan beliefs had assumed command. With a kind of sensuous pleasure he let himself be conquered.

And snow that night seemed in everybody's thoughts. The dancing couples talked of it; the hotel proprietors congratulated one another; it meant good sport and satisfied their guests; every one was planning trips and expeditions, talking of slopes and telemarks, of flying speed and distance, of drifts and crust and frost. Vitality and enthusiasm pulsed in the very air; all were alert and active, positive, radiating currents of creative life even into the stuffy atmosphere of that crowded ball-room. And the snow had caused it, the snow had brought it; all this discharge of eager sparkling energy was due primarily to the – Snow.

But in the mind of Hibbert, by some swift alchemy of his pagan yearnings, this energy became transmuted. It rarefied itself, gleaming in white and crystal currents of passionate anticipation, which he transferred, as by a species of electrical imagination, into the personality of the girl – the Girl of the Snow. She somewhere was waiting for him, expecting him, calling to him softly from those leagues of moonlit mountain. He remembered the touch of that cool, dry hand; the soft and icy breath against his cheek; the hush and softness of her presence in the way she came and the way she had gone again – like a flurry of snow the wind sent gliding up the slopes. She, like himself, belonged out there. He fancied that he heard her little windy voice come sifting to him through the snowy branches of the trees, calling his name … that haunting little voice that dived straight to the centre of his life as once, long years ago, two other voices used to do …

But nowhere among the costumed dancers did he see her slender figure. He danced with one and all, distrait and absent, a stupid partner as each girl discovered, his eyes ever turning towards the door and windows, hoping to catch the luring face, the vision that did not come … and at length, hoping even against hope. For the ball-room thinned; groups left one by one, going home to their hotels and châlets; the band tired obviously; people sat drinking lemon-squashes at the little tables, the men mopping their foreheads, everybody ready for bed.

It was close on midnight. As Hibbert passed through the hall to get his overcoat and snow-boots, he saw men in the passage by the 'sport-room', greasing their ski against an early start. Knapsack luncheons were being ordered by the kitchen swing doors. He sighed. Lighting a cigarette a friend offered him, he returned a confused reply to some question as to whether he could join their party in the morning. It seemed he did not hear it properly. He passed through the outer vestibule between the double glass doors, and went into the night.

The man who asked the question watched him go, an expression of anxiety momentarily in his eyes.

'Don't think he heard you,' said another, laughing. 'You've got to shout to Hibbert, his mind's so full of his work.'

'He works too hard,' suggested the first, 'full of queer ideas and dreams.'

But Hibbert's silence was not rudeness. He had not caught the invitation, that was all. The call of the hotel world had faded. He no longer heard it. Another wilder call was sounding in his ears.

For up the street he had seen a little figure moving. Close against the shadows of the baker's shop it glided – white, slim, enticing.

6

And at once into his mind passed the hush and softness of the snow – yet with it a searching, crying wildness for the heights. He knew by some incalculable, swift instinct she would not meet him in the village street. It was not there, amid crowding houses, she would speak to him. Indeed, already she had disappeared, melted from view up the white vista of the moonlit road. Yonder, he divined, she waited where the highway narrowed abruptly into the mountain path beyond the châlets.

It did not even occur to him to hesitate; mad though it seemed, and was – this sudden craving for the heights with her, at least for open spaces where the snow lay thick and fresh – it was too imperious to be denied. He does not remember going up to his room, putting the sweater over his evening clothes, and getting into the fur gauntlet gloves and the helmet cap of wool. Most certainly he has no recollection of fastening on his ski; he must have done it automatically. Some faculty of normal observation was in abeyance, as it were. His mind was out beyond the village – out with the snowy mountains and the moon.

Henri Défago, putting up the shutters over his *café* windows, saw him pass, and wondered mildly: 'Un monsieur qui fait du ski à cette heure! Il est Anglais, donc . . . !' He shrugged his shoulders, as though a man had the right to choose his own way of death. And Marthe Perotti, the hunchback wife of the shoemaker, looking by chance from her window, caught his figure moving swiftly up the road. She had other thoughts, for she knew and believed the old traditions of the witches and snow-beings that steal the souls of men. She had even heard, 'twas said, the dreaded 'synagogue' pass roaring down the street at night, and now, as then, she hid her eyes. 'They've called to him ... and he must go,' she murmured, making the sign of the cross.

But no one sought to stop him. Hibbert recalls only a single incident until he found himself beyond the houses, searching for her along the fringe of forest where the moonlight met the snow in a bewildering frieze of fantastic shadows. And the incident was simply this – that he remembered passing the church. Catching the outline of its tower against the stars, he was aware of a faint sense of hesitation. A vague uneasiness came and went – jarred unpleasantly across the flow of his excited feelings, chilling exhilaration. He caught the instant's discord, dismissed it, and – passed on. The seduction of the snow smothered the hint before he realised that it had brushed the skirts of warning.

And then he saw her. She stood there waiting in a little clear space of shining snow, dressed all in white, part of the moonlight and the glistening background, her slender figure just discernible.

'I waited, for I knew you would come,' the silvery little voice of windy beauty floated down to him. 'You *had* to come.'

'I'm ready,' he answered, 'I knew it too.'

The world of Nature caught him to its heart in those few words – the wonder and the glory of the night and snow. Life leaped within him. The passion of his pagan soul exulted, rose in joy, flowed out to her. He neither reflected nor considered, but let himself go like the veriest schoolboy in the wildness of first love.

'Give me your hand,' he cried, 'I'm coming …!'

'A little farther on, a little higher,' came her delicious answer. 'Here it is too near the village – and the church.'

And the words seemed wholly right and natural; he did not dream of questioning them; he understood that, with this little touch of civilisation in sight, the familiarity he suggested was impossible. Once out upon the open mountains, 'mid the freedom of huge slopes and towering peaks, the stars and moon to witness and the wilderness of snow to watch, they could taste an innocence of happy intercourse free from the dead conventions that imprison literal minds.

He urged his pace, yet did not quite overtake her. The girl kept always just a little bit ahead of his best efforts … And soon they left the trees behind and passed on to the enormous slopes of the sea of snow that rolled in mountainous terror and beauty to the stars. The wonder of the white world caught him away. Under the steady moonlight it was more than haunting. It was a living, white, bewildering power that deliciously confused the senses and laid a spell of wild perplexity upon the heart. It was a personality that cloaked, and yet revealed, itself through all this sheeted whiteness of snow. It rose, went with him, fled before, and followed after. Slowly it dropped lithe, gleaming arms about his neck, gathering him in …

Certainly some soft persuasion coaxed his very soul, urging him ever forwards, upwards, on towards the higher icy slopes. Judgment and reason left their throne, it seemed, completely, as in the madness of intoxication. The girl, slim and seductive, kept always just ahead, so that he never quite came up with her. He saw the white enchantment of her face and figure, something that streamed about her neck flying like a wreath of snow in the wind, and heard the alluring accents of her whispering voice that called from time to time: 'A little farther on, a little higher … Then we'll run home together!'

Sometimes he saw her hand stretched out to find his own, but each time, just as he came up with her, he saw her still in front, the hand and arm withdrawn. They took a gentle angle of ascent. The toil seemed nothing. In this crystal, wine-like air fatigue vanished. The sishing of the ski through the powdery surface of the snow was the only sound that broke the stillness; this, with his breathing and the rustle of her skirts, was all he heard. Cold moonshine, snow, and silence held the world. The sky was black, and the peaks beyond cut into it like frosted wedges of iron and steel. Far below the valley slept, the village long since hidden out of sight. He felt that he could never tire … The sound of the church clock rose from time to time faintly through the air – more and more distant.

'Give me your hand. It's time now to turn back.'

'Just one more slope,' she laughed. 'That ridge above us. Then we'll make for home.' And her low voice mingled pleasantly with the purring of their ski. His own seemed harsh and ugly by comparison.

'But I have never come so high before. It's glorious! This world of silent snow and moonlight – and *you*. You're a child of the snow, I swear. Let me come up – closer – to see your face – and touch your little hand.'

Her laughter answered him.

'Come on! A little higher. Here we're quite alone together.'

'It's magnificent,' he cried. 'But why did you hide away so long? I've looked and searched for you in vain ever since we skated —' he was going to say 'ten days ago', but the accurate memory of time had gone from him; he was not sure whether it was days or years or minutes. His thoughts of earth were scattered and confused.

'You looked for me in the wrong places,' he heard her murmur just above him. 'You looked in places where I never go. Hotels and houses kill me. I avoid them.' She laughed – a fine, shrill, windy little laugh.

'I loathe them too —'

He stopped. The girl had suddenly come quite close. A breath of ice passed through his very soul. She had touched him.

'But this awful cold!' he cried out, sharply, 'this freezing cold that takes me. The wind is rising; it's a wind of ice. Come, let us turn …!'

But when he plunged forward to hold her, or at least to look, the girl was gone again. And something in the way she stood there a few feet beyond, and stared down into his eyes so steadfastly in silence, made him shiver. The moonlight was behind her, but in some odd way he could not focus sight upon her face, although so close. The gleam of eyes he caught, but all the rest seemed white and snowy as though he looked beyond her – out into space …

The sound of the church bell came up faintly from the valley far below, and he counted the strokes – five. A sudden, curious weakness seized him as he listened. Deep within it was, deadly yet somehow sweet, and hard to resist. He felt like sinking down upon the snow and lying there … They had been climbing for five hours … It was, of course, the warning of complete exhaustion.

With a great effort he fought and overcame it. It passed away as suddenly as it came.

'We'll turn,' he said with a decision he hardly felt. 'It will be dawn before we reach the village again. Come at once. It's time for home.'

The sense of exhilaration had utterly left him. An emotion that was akin to fear swept coldly through him. But her whispering answer turned it instantly to terror – a terror that gripped him horribly and turned him weak and unresisting.

'Our home is – *here*!' A burst of wild, high laughter, loud and shrill, accompanied the words. It was like a whistling wind. The wind *had* risen, and clouds obscured the moon. 'A little higher – where we cannot hear the wicked bells,' she cried, and for the first time seized him deliberately by the hand. She moved, was suddenly close against his face. Again she touched him.

And Hibbert tried to turn away in escape, and so trying, found for the first time that the power of the snow – that other power which does not exhilarate but deadens effort – was upon him. The suffocating weakness that it brings to exhausted men, luring them to the sleep of death in her clinging soft embrace, lulling the will and conquering all desire for life – this was awfully upon him. His feet were heavy and entangled. He could not turn or move.

The girl stood in front of him, very near; he felt her chilly breath upon his cheeks; her hair passed blindingly across his eyes; and that icy wind came with her. He saw her whiteness close; again, it seemed, his sight passed through her into space as though she had no face. Her arms were round his neck. She drew him softly downwards to his knees. He sank; he yielded utterly; he obeyed. Her weight was upon him, smothering, delicious. The snow was to his waist ... She kissed him softly on the lips, the eyes, all over his face. And then she spoke his name in that voice of love and wonder, the voice that held the accent of two others – both taken over long ago by Death – the voice of his mother, and of the woman he had loved.

He made one more feeble effort to resist. Then, realising even while he struggled that this soft weight about his heart was sweeter than anything life could ever bring, he let his muscles relax, and sank back into the soft oblivion of the covering snow. Her wintry kisses bore him into sleep.

7

They say that men who know the sleep of exhaustion in the snow find no awakening on the hither side of death … The hours passed and the moon sank down below the white world's rim. Then, suddenly, there came a little crash upon his breast and neck, and Hibbert – woke.

He slowly turned bewildered, heavy eyes upon the desolate mountains, stared dizzily about him, tried to rise. At first his muscles would not act; a numbing, aching pain possessed him. He uttered a long, thin cry for help, and heard its faintness swallowed by the wind. And then he understood vaguely why he was only warm – not dead. For this very wind that took his cry had built up a sheltering mound of driven snow against his body while he slept. Like a curving wave it ran beside him. It was the breaking of its over-toppling edge that caused the crash, and the coldness of the mass against his neck that woke him.

Dawn kissed the eastern sky; pale gleams of gold shot every peak with splendour; but ice was in the air, and the dry and frozen snow blew like powder from the surface of the slopes. He saw the points of his ski projecting just below him. Then he – remembered. It seems he had just strength enough to realise that, could he but rise and stand, he might fly with terrific impetus towards the woods and village far beneath. The ski would carry him. But if he failed and fell …!

How he contrived it Hibbert never knew; this fear of death somehow called out his whole available reserve force. He rose slowly, balanced a moment, then, taking the angle of an immense zigzag, started down the awful slopes like an arrow from a bow. And automatically the splendid muscles of the practised ski-er and athlete saved and guided him, for he was hardly conscious of controlling either speed or direction. The snow stung face and eyes like fine steel shot; ridge after ridge flew past; the summits raced across the sky; the valley leaped up with bounds to meet him. He scarcely felt the ground beneath his feet as the huge slopes and distance melted before the lightning speed of that descent from death to life.

He took it in four mile-long zigzags, and it was the turning at each corner that nearly finished him, for then the strain of balancing taxed to the verge of collapse the remnants of his strength.

Slopes that have taken hours to climb can be descended in a short half-hour on ski, but Hibbert had lost all count of time. Quite other thoughts and feelings mastered him in that wild, swift dropping through the air that was like the flight of a bird. For ever close upon his heels came following forms and voices with the whirling snow-dust. He heard that little silvery voice of death and laughter at his back. Shrill and wild, with the whistling of the wind past his ears, he caught its pursuing tones; but in anger now, no longer soft and coaxing. And it was accompanied; she did not follow alone. It seemed a host of these flying figures of the snow chased madly just behind him. He felt them furiously smite his neck and cheeks, snatch at his hands and try to entangle his feet and ski in drifts. His eyes they blinded, and they caught his breath away.

The terror of the heights and snow and winter desolation urged him forward in the maddest race with death a human being ever knew; and so terrific was the speed that before the gold and crimson had left the summits to touch the ice-lips of the lower glaciers, he saw the friendly forest far beneath swing up and welcome him.

And it was then, moving slowly along the edge of the woods, he saw a light. A man was carrying it. A procession of human figures was passing in a dark line laboriously through the snow. And – he heard the sound of chanting.

Instinctively, without a second's hesitation, he changed his course. No longer flying at an angle as before, he pointed his ski straight down the mountain-side. The dreadful steepness did not frighten him. He knew full well it meant a crashing tumble at the bottom, but he also knew it meant a doubling of his speed – with safety at the end. For, though no definite thought passed through his mind, he understood that it was the village *curé* who carried that little gleaming lantern in the dawn, and that he was taking the Host to a châlet on the lower slopes – to some peasant *in extremis*. He remembered her terror of the church and bells. She feared the holy symbols.

There was one last wild cry in his ears as he started, a shriek of the wind before his face, and a rush of stinging snow against closed eyelids – and then he dropped through empty space. Speed took sight from him. It seemed he flew off the surface of the world.

❄

Indistinctly he recalls the murmur of men's voices, the touch of strong arms that lifted him, and the shooting pains as the ski were unfastened from the twisted ankle … for when he opened his eyes again to normal life he found himself lying in his bed at the post office with the doctor at his side. But for years to come the story of 'mad Hibbert's' ski-ing at night is recounted in that mountain village. He went, it seems, up slopes, and to a height that no man in his senses ever tried before. The tourists were agog about it for the rest of the season, and the very same day two of the bolder men went over the actual ground and photographed the slopes. Later Hibbert saw these photographs. He noticed one curious thing about them – though he did not mention it to any one:

There was only a single track.

The Sacrifice (1913)

1

Limasson was a religious man, though of what depth and quality were unknown, since no trial of ultimate severity had yet tested him. An adherent of no particular creed, he yet had his gods; and his self-discipline was probably more rigorous than his friends conjectured. He was so reserved. Few guessed, perhaps, the desires conquered, the passions regulated, the inner tendencies trained and schooled – not by denying their expression, but by transmuting them alchemically into nobler channels. He had in him the makings of an enthusiastic devotee, and might have become such but for two limitations that prevented. He loved his wealth, labouring to increase it to the neglect of other interests; and, secondly, instead of following up one steady line of search, he scattered himself upon many picturesque theories, like an actor who wants to play all parts rather than concentrate on one. And the more picturesque the part, the more he was attracted. Thus, though he did his duty unshrinkingly and with a touch of love, he accused himself sometimes of merely gratifying a sensuous taste in spiritual sensations. There was this unbalance in him that argued want of depth.

As for his gods – in the end he discovered their reality by first doubting, then denying their existence.

It was this denial and doubt that restored them to their thrones, converting his dilettante skirmishes into genuine, deep belief; and the proof came to him one summer in early June when he was making ready to leave town for his annual month among the mountains.

With Limasson mountains, in some inexplicable sense, were a passion almost, and climbing so deep a pleasure that the ordinary scrambler hardly understood it. Grave as a kind of worship it was to him; the preparations for an ascent, the ascent itself in particular, involved a concentration that seemed symbolical as of a ritual. He not only loved the heights, the massive grandeur, the splendour of vast proportions blocked in space, but loved them with a respect that held a touch of awe. The emotion mountains stirred in him, one might say, was of that profound, incalculable kind that held kinship with his religious feelings, half realised though these were. His gods had their invisible thrones somewhere among the grim, forbidding heights. He prepared himself for this annual mountaineering with the same earnestness that a holy man might approach a solemn festival of his church.

And the impetus of his mind was running with big momentum in this direction, when there fell upon him, almost on the eve of starting, a swift series of disasters that shook his being to its last foundations, and left him stunned among the ruins. To describe these is unnecessary. People said, 'One thing after another like that! What appalling luck! Poor wretch!' then wondered, with the curiosity of children, how in the world he would take it. Due to no apparent fault of his own, these disasters were so sudden that life seemed in a moment shattered, and his interest in existence almost ceased. People shook their heads and thought of the emergency exit. But Limasson was too vital a man to dream of annihilation. Upon him it had a different effect – he turned and questioned what he called his gods. They did not answer or explain. For the first time in his life he doubted. A hair's breadth beyond lay definite denial.

The ruin in which he sat, however, was not material; no man of his age, possessed of courage and a working scheme of life, would permit disaster of a material order to overwhelm him. It was collapse of a mental, spiritual kind, an assault upon the roots of character and temperament. Moral duties laid suddenly upon him threatened to crush. His *personal* existence was assailed, and apparently must end. He must spend the remainder of his life caring for others who were nothing to him. No outlet showed, no way of escape, so diabolically complete was the combination of events that rushed his inner trenches. His faith was shaken. A man can but endure so much, and remain human. For him the saturation point seemed reached. He experienced the spiritual equivalent of that physical numbness which supervenes when pain has touched the limit of endurance. He laughed, grew callous, then mocked his silent gods.

It is said that upon this state of blank negation there follows sometimes a condition of lucidity which mirrors with crystal clearness the forces driving behind life at a given moment, a kind of clairvoyance that brings explanation and therefore peace. Limasson looked for this in vain. There was the doubt that questioned, there was the sneer that mocked the silence into which his questions fell; but there was neither answer nor explanation, and certainly not peace. There was no relief. In this tumult of revolt he did none of the things his friends suggested or expected; he merely followed the line of least resistance. He yielded to the impetus that was upon him when the catastrophe came. To their indignant amazement he went out to his mountains.

All marvelled that at such a time he could adopt so trivial a line of action, neglecting duties that seemed paramount; they disapproved. Yet in reality he was taking no definite action at all, but merely drifting with the momentum that had been acquired just before. He was bewildered with so much pain, confused with suffering, stunned with the crash that flung him helpless amid undeserved calamity. He turned to the mountains as a child to its mother, instinctively. Mountains had never failed to bring him consolation, comfort, peace. Their grandeur restored proportion whenever disorder threatened life. No calculation, properly speaking, was in his move at all; but a blind desire for a violent physical reaction such as climbing brings. And the instinct was more wholesome than he knew.

In the high upland valley among lonely peaks whither Limasson then went, he found in some measure the proportion he had lost. He studiously avoided thinking; he lived in his muscles recklessly. The region with its little Inn was familiar to him; peak after peak he attacked, sometimes with, but more often without a guide, until his reputation as a sane climber, a laurelled member of all the foreign Alpine Clubs, was seriously in danger. That he overdid it physically is beyond question, but that the mountains breathed into him some portion of their enormous calm and deep endurance is also true. His gods, meanwhile, he neglected utterly for the first time in his life. If he thought of them at all, it was as tinsel figures imagination had created, figures upon a stage that merely decorated life for those whom pretty pictures pleased. Only – he had left the theatre and their make-believe no longer hypnotised his mind. He realised their impotence and disowned them. This attitude, however, was subconscious; he lent to it no substance, either of thought or speech. He ignored rather than challenged their existence.

And it was somewhat in this frame of mind – thinking little, feeling even less – that he came out into the hotel vestibule after dinner one evening, and took mechanically the bundle of letters the porter handed to him. They had no possible interest for him; in a corner where the big steam-heater mitigated the chilliness of the hall, he idly sorted them. The score or so of other guests, chiefly expert climbing men, were trailing out in twos and threes from the dining-room; but he felt as little interest in them as in his letters: no conversation could alter facts, no written phrases change his circumstances. At random, then, he opened a business letter with a typewritten address – it would probably be impersonal, less of a mockery, therefore, than the others with their tiresome sham condolences. And, in a sense, it was impersonal; sympathy from a solicitor's office is mere formula, a few extra ticks upon the universal keyboard of a Remington. But as he read it, Limasson made a discovery that startled him into acute and bitter sensation. He had imagined the limit of bearable suffering and disaster already reached. Now, in a few dozen words, his error was proved convincingly. The fresh blow was dislocating.

This culminating news of additional catastrophe disclosed within him entirely new reaches of pain, of biting, resentful fury. Limasson experienced a momentary stopping of the heart as he took it in, a dizziness, a violent sensation of revolt whose impotence induced almost physical nausea. He felt like – death.

'Must I suffer all things?' flashed through his arrested intelligence in letters of fire.

There was a sullen rage in him, a dazed bewilderment, but no positive suffering as yet. His emotion was too sickening to include the smaller pains of disappointment; it was primitive, blind anger that he knew. He read the letter calmly, even to the neat paragraph of machine-made sympathy at the last, then placed it in his inner pocket. No outward sign of disturbance was upon him; his breath came slowly; he reached over to the table for a match, holding it at arm's length lest the sulphur fumes should sting his nostrils.

And in that moment he made his second discovery. The fact that further suffering was still possible included also the fact that some touch of resignation had been left in him, and therefore some vestige of belief as well. Now, as he felt the crackling sheet of stiff paper in his pocket, watched the sulphur die, and saw the wood ignite, this remnant faded utterly away. Like the blackened end of the match, it shrivelled and dropped off. It vanished. Savagely, yet with an external calmness that enabled him to light his pipe with untrembling hand, he addressed his futile deities. And once more in fiery letters there flashed across the darkness of his passionate thought:

'Even this you demand of me – this cruel, ultimate sacrifice?'

And he rejected them, bag and baggage; for they were a mockery and a lie. With contempt he repudiated them for ever. The stage of doubt had passed. He denied his gods. Yet, with a smile upon his lips; for what were they after all but the puppets his religious fancy had imagined? They never had existed. Was it, then, merely the picturesque, sensational aspect of his devotional temperament that had created them? That side of his nature, in any case, was dead now, killed by a single devastating blow. The gods went with it.

Surveying what remained of his life, it seemed to him like a city that an earthquake has reduced to ruins. The inhabitants think no worse thing could happen. Then comes the fire.

❄

Two lines of thought, it seems, then developed parallel in him and simultaneously, for while underneath he stormed against this culminating blow, his upper mind dealt calmly with the project of a great expedition he would make at dawn. He had engaged no guide. As an experienced mountaineer, he knew the district well; his name was tolerably familiar, and in half an hour he could have settled all details, and retired to bed with instructions to be called at two. But, instead, he sat there waiting, unable to stir, a human volcano that any moment might break forth into violence. He smoked his pipe as quietly as though nothing had happened, while through the blazing depths of him ran ever this one self-repeating statement: 'Even this you demand of me, this cruel, ultimate sacrifice! . . .' His self-control, dynamically estimated, just then must have been very great and, thus repressed, the store of potential energy accumulated enormously.

With thought concentrated largely upon this final blow, Limasson had not noticed the people who streamed out of the *salle à manger* and scattered themselves in groups about the hall. Some individual, now and again, approached his chair with the idea of conversation, then, seeing his absorption, turned away. Even when a climber whom he slightly knew reached across him with a word of apology for the matches, Limasson made no response, for he did not see him. He noticed nothing. In particular he did not notice two men who, from an opposite corner, had for some time been observing him. He now looked up – by chance? – and was vaguely aware that they were discussing him. He met their eyes across the hall, and started.

For at first he thought he knew them. Possibly he had seen them about in the hotel – they seemed familiar – yet he certainly had never spoken with them. Aware of his mistake, he turned his glance elsewhere, though still vividly conscious of their attention. One was a clergyman or a priest; his face wore an air of gravity touched by sadness, a sternness about the lips counteracted by a kindling beauty in the eyes that betrayed enthusiasm nobly regulated. There was a suggestion of stateliness in the man that made the impression very sharp. His clothing emphasised it. He wore a dark tweed suit that was strict in its simplicity. There was austerity in him somewhere.

His companion, perhaps by contrast, seemed inconsiderable in his conventional evening dress. A good deal younger than his friend, his hair, always a tell-tale detail, was a trifle long; the thin fingers that flourished a cigarette wore rings; the face, though picturesque, was flippant, and his entire attitude conveyed a certain insignificance. Gesture, that faultless language which challenges counterfeit, betrayed unbalance somewhere. The impression he produced, however, was shadowy compared to the sharpness of the other. 'Theatrical' was the word in Limasson's mind, as he turned his glance elsewhere. But as he looked away he fidgeted. The interior darkness caused by the dreadful letter rose about him. It engulfed him. Dizziness came with it …

Far away the blackness was fringed with light, and through this light, stepping with speed and carelessness as from gigantic distance, the two men, suddenly grown large, came at him. Limasson, in self-protection, turned to meet them. Conversation he did not desire. Somehow he had expected this attack.

Yet the instant they began to speak – it was the priest who opened fire – it was all so natural and easy that he almost welcomed the diversion. A phrase by way of introduction – and he was speaking of the summits. Something in Limasson's mind turned over. The man was a serious climber, one of his own species. The sufferer felt a certain relief as he heard the invitation, and realised, though dully, the compliment involved.

'If you felt inclined to join us – if you would honour us with your company,' the man was saying quietly, adding something then about 'your great experience' and 'invaluable advice and judgment'.

Limasson looked up, trying hard to concentrate and understand.

'The Tour du Néant?' he repeated, mentioning the peak proposed. Rarely attempted, never conquered, and with an ominous record of disaster, it happened to be the very summit he had meant to attack himself next day.

'You have engaged guides?' He knew the question foolish.

'No guide will try it,' the priest answered, smiling, while his companion added with a flourish, 'but we – we need no guide – if *you* will come.'

'You are unattached, I believe? You are alone?' the priest enquired, moving a little in front of his friend, as though to keep him in the background.

'Yes,' replied Limasson. 'I am quite alone.'

He was listening attentively, but with only part of his mind. He realised the flattery of the invitation. Yet it was like flattery addressed to some one else. He felt himself so indifferent, so – dead. These men wanted his skilful body, his experienced mind; and it was his body and mind that talked with them, and finally agreed to go. Many a time expeditions had been planned in just this way, but to-night he felt there was a difference. Mind and body signed the agreement, but his soul, listening elsewhere and looking on, was silent. With his rejected gods it had left him, though hovering close still. It did not interfere; it did not warn; it even approved; it sang to him from great distance that this expedition cloaked another. He was bewildered by the clashing of his higher and his lower mind.

'At one in the morning, then, if that will suit you …' the older man concluded.

'I'll see to the provisions,' exclaimed the younger enthusiastically, 'and I shall take my telephoto for the summit. The porters can come as far as the Great Tower. We're over six thousand feet here already, you see, so …' and his voice died away in the distance as his companion led him off.

Limasson saw him go with relief. But for the other man he would have declined the invitation. At heart he was indifferent enough. What decided him really was the coincidence that the Tour du Néant was the very peak he had intended to attack himself *alone*, and the curious feeling that this expedition cloaked another somehow – almost that these men had a hidden motive. But he dismissed the idea – it was not worth thinking about. A moment later he followed them to bed. So careless was he of the affairs of the world, so dead to mundane interests, that he tore up his other letters and tossed them into a corner of the room – unread.

2

Once in his chilly bedroom he realised that his upper mind had permitted him to do a foolish thing; he had drifted like a schoolboy into an unwise situation. He had pledged himself to an expedition with two strangers, an expedition for which normally he would have chosen his companions with the utmost caution. Moreover, he was guide; they looked to him for safety, while yet it was they who had arranged and planned it. But who were these men with whom he proposed to run grave bodily risks? He knew them as little as they knew him. Whence came, he wondered, the curious idea that this climb was really planned by another who was no one of them?

The thought slipped idly across his mind; going out by one door, it came back, however, quickly by another. He did not think about it more than to note its passage through the disorder that passed with him just then for thinking. Indeed, there was nothing in the whole world for which he cared a single brass farthing. As he undressed for bed, he said to himself: 'I shall be called at one … but why am I going with these two on this wild plan? … And who made the plan?' …

It seemed to have settled itself. It came about so naturally and easily, so quickly. He probed no deeper. He didn't care. And for the first time he omitted the little ritual, half prayer, half adoration, it had always been his custom to offer to his deities upon retiring to rest. He no longer recognised them.

How utterly broken his life was! How blank and terrible and lonely! He felt cold, and piled his overcoats upon the bed, as though his mental isolation involved a physical effect as well. Switching off the light by the door, he was in the act of crossing the floor in the darkness when a sound beneath the window caught his ear. Outside there were voices talking. The roar of falling water made them indistinct, yet he was sure they were voices, and that one of them he knew. He stopped still to listen. He heard his own name uttered – 'John Limasson'. They ceased. He stood a moment shivering on the boards, then crawled into bed beneath the heavy clothing. But in the act of settling down, they began again. He raised himself again hurriedly to listen. What little wind there was passed in that moment down the valley, carrying off the roar of falling water; and into the moment's space of silence dropped fragments of definite sentences:

'They are close, you say – close down upon the world?' It was the voice of the priest surely.

'For days they have been passing,' was the answer – a rough, deep tone that might have been a peasant's, and a kind of fear in it, 'for all my flocks are scattered.'

'The signs are sure? You know them?'

'Tumult,' was the answer in much lower tones. 'There has been tumult in the mountains ...'

There was a break then as though the voices sank too low to be heard. Two broken fragments came next, end of a question – beginning of an answer.

'... the opportunity of a lifetime?'

'... if he goes of his own free will, success is sure. For acceptance is ...'

And the wind, returning, bore back the sound of the falling water, so that Limasson heard no more ...

An indefinable emotion stirred in him as he turned over to sleep. He stuffed his ears lest he should hear more. He was aware of a sinking of the heart that was inexplicable. What in the world were they talking about, these two? What was the meaning of these disjointed phrases? There lay behind them a grave significance almost solemn. That 'tumult in the mountains' was somehow ominous, its suggestion terrible and mighty. He felt disturbed, uncomfortable, the first emotion that had stirred in him for days. The numbness melted before its faint awakening. Conscience was in it – he felt vague prickings – but it was deeper far than conscience. Somewhere out of sight, in a region life had as yet not plumbed, the words sank down and vibrated like pedal notes. They rumbled away into the night of undecipherable things. And, though explanation failed him, he felt they had reference somehow to the morrow's expedition: how, what, wherefore, he knew not; his name had been spoken – then these curious sentences; that was all. Yet to-morrow's expedition, what was it but an expedition of impersonal kind, not even planned by himself? Merely his own plan taken and altered by others – made over? His personal business, his personal life, were not really in it at all.

The thought startled him a moment. He had no personal life ...!

Struggling with sleep, his brain played the endless game of disentanglement without winning a single point, while the under-mind in him looked on and smiled – because it *knew*. Then, suddenly, a great peace fell over him. Exhaustion brought it perhaps. He fell asleep; and next moment, it seemed, he was aware of a thundering at the door and an unwelcome growling voice, '*'s ist bald ein Uhr, Herr! Aufstehen!*'

Rising at such an hour, unless the heart be in it, is a sordid and depressing business; Limasson dressed without enthusiasm, conscious that thought and feeling were exactly where he had left them on going to sleep. The same confusion and bewilderment were in him; also the same deep solemn emotion stirred by the whispering voices. Only long habit enabled him to attend to detail, and ensured that nothing was forgotten. He felt heavy and oppressed, a kind of anxiety about him; the routine of preparation he followed gravely, utterly untouched by the customary joy; it was mechanical. Yet through it ran the old familiar sense of ritual, due to the practice of so many years, that cleansing of mind and body for a big Ascent – like initiatory rites that once had been as important to him as those of some priest who approached the worship of his deity in the temples of ancient time. He performed the ceremony with the same care as though no ghost of vanished faith still watched him, beckoning from the air as formerly ... His knapsack carefully packed, he took his ice-axe from beside the bed, turned out the light, and went down the creaking wooden stairs in stockinged feet, lest his heavy boots should waken the other sleepers. And in his head still rang the phrase he had fallen asleep on – as though just uttered:

'The signs are sure; for days they have been passing – close down upon the world. The flocks are scattered. There has been tumult – tumult in the mountains.' The other fragments he had forgotten. But who were 'they'? And why did the word bring a chill of awe into his blood?

And as the words rolled through him Limasson felt tumult in his thoughts and feelings too. There had been tumult in his life, and all his joys were scattered – joys that hitherto had fed his days. The signs were sure. Something was close down upon his little world – passing – sweeping. He felt a touch of terror.

Outside in the fresh darkness of very early morning the strangers stood waiting for him. Rather, they seemed to arrive in the same instant as himself, equally punctual. The clock in the church tower sounded one. They exchanged low greetings, remarked that the weather promised to hold good, and started off in single file over soaking meadows towards the first belt of forest. The porter – mere peasant, unfamiliar of face and not connected with the hotel – led the way with a hurricane lantern. The air was marvellously sweet and fragrant. In the sky overhead the stars shone in their thousands. Only the noise of falling water from the heights, and the regular thud of their heavy boots broke the stillness. And, black against the sky, towered the enormous pyramid of the Tour du Néant they meant to conquer.

Perhaps the most delightful portion of a big ascent is the beginning in the scented darkness while the thrill of possible conquest lies still far off. The hours stretch themselves queerly; last night's sunset might be days ago; sunrise and the brilliance coming seem in another week, part of dim futurity like children's holidays. It is difficult to realise that this biting cold before the dawn, and the blazing heat to come, both belong to the same to-day.

There were no sounds as they toiled slowly up the zigzag path through the first fifteen hundred feet of pine-woods; no one spoke; the clink of nails and ice-axe points against the stones was all they heard. For the roar of water was felt rather than heard; it beat against the ears and the skin of the whole body at once. The deeper notes were below them now in the sleeping valley; the shriller ones sounded far above, where streams just born out of ponderous snow-beds tinkled sharply …

The change came delicately. The stars turned a shade less brilliant, a softness in them as of human eyes that say farewell. Between the highest branches the sky grew visible. A sighing air smoothed all their crests one way; moss, earth, and open spaces brought keen perfumes; and the little human procession, leaving the forest, stepped out into the vastness of the world above the tree-line. They paused while the porter stooped to put his lantern out. In the eastern sky was colour. The peaks and crags rushed closer.

Was it the Dawn? Limasson turned his eyes from the height of sky where the summits pierced a path for the coming day, to the faces of his companions, pale and wan in the early twilight. How small, how insignificant they seemed amid this hungry emptiness of desolation. The stupendous cliffs fled past them, led by headstrong peaks crowned with eternal snows. Thin lines of cloud, trailing half way up precipice and ridge, seemed like the swish of movement – as though he caught the earth turning as she raced through space. The four of them, timid riders on the gigantic saddle, clung for their lives against her titan ribs, while currents of some majestic life swept up at them from every side. He drew deep draughts of the rarefied air into his lungs. It was very cold. Avoiding the pallid, insignificant faces of his companions, he pretended interest in the porter's operations; he stared fixedly on the ground. It seemed twenty minutes before the flame was extinguished, and the lantern fastened to the pack behind. This Dawn was unlike any he had seen before.

For, in reality, all the while, Limasson was trying to bring order out of the extraordinary thoughts and feelings that had possessed him during the slow forest ascent, and the task was not crowned with much success. The Plan, made by others, had taken charge of him, he felt; and he had thrown the reins of personal will and interest loosely upon its steady gait. He had abandoned himself carelessly to what might come. Knowing that he was leader of the expedition, he yet had suffered the porter to go first, taking his own place as it was appointed to him, behind the younger man, but before the priest. In this order, they had plodded, as only experienced climbers plod, for hours without a rest, until half way up a change had taken place. He had wished it, and instantly it was effected. The priest moved past him, while his companion dropped to the rear – the companion who forever stumbled in his speed, whereas the older man climbed surely, confidently. And thereafter Limasson walked more easily – as though the relative positions of the three were of importance somehow. The steep ascent of smothering darkness through the woods became less arduous. He was glad to have the younger man behind him.

For the impression had strengthened as they climbed in silence that this ascent pertained to some significant Ceremony, and the idea had grown insistently, almost stealthily, upon him. The movements of himself and his companions, especially the positions each occupied relatively to the other, established some kind of intimacy that resembled speech, suggesting even question and answer. And the entire performance, while occupying hours by his watch, it seemed to him more than once, had been in reality briefer than the flash of a passing thought, so that he saw it within himself – pictorially. He thought of a picture worked in colours upon a strip of elastic. Some one pulled the strip, and the picture stretched. Or some one released it again, and the picture flew back, reduced to a mere stationary speck. All happened in a single speck of time.

And the little change of position, apparently so trivial, gave point to this singular notion working in his undermind – that this ascent was a ritual and a ceremony as in older days, its significance approaching revelation, however, for the first time – now. Without language, this stole over him; no words could quite describe it. For it came to him that these three formed a unit, himself being in some fashion yet the acknowledged principal, the leader. The labouring porter had no place in it, for this first toiling through the darkness was a preparation, and when the actual climb began, he would disappear, while Limasson himself went first. This idea that they took part together in a Ceremony established itself firmly in him, with the added wonder that, though so often done, he performed it now for the first time with full comprehension, knowledge, truth. Empty of personal desire, indifferent to an ascent that formerly would have thrilled his heart with ambition and delight, he understood that climbing had ever been a ritual for his soul and of his soul, and that power must result from its sincere accomplishment. It was a symbolical ascent.

In words this did not come to him. He felt it, never criticising. That is, he neither rejected nor accepted. It stole most sweetly, grandly, over him. It floated into him while he climbed, yet so convincingly that he had felt his relative position must be changed. The younger man held too prominent a post, or at least a wrong one – in advance. Then, after the change, effected mysteriously as though all recognised it, this line of certainty increased, and there came upon him the big, strange knowledge that all of life is a Ceremony on a giant scale, and that by performing the movements accurately, with sincere fidelity, there may come – knowledge. There was gravity in him from that moment.

This ran in his mind with certainty. Though his thought assumed no form of little phrases, his brain yet furnished detailed statements that clinched the marvellous thing with simile and incident which daily life might apprehend: That knowledge arises from action; that to do the thing invites the teaching and explains it. Action, moreover, is symbolical; a group of men, a family, an entire nation, engaged in those daily movements which are the working out of their destiny, perform a Ceremony which is in direct relation somewhere to the pattern of greater happenings which are the teachings of the Gods. Let the body imitate, reproduce – in a bedroom, in a wood – anywhere – the movements of the stars, and the meaning of those stars shall sink down into the heart. The movements constitute a script, a language. To mimic the gestures of a stranger is to understand his mood, his point of view – to establish a grave and solemn intimacy. Temples are everywhere, for the entire earth is a temple, and the body, House of Royalty, is the biggest temple of them all. To ascertain the pattern its movements trace in daily life, *could* be to determine the relation of that particular ceremony to the Cosmos, and so learn power. The entire system of Pythagoras, he realised, could be taught without a single word – by movements; and in everyday life even the commonest act and vulgarest movement are part of some big Ceremony – a message from the Gods. Ceremony, in a word, is three-dimensional language, and action, therefore, is the language of the Gods. The Gods he had denied were speaking to him … passing with tumult close across his broken life … Their passage it was, indeed, that had caused the breaking!

In this cryptic, condensed fashion the great fact came over him – that he and these other two, here and now, took part in some great Ceremony of whose ultimate object as yet he was in ignorance. The impact with which it dropped upon his mind was tremendous. He realised it most fully when he stepped from the darkness of the forest and entered the expanse of glimmering, early light; up till this moment his mind was being prepared only, whereas now he knew. The innate desire to worship which all along had been his, the momentum his religious temperament had acquired during forty years, the yearning to have proof, in a word, that the Gods he once acknowledged were really true, swept back upon him with that violent reaction which denial had aroused.

He wavered where he stood …

Looking about him, then, while the others rearranged burdens the returning porter now discarded, he perceived the astonishing beauty of the time and place, feeling it soak into him as by the very pores of his skin. From all sides this beauty rushed upon him. Some radiant, wingéd sense of wonder sped past him through the silent air. A thrill of ecstasy ran down every nerve. The hair of his head stood up. It was far from unfamiliar to him, this sight of the upper mountain world awakening from its sleep of the summer night, but never before had he stood shuddering thus at its exquisite cold glory, nor felt its significance as now, so mysteriously *within himself.* Some transcendent power that held sublimity was passing across this huge desolate plateau, far more majestic than the mere sunrise among mountains he had so often witnessed. There was Movement. He understood why he had seen his companions insignificant. Again he shivered and looked about him, touched by a solemnity that held deep awe.

Personal life, indeed, was wrecked, destroyed, but something greater was on the way. His fragile alliance with a spiritual world was strengthened. He realised his own past insolence. He became afraid.

3

The treeless plateau, littered with enormous boulders, stretched for miles to right and left, grey in the dusk of very early morning. Behind him dropped thick guardian pine-woods into the sleeping valley that still detained the darkness of the night. Here and there lay patches of deep snow, gleaming faintly through thin rising mist; singing streams of icy water spread everywhere among the stones, soaking the coarse rough grass that was the only sign of vegetation. No life was visible; nothing stirred; nor anywhere was movement, but of the quiet trailing mist and of his own breath that drifted past his face like smoke. Yet through the splendid stillness there *was* movement; that sense of absolute movement which results in stillness – it was owing to the stillness that he became aware of it – so vast, indeed, that only immobility could express it. Thus, on the calmest day in summer, may the headlong rushing of the earth through space seem more real than when the tempest shakes the trees and water on its surface; or great machinery turn with such vertiginous velocity that it appears steady to the deceived function of the eye. For it was not through the eye that this solemn Movement made itself known, but rather through a massive sensation that owned his entire body as its organ. Within the league-long amphitheatre of enormous peaks and precipices that enclosed the plateau, piling themselves upon the horizon, Limasson felt the outline of a Ceremony extended. The pulses of its grandeur poured into him where he stood. Its vast design was knowable because they themselves had traced – were even then tracing – its earthly counterpart in little. And the awe in him increased.

'This light is false. We have an hour yet before the true dawn,' he heard the younger man say lightly. 'The summits still are ghostly. Let us enjoy the sensation, and see what we can make of it.'

And Limasson, looking up startled from his reverie, saw that the far-away heights and towers indeed were heavy with shadow, faint still with the light of stars. It seemed to him they bowed their awful heads and that their stupendous shoulders lowered. They drew together, shutting out the world.

'True,' said his companion, 'and the upper snows still wear the spectral shine of night. But let us now move faster, for we travel very light. The sensations you propose will but delay and weaken us.'

He handed a share of the burdens to his companion and to Limasson. Slowly they all moved forward, and the mountains shut them in.

And two things Limasson noted then, as he shouldered his heavier pack and led the way: first, that he suddenly knew their destination though its purpose still lay hidden; and, secondly, that the porter's leaving before the ascent proper began signified finally that ordinary climbing was not their real objective. Also – the dawn was a lifting of inner veils from off his mind, rather than a brightening of the visible earth due to the nearing sun. Thick darkness, indeed, draped this enormous, lonely amphitheatre where they moved.

'You lead us well,' said the priest a few feet behind him, as he picked his way unfalteringly among the boulders and the streams.

'Strange that I do so,' replied Limasson in a low tone, 'for the way is new to me, and the darkness grows instead of lessening.' The language seemed hardly of his choosing. He spoke and walked as in a dream.

Far in the rear the voice of the younger man called plaintively after them: 'You go so fast, I can't keep up with you,' and again he stumbled and dropped his ice-axe among the rocks. He seemed for ever stooping to drink the icy water, or clambering off the trail to test the patches of snow as to quality and depth. 'You're missing all the excitement,' he cried repeatedly. 'There are a hundred pleasures and sensations by the way.'

They paused a moment for him to overtake them; he came up panting and exhausted, making remarks about the fading stars, the wind upon the heights, new routes he longed to try up dangerous couloirs, about everything, it seemed, except the work in hand. There was eagerness in him, the kind of excitement that saps energy and wastes the nervous force, threatening a probable collapse before the arduous object is attained.

'Keep to the thing in hand,' replied the priest sternly. 'We are not really going fast; it is you who are scattering yourself to no purpose. It wears us all. We must husband our resources,' and he pointed significantly to the pyramid of the Tour du Néant that gleamed above them at an incredible altitude.

'We are here to amuse ourselves; life is a pleasure, a sensation, or it is nothing,' grumbled his companion; but there was a gravity in the tone of the older man that discouraged argument and made resistance difficult. The other arranged his pack for the tenth time, twisting his axe through an ingenious scheme of straps and string, and fell silently into line behind his leaders. Limasson moved on again … and the darkness at length began to lift. Far overhead, at first, the snowy summits shone with a hue less spectral; a delicate pink spread softly from the east; there was a freshening of the chilly wind; then suddenly the highest peak that topped the others by a thousand feet of soaring rock, stepped sharply into sight, half golden and half rose. At the same instant, the vast Movement of the entire scene slowed down; there came one or two terrific gusts of wind in quick succession; a roar like an avalanche of falling stones boomed distantly – and Limasson stopped dead and held his breath.

For something blocked the way before him, something he knew he could not pass. Gigantic and unformed, it seemed part of the architecture of the desolate waste about him, while yet it bulked there, enormous in the trembling dawn, as belonging neither to plain nor mountain. Suddenly it was there, where a moment before had been mere emptiness of air. Its massive outline shifted into visibility as though it had risen from the ground. He stood stock still. A cold that was not of this world turned him rigid in his tracks. A few yards behind him the priest had halted too. Farther in the rear they heard the stumbling tread of the younger man, and the faint calling of his voice – a feeble broken sound as of a man whom sudden fear distressed to helplessness.

'We're off the track, and I've lost my way,' the words came on the still air. 'My axe is gone … let us put on the rope! … Hark! Do you hear that roar?' And then a sound as though he came slowly groping on his hands and knees.

'You have exhausted yourself too soon,' the priest answered sternly. 'Stay where you are and rest, for we go no farther. This is the place we sought.'

There was in his tone a kind of ultimate solemnity that for a moment turned Limasson's attention from the great obstacle that blocked his farther way. The darkness lifted veil by veil, not gradually, but by a series of leaps as when some one inexpertly turns a wick. He perceived then that not a single Grandeur loomed in front, but that others of similar kind, some huger than the first, stood all about him, forming an enclosing circle that hemmed him in.

Then, with a start, he recovered himself. Equilibrium and common sense returned. The trick that sight had played upon him, assisted by the rarefied atmosphere of the heights and by the witchery of dawn, was no uncommon one, after all. The long straining of the eyes to pick the way in an uncertain light so easily deceives perspective. Delusion ever follows abrupt change of focus. These shadowy encircling forms were but the rampart of still distant precipices whose giant walls framed the tremendous amphitheatre to the sky.

Their closeness was a mere gesture of the dusk and distance.

The shock of the discovery produced an instant's unsteadiness in him that brought bewilderment. He straightened up, raised his head, and looked about him. The cliffs, it seemed to him, shifted back instantly to their accustomed places; as though after all they *had* been close; there was a reeling among the topmost crags; they balanced fearfully, then stood still against a sky already faintly crimson. The roar he heard, that might well have seemed the tumult of their hurrying speed, was in reality but the wind of dawn that rushed against their ribs, beating the echoes out with angry wings. And the lines of trailing mist, streaking the air like proofs of rapid motion, merely coiled and floated in the empty spaces.

He turned to the priest, who had moved up beside him.

'How strange,' he said, 'is this beginning of new light. My sight went all astray for a passing moment. I thought the mountains stood right across my path. And when I looked up just now it seemed they all ran back.' His voice was small and lost in the great listening air.

The man looked fixedly at him. He had removed his slouch

hat, hot with the long ascent, and as he answered, a long thin shadow flitted across his features. A breadth of darkness dropped about them. It was as though a mask were forming. The face that now was covered had been – naked. He was so long in answering that Limasson heard his mind sharpening the sentence like a pencil.

He spoke very slowly. '*They* move perhaps even as Their powers move, and Their minutes are our years. Their passage ever is in tumult. There is disorder then among the affairs of men; there is confusion in their minds. There may be ruin and disaster, but out of the wreckage shall issue strong, fresh growth. For like a sea, They pass.'

There was in his mien a grandeur that seemed borrowed marvellously from the mountains. His voice was grave and deep; he made no sign or gesture; and in his manner was a curious steadiness that breathed through the language a kind of sacred prophecy.

Long, thundering gusts of wind passed distantly across the precipices as he spoke. The same moment, expecting apparently no rejoinder to his strange utterance, he stooped and began to unpack his knapsack. The change from the sacerdotal language to this commonplace and practical detail was singularly bewildering.

'It is the time to rest,' he added, 'and the time to eat. Let us prepare.' And he drew out several small packets and laid them in a row upon the ground. Awe deepened over Limasson as he watched, and with it a great wonder too. For the words seemed ominous, as though this man, upon the floor of some vast Temple, said: 'Let us prepare a sacrifice ...!' There flashed into him, out of depths that had hitherto concealed it, a lightning clue that hinted at explanation of the entire strange proceeding – of the abrupt meeting with the strangers, the impulsive acceptance of their project for the great ascent, their grave behaviour as though it were a Ceremonial of immense design, his change of position, the bewildering tricks of sight, and the solemn language, finally, of the older man that corroborated what he himself had deemed at first illusion. In a flying second of time this all swept through him – and with it the sharp desire to turn aside, retreat, to run away.

Noting the movement, or perhaps divining the emotion prompting it, the priest looked up quickly. In his tone was a coldness that seemed as though this scene of wintry desolation uttered words:

'You have come too far to think of turning back. It is not possible. You stand now at the gates of birth – and death. All that might hinder, you have so bravely cast aside. Be brave now to the end.'

And, as Limasson heard the words, there dropped suddenly into him a new and awful insight into humanity, a power that unerringly discovered the spiritual necessities of others, and therefore of himself. With a shock he realised that the younger man who had accompanied them with increasing difficulty as they climbed higher and higher – was but a shadow of reality. Like the porter, he was but an encumbrance who impeded progress. And he turned his eyes to search the desolate landscape.

'You will not find him,' said his companion, 'for he is gone. Never, unless you weakly call, shall you see him again, nor desire to hear his voice.' And Limasson realised that in his heart he had all the while disapproved of the man, disliked him for his theatrical fondness of sensation and effect, more, that he had even hated and despised him. Starvation might crawl upon him where he had fallen and eat his life away before he would stir a finger to save him. It was with the older man he now had dreadful business in hand.

'I am glad,' he answered, 'for in the end he must have proved my death – our death!'

And they drew closer round the little circle of food the priest had laid upon the rocky ground, an intimate understanding linking them together in a sympathy that completed Limasson's bewilderment. There was bread, he saw, and there was salt; there was also a little flask of deep red wine. In the centre of the circle was a miniature fire of sticks the priest had collected from the bushes of wild rhododendron. The smoke rose upwards in a thin blue line. It did not even quiver, so profound was the surrounding stillness of the mountain air, but far away among the precipices ran the boom of falling water, and behind it again, the muffled roar as of peaks and snow-fields that swept with a rolling thunder through the heavens.

'They are passing,' the priest said in a low voice, 'and They know that you are here. You have now the opportunity of a lifetime; for, if you yield acceptance of your own free will, success is sure. You stand before the gates of birth and death. They offer you life.'

'Yet … I denied Them!' He murmured it below his breath.

'Denial is evocation. You called to them, and They have come. The sacrifice of your little personal life is all They ask. Be brave – and yield it.'

He took the bread as he spoke, and, breaking it in three pieces, he placed one before Limasson, one before himself, and the third he laid upon the flame which first blackened and then consumed it.

'Eat it and understand,' he said, 'for it is the nourishment that shall revive your fading life.'

Next, with the salt, he did the same. Then, raising the flask of wine, he put it to his lips, offering it afterwards to his companion. When both had drunk there still remained the greater part of the contents. He lifted the vessel with both hands reverently towards the sky. He stood upright.

'The blood of your personal life I offer to Them in your name. By the renunciation which seems to you as death shall you pass through the gates of birth to the life of freedom beyond. For the ultimate sacrifice that They ask of you is – this.'

And bending low before the distant heights, he poured the wine upon the rocky ground.

For a period of time Limasson found no means of measuring, so terrible were the emotions in his heart, the priest remained in this attitude of worship and obeisance. The tumult in the mountains ceased. An absolute hush dropped down upon the world. There seemed a pause in the inner history of the universe itself. All waited – till he rose again. And, when he did so, the mask that had for hours now been spreading across his features, was accomplished. The eyes gazed sternly down into his own. Limasson looked – and recognised. He stood face to face with the man whom he knew best of all others in the world ... himself.

There had been death. There had also been that recovery of splendour which is birth and resurrection.

And the sun that moment, with the sudden surprise that mountains only know, rushed clear above the heights, bathing the landscape and the standing figure with a stainless glory. Into the vast Temple where he knelt, as into that greater inner Temple which is mankind's true House of Royalty, there poured the completing Presence which is – Light.

'For in this way, and in this way only, shall you pass from death to life,' sang a chanting voice he recognised also now for the first time as indubitably his own.

It was marvellous. But the birth of light is ever marvellous. It was anguish; but the pangs of resurrection since time began have been accomplished by the sweetness of fierce pain. For the majority still lie in the pre-natal stage, unborn, unconscious of a definite spiritual existence. In the womb they grope and stifle, depending ever upon another. Denial is ever the call to life, a protest against continued darkness for deliverance. Yet birth is the ruin of all that has hitherto been depended on. There comes then that standing alone which at first seems desolate isolation. The tumult of destruction precedes release.

Limasson rose to his feet, stood with difficulty upright, looked about him from the figure so close now at his side to the snowy summit of that Tour du Néant he would never climb. The roar and thunder of *Their* passage was resumed. It seemed the mountains reeled.

'They are passing,' sang the voice that was beside him and within him too, 'but They have known you, and your offering is accepted. When They come close upon the world there is ever wreckage and disaster in the affairs of men. They bring disorder and confusion into the mind, a confusion that seems final, a disorder that seems to threaten death. For there is tumult in Their Presence, and apparent chaos that seems the abandonment of order. Out of this vast ruin, then, there issues life in new design. The dislocation is its entrance, the dishevelment its strength. There has been birth …'

The sunlight dazzled his eyes. That distant roar, like a wind, came close and swept his face. An icy air, as from a passing star, breathed over him.

'Are you prepared?' he heard.

He knelt again. Without a sign of hesitation or reluctance, he bared his chest to the sun and wind. The flash came swiftly, instantly, descending into his heart with unerring aim. He saw the gleam in the air, he felt the fiery impact of the blow, he even saw the stream gush forth and sink into the rocky ground, far redder than the wine …

❄

He gasped for breath a moment, staggered, reeled, collapsed ... and within the moment, so quickly did all happen, he was aware of hands that supported him and helped him to his feet. But he was too weak to stand. They carried him up to bed. The porter, and the man who had reached across him for the matches five minutes before, intending conversation, stood, one at his feet and the other at his head. As he passed through the vestibule of the hotel, he saw the people staring, and in his hand he crumpled up the unopened letters he had received so short a time ago.

'I really think – I can manage alone,' he thanked them. 'If you will set me down I can walk. I felt dizzy for a moment.'

'The heat in the hall —' the gentleman began in a quiet, sympathetic voice.

They left him standing on the stairs, watching a moment to see that he had quite recovered. Limasson walked up the two flights to his room without faltering. The momentary dizziness had passed. He felt quite himself again, strong, confident, able to stand alone, able to move forward, able to *climb.*

Reincarnation

On Reincarnation (1930)

Towards the end of a long life, filled with reading, thinking, searching for its explanation, I have yet to find a solution that solves its problems better than the explanation of reincarnation. No saner solution, covering all the facts, presents itself. A few years ago, talking in the shadow of the pyramids with one of the clearest minds in England, in Europe for that matter, his words come back to me in this connection. The insistence of the ancient Egyptians on the afterlife had been under discussion, when my friend said suddenly: 'We have no proof, nor ever shall have. Survival must always remain a subject for speculation. I have no creed, no faith, myself. Of all the systems the world has yet devised, I know one only that offers a satisfactory explanation of the complex problems of existence – reincarnation. It is logical, just, complete. It holds water.'

I asked him why, then, he could not accept it, and he had no answer. He talked a lot, that is to say, but what he said was not an answer.

Enough has been written on this subject to fill a library, and the evidence, such as it is, lies heavily in its favour. A considerable majority of the planet's population accept it, and the older, the deeper the wisdom of a race, the more its teaching is acceptable. In the West, during the last twenty-five years, the leaning towards it has increased enormously. It is considered, written and thought about; in many circles it is popular; it flatters the importance of the ego, it offers an excuse for present insignificance, it explains first love, first hate, instantaneous sympathies and antipathies; it assists lovers; it offers admirable excuses for a thousand weaknesses. It is a popular belief especially among the unthinking, and its appeal to the imagination is limitless. 'Did I not sing to thee in Babylon, or did we set a sail in Carthage Bay?' pertains to the modern cinema atmosphere.

As a boy, as a young man, I remember, I accepted the theory of reincarnation without reserve. Karma, cause and effect, Devachan, the uselessness of definite memory, the justice, logic, fairness of the conception, with all the rest, found no opposition in my mind. Writers like E D Walker and Mrs Besant presented it all in unanswerable form. Something, too, deeper than my reason held it as true. It certainly became a guiding principle, and 'we reap what we sow' was not a bad star to hitch one's waggon to. A Christian upbringing was soothed by M'Taggart of Cambridge (*Some Dogmas of Religion*): 'There seems nothing in pre-existence incompatible with any of the dogmas which are generally accepted as fundamental to Christianity.' Our forgetting of the actual circumstances in which we acquired love, virtue, wisdom, the same admirable thinker shows to be a gain rather than a loss. And the clinching statement of the Ancient Wisdom expressed my own feelings adequately: Souls without a past behind them, springing suddenly into existence, out of nothing, with marked mental and moral peculiarities, are a conception as monstrous as would be the corresponding conception of babies suddenly appearing from nowhere, unrelated to anybody, but showing marked racial and family types. The theme was used by me in several novels and in many a short story.

Well – it may be true; personally, I hope it is. Its consolation, to begin with, is immense. The 'winzas', described by Fielding Hall's *Soul of a People*, may have actually brought memory over with them from previous and recent incarnations. If any real proof of a Faith existed, however, that Faith would no longer be a faith, but a certainty. And reincarnation, for the race as a whole, is certainly not a certainty. If one single hairdresser discovered a means of making hair grow, the certainty would convince the whole world of bald-headed men in a few weeks. Some hold that, in our normal state, we possess no faculty for knowing, recognizing truth, and that only in abnormal states of consciousness can it be perceived even, and then only be communicated to others in similar abnormal states. This means that only to individuals, never to a race as a whole, is truth perceptible. We edge very deep waters here … and shall be wiser to stick to the point, *viz*, that a theory, however complete, is still a theory. Personally, I know no proof that reincarnation is true. My youthful acceptance has disappeared. Doubts have crept in since that happy ardent period.

To catch a doubt and label it is no easy matter. The best doubts, so to call them, the most valid probably, have their mysterious origin, it seems, in the profoundest layers of the subconscious region. An intellectual doubt can be grappled with, faced, perhaps destroyed; not so those gnawing, haunting uncertainties whose actual birth lies beyond the reach of what are termed the reasoning faculties. The philosophic argument, chief support of reincarnation, remains as strong as ever it was, and it is, indeed, so strong that many consider it unassailable. Physical proof, it seems to me, we shall never have, yet I realize perfectly that to rely upon physical proof in a question of faith argues a lack of sturdiness in that faith. The first flutter of wavering comes back to me, though not the growth of question that followed; and this first flutter arose with the suggestion, much talked and written about, of reincarnation being true only in a limited sense: that some, not all, would be re-born. There could be no question of reincarnating unless, and until, there was something to reincarnate – something real, its right to permanency established by development. Did the majority of human beings possess that real 'something', had they developed anything that entitled them to claim the right to rebirth? The literature dealing with *what* it is that reincarnates became voluminous and confusing, and its consideration here would involve far too much space, though the question is of vital interest. If, however, rebirth was not true for everybody, for even the least significant individual (yet what constitutes an 'individual'!), the main justice, sweetness, consolation in the theory disappeared.

With regard to that large, even important, body of evidence that concerns the memory of former lives claimed by many, the advance of recent years in psychology has something of interest to say. The powers of the subliminal self, heralded by Myers long ago in his *Human Personality and its Survival of Bodily Death*, and since dealt with in numerous volumes of valuable observation and experiment, need no detailed mention to readers of this magazine. Their apparently limitless nature, both Past and Future open to them, seems established. And Dr Osty, in one of the best books that exist in the subject, speaks of even a higher range of powers in us, a 'transcendental modality,' as I think he terms it, approaching here perhaps to the possibilities contained in Yoga, since he remarks that there is a 'physiological barrier' to be overcome before their attainment is feasible. The point here, however, is that to these powers nothing that is past is inaccessible, and that all memories – family, racial, planetary – can, so to speak, be tapped. Nor can the 'tapper', obviously, claim his right to particular memories as his own. The German writer and critic, Gurthis, has much of interest to report in this connection in his volume, *Voices from the Other Side*; and Prof Flournoy, of Geneva, is even more illuminating in his account of Helene Smith (*From India to Planet Mars*), where the subject, remembering a former life on Mars, reproduced without a moment's hesitation the Martian alphabet, clearly a creation of subconscious fantasy, since it was shown to be based entirely upon her own native language – French. Colonel de Rochas, again, reports a case of value with the subject whose pre-natal life and memories he sought under hypnosis. The immediate experiment in hand being over, the subject offered detailed memories of some four 'earlier lives', in one of which she was a man, yet all of which, upon such investigation as was possible later, proving unverifiable. With such powers latent in our deeper being, it becomes difficult, in any case, for an individual to establish his claim to recovered incidents as his own in a former life. Proof will hardly be found in this direction.

Personally, however, and whatever doubt may whisper, I find myself hoping that reincarnation is the true explanation of life and its inequalities on every plane. There seems no sounder guiding principle, no juster, no more all-inclusive system. This bugbear of 'not remembering' is not, after all, of real importance. Imagination is memory; a talent, a virtue, a weakness, these, too, are memories, and the best form of memory. 'Can we be wiser by reason of something which we have forgotten?' Unquestionably we can. A man who dies after acquiring knowledge – and all men acquire some – might enter his new life, deprived indeed of his knowledge, but not deprived of the increased strength and delicacy of mind which he had gained in acquiring the knowledge. And if so, he will be wiser in the second life because of what has happened in the first. Of course he loses something in losing the actual knowledge. But is not even this loss a gain? For the mere accumulation of knowledge, if memory never ceased, would soon become overwhelming, and worse than useless. 'What better fate,' asks Professor M'Taggart, 'would we sigh for than to leave such accumulations behind us, preserving their greatest value in the *mental faculties* which have been strengthened by their acquisition.'

The Insanity of Jones (A Study in Reincarnation) (1907)

1

Adventures come to the adventurous, and mysterious things fall in the way of those who, with wonder and imagination, are on the watch for them; but the majority of people go past the doors that are half ajar, thinking them closed, and fail to notice the faint stirrings of the great curtain that hangs ever in the form of appearances between them and the world of causes behind.

For only to the few whose inner senses have been quickened, perchance by some strange suffering in the depths, or by a natural temperament bequeathed from a remote past, comes the knowledge, not too welcome, that this greater world lies ever at their elbow, and that any moment a chance combination of moods and forces may invite them to cross the shifting frontier.

Some, however, are born with this awful certainty in their hearts, and are called to no apprenticeship, and to this select company Jones undoubtedly belonged.

All his life he had realised that his senses brought to him merely a more or less interesting set of sham appearances; that space, as men measure it, was utterly misleading; that time, as the clock ticked it in a succession of minutes, was arbitrary nonsense; and, in fact, that all his sensory perceptions were but a clumsy representation of *real* things behind the curtain – things he was for ever trying to get at, and that sometimes he actually did get at.

He had always been tremblingly aware that he stood on the borderland of another region, a region where time and space were merely forms of thought, where ancient memories lay open to the sight, and where the forces behind each human life stood plainly revealed and he could see the hidden springs at the very heart of the world. Moreover, the fact that he was a clerk in a fire insurance office, and did his work with strict attention, never allowed him to forget for one moment that, just beyond the dingy brick walls where the hundred men scribbled with pointed pens beneath the electric lamps, there existed this glorious region where the important part of himself dwelt and moved and had its being. For in this region he pictured himself playing the part of a spectator to his ordinary workaday life, watching, like a king, the stream of events, but untouched in his own soul by the dirt, the noise, and the vulgar commotion of the outer world.

And this was no poetic dream merely. Jones was not playing prettily with idealism to amuse himself. It was a living, working belief. So convinced was he that the external world was the result of a vast deception practised upon him by the gross senses, that when he stared at a great building like St Paul's he felt it would not very much surprise him to see it suddenly quiver like a shape of jelly and then melt utterly away, while in its place stood all at once revealed the mass of colour, or the great intricate vibrations, or the splendid sound – the spiritual idea – which it represented in stone.

For something in this way it was that his mind worked.

Yet, to all appearances, and in the satisfaction of all business claims, Jones was normal and unenterprising. He felt nothing but contempt for the wave of modern psychism. He hardly knew the meaning of such words as 'clairvoyance' and 'clairaudience'. He had never felt the least desire to join the Theosophical Society and to speculate in theories of astral-plane life, or elementals. He attended no meetings of the Psychical Research Society, and knew no anxiety as to whether his 'aura' was black or blue; nor was he conscious of the slightest wish to mix in with the revival of cheap occultism which proves so attractive to weak minds of mystical tendencies and unleashed imaginations.

There were certain things he *knew*, but none he cared to argue about; and he shrank instinctively from attempting to put names to the contents of this other region, knowing well that such names could only limit and define things that, according to any standards in use in the ordinary world, were simply undefinable and illusive.

So that, although this was the way his mind worked, there was clearly a very strong leaven of common sense in Jones. In a word, the man the world and the office knew as Jones *was* Jones. The name summed him up and labelled him correctly – John Enderby Jones.

Among the things that he *knew*, and therefore never cared to speak or speculate about, one was that he plainly saw himself as the inheritor of a long series of past lives, the net result of painful evolution, always as himself, of course, but in numerous different bodies each determined by the behaviour of the preceding one. The present John Jones was the last result to date of all the previous thinking, feeling, and doing of John Jones in earlier bodies and in other centuries. He pretended to no details, nor claimed distinguished ancestry, for he realised his past must have been utterly commonplace and insignificant to have produced his present; but he was just as sure he had been at this weary game for ages as that he breathed, and it never occurred to him to argue, to doubt, or to ask questions. And one result of this belief was that his thoughts dwelt upon the past rather than upon the future; that he read much history, and felt specially drawn to certain periods whose spirit he understood instinctively as though he had lived in them; and that he found all religions uninteresting because, almost without exception, they start from the present and speculate ahead as to what men shall become, instead of looking back and speculating why men have got here as they are.

In the insurance office he did his work exceedingly well, but without much personal ambition. Men and women he regarded as the impersonal instruments for inflicting upon him the pain or pleasure he had earned by his past workings, for chance had no place in his scheme of things at all; and while he recognised that the practical world could not get along unless every man did his work thoroughly and conscientiously, he took no interest in the accumulation of fame or money for himself, and simply, therefore, did his plain duty, with indifference as to results.

In common with others who lead a strictly impersonal life, he possessed the quality of utter bravery, and was always ready to face any combination of circumstances, no matter how terrible, because he saw in them the just working-out of past causes he had himself set in motion which could not be dodged or modified. And whereas the majority of people had little meaning for him, either by way of attraction or repulsion, the moment he met some one with whom he felt his past had been *vitally* interwoven his whole inner being leapt up instantly and shouted the fact in his face, and he regulated his life with the utmost skill and caution, like a sentry on watch for an enemy whose feet could already be heard approaching.

Thus, while the great majority of men and women left him uninfluenced – since he regarded them as so many souls merely passing with him along the great stream of evolution – there were, here and there, individuals with whom he recognised that his smallest intercourse was of the gravest importance. These were persons with whom he knew in every fibre of his being he had accounts to settle, pleasant or otherwise, arising out of dealings in past lives; and into his relations with these few, therefore, he concentrated as it were the efforts that most people spread over their intercourse with a far greater number. By what means he picked out these few individuals only those conversant with the startling processes of the subconscious memory may say, but the point was that Jones believed the main purpose, if not quite the entire purpose, of his present incarnation lay in his faithful and thorough settling of these accounts, and that if he sought to evade the least detail of such settling, no matter how unpleasant, he would have lived in vain, and would return to his next incarnation with this added duty to perform. For according to his beliefs there was no Chance, and could be no ultimate shirking, and to avoid a problem was merely to waste time and lose opportunities for development.

And there was one individual with whom Jones had long understood clearly he had a very large account to settle, and towards the accomplishment of which all the main currents of his being seemed to bear him with unswerving purpose. For, when he first entered the insurance office as a junior clerk ten years before, and through a glass door had caught sight of this man seated in an inner room, one of his sudden overwhelming flashes of intuitive memory had burst up into him from the depths, and he had seen, as in a flame of blinding light, a symbolical picture of the future rising out of a dreadful past, and he had, without any act of definite volition, marked down this man for a real account to be settled.

'With *that* man I shall have much to do,' he said to himself, as he noted the big face look up and meet his eye through the glass. 'There is something I cannot shirk – a vital relation out of the past of both of us.'

And he went to his desk trembling a little, and with shaking knees, as though the memory of some terrible pain had suddenly laid its icy hand upon his heart and touched the scar of a great horror. It was a moment of genuine terror when their eyes had met through the glass door, and he was conscious of an inward shrinking and loathing that seized upon him with great violence and convinced him in a single second that the settling of this account would be almost, perhaps, more than he could manage.

The vision passed as swiftly as it came, dropping back again into the submerged region of his consciousness; but he never forgot it, and the whole of his life thereafter became a sort of natural though undeliberate preparation for the fulfilment of the great duty when the time should be ripe.

In those days – ten years ago – this man was the Assistant Manager, but had since been promoted as Manager to one of the company's local branches; and soon afterwards Jones had likewise found himself transferred to this same branch. A little later, again, the branch at Liverpool, one of the most important, had been in peril owing to mismanagement and defalcation, and the man had gone to take charge of it, and again, by mere chance apparently, Jones had been promoted to the same place. And this pursuit of the Assistant Manager had continued for several years, often, too, in the most curious fashion; and though Jones had never exchanged a single word with him, or been so much as noticed indeed by the great man, the clerk understood perfectly well that these moves in the game were all part of a definite purpose. Never for one moment did he doubt that the Invisibles behind the veil were slowly and surely arranging the details of it all so as to lead up suitably to the climax demanded by justice, a climax in which himself and the Manager would play the leading *rôles*.

'It is inevitable,' he said to himself, 'and I feel it may be terrible; but when the moment comes I shall be ready, and I pray God that I may face it properly and act like a man.'

Moreover, as the years passed, and nothing happened, he felt the horror closing in upon him with steady increase, for the fact was Jones hated and loathed the Manager with an intensity of feeling he had never before experienced towards any human being. He shrank from his presence, and from the glance of his eyes, as though he remembered to have suffered nameless cruelties at his hands; and he slowly began to realise, moreover, that the matter to be settled between them was one of very ancient standing, and that the nature of the settlement was a discharge of accumulated punishment which would probably be very dreadful in the manner of its fulfilment.

When, therefore, the chief cashier one day informed him that the man was to be in London again – this time as General Manager of the head office – and said that he was charged to find a private secretary for him from among the best clerks, and further intimated that the selection had fallen upon himself, Jones accepted the promotion quietly, fatalistically, yet with a degree of inward loathing hardly to be described. For he saw in this merely another move in the evolution of the inevitable Nemesis which he simply dared not seek to frustrate by any personal consideration; and at the same time he was conscious of a certain feeling of relief that the suspense of waiting might soon be mitigated. A secret sense of satisfaction, therefore, accompanied the unpleasant change, and Jones was able to hold himself perfectly well in hand when it was carried into effect and he was formally introduced as private secretary to the General Manager.

Now the Manager was a large, fat man, with a very red face and bags beneath his eyes. Being short-sighted, he wore glasses that seemed to magnify his eyes, which were always a little bloodshot. In hot weather a sort of thin slime covered his cheeks, for he perspired easily. His head was almost entirely bald, and over his turn-down collar his great neck folded in two distinct reddish collops of flesh. His hands were big and his fingers almost massive in thickness.

He was an excellent business man, of sane judgment and firm will, without enough imagination to confuse his course of action by showing him possible alternatives; and his integrity and ability caused him to be held in universal respect by the world of business and finance. In the important regions of a man's character, however, and at heart, he was coarse, brutal almost to savagery, without consideration for others, and as a result often cruelly unjust to his helpless subordinates.

In moments of temper, which were not infrequent, his face turned a dull purple, while the top of his bald head shone by contrast like white marble, and the bags under his eyes swelled till it seemed they would presently explode with a pop. And at these times he presented a distinctly repulsive appearance.

But to a private secretary like Jones, who did his duty regardless of whether his employer was beast or angel, and whose mainspring was principle and not emotion, this made little difference. Within the narrow limits in which any one *could* satisfy such a man, he pleased the General Manager; and more than once his piercing intuitive faculty, amounting almost to clairvoyance, assisted the chief in a fashion that served to bring the two closer together than might otherwise have been the case, and caused the man to respect in his assistant a power of which he possessed not even the germ himself. It was a curious relationship that grew up between the two, and the cashier, who enjoyed the credit of having made the selection, profited by it indirectly as much as any one else.

So for some time the work of the office continued normally and very prosperously. John Enderby Jones received a good salary, and in the outward appearance of the two chief characters in this history there was little change noticeable, except that the Manager grew fatter and redder, and the secretary observed that his own hair was beginning to show rather greyish at the temples.

There were, however, two changes in progress, and they both had to do with Jones, and are important to mention.

One was that he began to dream evilly. In the region of deep sleep, where the possibility of significant dreaming first develops itself, he was tormented more and more with vivid scenes and pictures in which a tall thin man, dark and sinister of countenance, and with bad eyes, was closely associated with himself. Only the setting was that of a past age, with costumes of centuries gone by, and the scenes had to do with dreadful cruelties that could not belong to modern life as he knew it.

The other change was also significant, but is not so easy to describe, for he had in fact become aware that some new portion of himself, hitherto unawakened, had stirred slowly into life out of the very depths of his consciousness. This new part of himself amounted almost to another personality, and he never observed its least manifestation without a strange thrill at his heart.

For he understood that it had begun to *watch* the Manager!

2

It was the habit of Jones, since he was compelled to work among conditions that were utterly distasteful, to withdraw his mind wholly from business once the day was over. During office hours he kept the strictest possible watch upon himself, and turned the key on all inner dreams, lest any sudden uprush from the deeps should interfere with his duty. But, once the working day was over, the gates flew open, and he began to enjoy himself.

He read no modern books on the subjects that interested him, and, as already said, he followed no course of training, nor belonged to any society that dabbled with half-told mysteries; but, once released from the office desk in the Manager's room, he simply and naturally entered the other region, because he was an old inhabitant, a rightful denizen, and because he belonged there. It was, in fact, really a case of dual personality; and a carefully drawn agreement existed between Jones-of-the-fire-insurance-office and Jones-of-the-mysteries, by the terms of which, under heavy penalties, neither region claimed him out of hours.

For the moment he reached his rooms under the roof in Bloomsbury, and had changed his city coat to another, the iron doors of the office clanged far behind him, and in front, before his very eyes, rolled up the beautiful gates of ivory, and he entered into the places of flowers and singing and wonderful veiled forms. Sometimes he quite lost touch with the outer world, forgetting to eat his dinner or go to bed, and lay in a state of trance, his consciousness working far out of the body. And on other occasions he walked the streets on air, half-way between the two regions, unable to distinguish between incarnate and discarnate forms, and not very far, probably, beyond the strata where poets, saints, and the greatest artists have moved and thought and found their inspiration. But this was only when some insistent bodily claim prevented his full release, and more often than not he was entirely independent of his physical portion and free of the real region, without let or hindrance.

One evening he reached home utterly exhausted after the burden of the day's work. The Manager had been more than usually brutal, unjust, ill-tempered, and Jones had been almost persuaded out of his settled policy of contempt into answering back. Everything seemed to have gone amiss, and the man's coarse, underbred nature had been in the ascendant all day long: he had thumped the desk with his great fists, abused, found fault unreasonably, uttered outrageous things, and behaved generally as he actually was – beneath the thin veneer of acquired business varnish. He had done and said everything to wound all that was woundable in an ordinary secretary, and though Jones fortunately dwelt in a region from which he looked down upon such a man as he might look down on the blundering of a savage animal, the strain had nevertheless told severely upon him, and he reached home wondering for the first time in his life whether there was perhaps a point beyond which he would be unable to restrain himself any longer.

For something out of the usual had happened. At the close of a passage of great stress between the two, every nerve in the secretary's body tingling from undeserved abuse, the Manager had suddenly turned full upon him, in the corner of the private room where the safes stood, in such a way that the glare of his red eyes, magnified by the glasses, looked straight into his own. And at this very second that other personality in Jones – the one that was ever *watching* – rose up swiftly from the deeps within and held a mirror to his face.

A moment of flame and vision rushed over him, and for one single second – one merciless second of clear sight – he saw the Manager as the tall dark man of his evil dreams, and the knowledge that he had suffered at his hands some awful injury in the past crashed through his mind like the report of a cannon.

It all flashed upon him and was gone, changing him from fire to ice, and then back again to fire; and he left the office with the certain conviction in his heart that the time for his final settlement with the man, the time for the inevitable retribution, was at last drawing very near.

According to his invariable custom, however, he succeeded in putting the memory of all this unpleasantness out of his mind with the changing of his office coat, and after dozing a little in his leather chair before the fire, he started out as usual for dinner in the Soho French restaurant, and began to dream himself away into the region of flowers and singing, and to commune with the Invisibles that were the very sources of his real life and being.

For it was in this way that his mind worked, and the habits of years had crystallised into rigid lines along which it was now necessary and inevitable for him to act.

At the door of the little restaurant he stopped short, a half-remembered appointment in his mind. He had made an engagement with some one, but where, or with whom, had entirely slipped his memory. He thought it was for dinner, or else to meet just after dinner, and for a second it came back to him that it had something to do with the office, but, whatever it was, he was quite unable to recall it, and a reference to his pocket engagement book showed only a blank page. Evidently he had even omitted to enter it; and after standing a moment vainly trying to recall either the time, place, or person, he went in and sat down.

But though the details had escaped him, his subconscious memory seemed to know all about it, for he experienced a sudden sinking of the heart, accompanied by a sense of foreboding anticipation, and felt that beneath his exhaustion there lay a centre of tremendous excitement. The emotion caused by the engagement was at work, and would presently cause the actual details of the appointment to reappear.

Inside the restaurant the feeling increased, instead of passing: some one was waiting for him somewhere – some one whom he had definitely arranged to meet. He was expected by a person that very night and just about that very time. But by whom? Where? A curious inner trembling came over him, and he made a strong effort to hold himself in hand and to be ready for anything that might come.

And then suddenly came the knowledge that the place of appointment was this very restaurant, and, further, that the person he had promised to meet was already here, waiting somewhere quite close beside him.

He looked up nervously and began to examine the faces round him. The majority of the diners were Frenchmen, chattering loudly with much gesticulation and laughter; and there was a fair sprinkling of clerks like himself who came because the prices were low and the food good, but there was no single face that he recognised until his glance fell upon the occupant of the corner seat opposite, generally filled by himself.

'There's the man who's waiting for me!' thought Jones instantly.

He knew it at once. The man, he saw, was sitting well back into the corner, with a thick overcoat buttoned tightly up to the chin. His skin was very white, and a heavy black beard grew far up over his cheeks. At first the secretary took him for a stranger, but when he looked up and their eyes met, a sense of familiarity flashed across him, and for a second or two Jones imagined he was staring at a man he had known years before. For, barring the beard, it was the face of an elderly clerk who had occupied the next desk to his own when he first entered the service of the insurance company, and had shown him the most painstaking kindness and sympathy in the early difficulties of his work. But a moment later the illusion passed, for he remembered that Thorpe had been dead at least five years. The similarity of the eyes was obviously a mere suggestive trick of memory.

The two men stared at one another for several seconds, and then Jones began to act *instinctively*, and because he had to. He crossed over and took the vacant seat at the other's table, facing him; for he felt it was somehow imperative to explain why he was late, and how it was he had almost forgotten the engagement altogether.

No honest excuse, however, came to his assistance, though his mind had begun to work furiously.

'Yes, you *are* late,' said the man quietly, before he could find a single word to utter. 'But it doesn't matter. Also, you had forgotten the appointment, but that makes no difference either.'

'I knew – that there was an engagement,' Jones stammered, passing his hand over his forehead; 'but somehow —'

'You will recall it presently,' continued the other in a gentle voice, and smiling a little. 'It was in deep sleep last night we arranged this, and the unpleasant occurrences of to-day have for the moment obliterated it.'

A faint memory stirred within him as the man spoke, and a grove of trees with moving forms hovered before his eyes and then vanished again, while for an instant the stranger seemed to be capable of self-distortion and to have assumed vast proportions, with wonderful flaming eyes.

'Oh!' he gasped. 'It was there – in the other region?'

'Of course,' said the other, with a smile that illumined his whole face. 'You will remember presently, all in good time, and meanwhile you have no cause to feel afraid.'

There was a wonderful soothing quality in the man's voice, like the whispering of a great wind, and the clerk felt calmer at once. They sat a little while longer, but he could not remember that they talked much or ate anything. He only recalled afterwards that the head waiter came up and whispered something in his ear, and that he glanced round and saw the other people were looking at him curiously, some of them laughing, and that his companion then got up and led the way out of the restaurant.

They walked hurriedly through the streets, neither of them speaking; and Jones was so intent upon getting back the whole history of the affair from the region of deep sleep, that he barely noticed the way they took. Yet it was clear he knew where they were bound for just as well as his companion, for he crossed the streets often ahead of him, diving down alleys without hesitation, and the other followed always without correction.

The pavements were very full, and the usual night crowds of London were surging to and fro in the glare of the shop lights, but somehow no one impeded their rapid movements, and they seemed to pass through the people as if they were smoke. And, as they went, the pedestrians and traffic grew less and less, and they soon passed the Mansion House and the deserted space in front of the Royal Exchange, and so on down Fenchurch Street and within sight of the Tower of London, rising dim and shadowy in the smoky air.

Jones remembered all this perfectly well, and thought it was his intense preoccupation that made the distance seem so short. But it was when the Tower was left behind and they turned northwards that he began to notice how altered everything was, and saw that they were in a neighbourhood where houses were suddenly scarce, and lanes and fields beginning, and that their only light was the stars overhead. And, as the deeper consciousness more and more asserted itself to the exclusion of the surface happenings of his mere body during the day, the sense of exhaustion vanished, and he realised that he was moving somewhere in the region of causes behind the veil, beyond the gross deceptions of the senses, and released from the clumsy spell of space and time.

Without great surprise, therefore, he turned and saw that his companion had altered, had shed his overcoat and black hat, and was moving beside him absolutely *without sound*. For a brief second he saw him, tall as a tree, extending through space like a great shadow, misty and wavering of outline, followed by a sound like wings in the darkness; but, when he stopped, fear clutching at his heart, the other resumed his former proportions, and Jones could plainly see his normal outline against the green field behind.

Then the secretary saw him fumbling at his neck, and at the same moment the black beard came away from the face in his hand.

'Then you *are* Thorpe!' he gasped, yet somehow without overwhelming surprise.

They stood facing one another in the lonely lane, trees meeting overhead and hiding the stars, and a sound of mournful sighing among the branches.

'I am Thorpe,' was the answer in a voice that almost seemed part of the wind. 'And I have come out of our far past to help you, for my debt to you is large, and in this life I had but small opportunity to repay.'

Jones thought quickly of the man's kindness to him in the office, and a great wave of feeling surged through him as he began to remember dimly the friend by whose side he had already climbed, perhaps through vast ages of his soul's evolution.

'To help me *now*?' he whispered.

'You will understand me when you enter into your real memory and recall how great a debt I have to pay for old faithful kindnesses of long ago,' sighed the other in a voice like falling wind.

'Between us, though, there can be no question of *debt*,' Jones heard himself saying, and remembered the reply that floated to him on the air and the smile that lightened for a moment the stern eyes facing him.

'Not of debt, indeed, but of privilege.'

Jones felt his heart leap out towards this man, this old friend, tried by centuries and still faithful. He made a movement to seize his hand. But the other shifted like a thing of mist, and for a moment the clerk's head swam and his eyes seemed to fail.

'Then you are *dead*?' he said under his breath with a slight shiver.

'Five years ago I left the body you knew,' replied Thorpe. 'I tried to help you then instinctively, not fully recognising you. But now I can accomplish far more.'

With an awful sense of foreboding and dread in his heart, the secretary was beginning to understand.

'It has to do with – with ––?'

'Your past dealings with the Manager,' came the answer, as the wind rose louder among the branches overhead and carried off the remainder of the sentence into the air.

Jones's memory, which was just beginning to stir among the deepest layers of all, shut down suddenly with a snap, and he followed his companion over fields and down sweet-smelling lanes where the air was fragrant and cool, till they came to a large house, standing gaunt and lonely in the shadows at the edge of a wood. It was wrapped in utter stillness, with windows heavily draped in black, and the clerk, as he looked, felt such an overpowering wave of sadness invade him that his eyes began to burn and smart, and he was conscious of a desire to shed tears.

The key made a harsh noise as it turned in the lock, and when the door swung open into a lofty hall they heard a confused sound of rustling and whispering, as of a great throng of people pressing forward to meet them. The air seemed full of swaying movement, and Jones was certain he saw hands held aloft and dim faces claiming recognition, while in his heart, already oppressed by the approaching burden of vast accumulated memories, he was aware of the *uncoiling of something* that had been asleep for ages.

As they advanced he heard the doors close with a muffled thunder behind them, and saw that the shadows seemed to retreat and shrink away towards the interior of the house, carrying the hands and faces with them. He heard the wind singing round the walls and over the roof, and its wailing voice mingled with the sound of deep, collective breathing that filled the house like the murmur of a sea; and as they walked up the broad staircase and through the vaulted rooms, where pillars rose like the stems of trees, he knew that the building was crowded, row upon row, with the thronging memories of his own long past.

'This is the *House of the Past*,' whispered Thorpe beside him, as they moved silently from room to room; 'the house of *your* past. It is full from cellar to roof with the memories of what you have done, thought, and felt from the earliest stages of your evolution until now.

'The house climbs up almost to the clouds, and stretches back into the heart of the wood you saw outside, but the remoter halls are filled with the ghosts of ages ago too many to count, and even if we were able to waken them you could not remember them now. Some day, though, they will come and claim you, and you must know them, and answer their questions, for they can never rest till they have exhausted themselves again through you, and justice has been perfectly worked out.

'But now follow me closely, and you shall see the particular memory for which I am permitted to be your guide, so that you may know and understand a great force in your present life, and may use the sword of justice, or rise to the level of a great forgiveness, according to your degree of power.'

Icy thrills ran through the trembling clerk, and as he walked slowly beside his companion he heard from the vaults below, as well as from more distant regions of the vast building, the stirring and sighing of the serried ranks of sleepers, sounding in the still air like a chord swept from unseen strings stretched somewhere among the very foundations of the house.

Stealthily, picking their way among the great pillars, they moved up the sweeping staircase and through several dark corridors and halls, and presently stopped outside a small door in an archway where the shadows were very deep.

'Remain close by my side, and remember to utter no cry,' whispered the voice of his guide, and as the clerk turned to reply he saw his face was stern to whiteness and even shone a little in the darkness.

The room they entered seemed at first to be pitchy black, but gradually the secretary perceived a faint reddish glow against the farther end, and thought he saw figures moving silently to and fro.

'Now watch!' whispered Thorpe, as they pressed close to the wall near the door and waited. 'But remember to keep absolute silence. It is a torture scene.'

Jones felt utterly afraid, and would have turned to fly if he dared, for an indescribable terror seized him and his knees shook; but some power that made escape impossible held him remorselessly there, and with eyes glued on the spots of light he crouched against the wall and waited.

The figures began to move more swiftly, each in its own dim light that shed no radiance beyond itself, and he heard a soft clanking of chains and the voice of a man groaning in pain. Then came the sound of a door closing, and thereafter Jones saw but one figure, the figure of an old man, naked entirely, and fastened with chains to an iron framework on the floor. His memory gave a sudden leap of fear as he looked, for the features and white beard were familiar, and he recalled them as though of yesterday.

The other figures had disappeared, and the old man became the centre of the terrible picture. Slowly, with ghastly groans, as the heat below him increased into a steady glow, the aged body rose in a curve of agony, resting on the iron frame only where the chains held wrists and ankles fast. Cries and gasps filled the air, and Jones felt exactly as though they came from his own throat, and as if the chains were burning into his own wrists and ankles, and the heat scorching the skin and flesh upon his own back. He began to writhe and twist himself.

'Spain!' whispered the voice at his side, 'and four hundred years ago.'

'And the purpose?' gasped the perspiring clerk, though he knew quite well what the answer must be.

'To extort the name of a friend, to his death and betrayal,' came the reply through the darkness.

A sliding panel opened with a little rattle in the wall immediately above the rack, and a face, framed in the same red glow, appeared and looked down upon the dying victim. Jones was only just able to choke a scream, for he recognised the tall dark man of his dreams. With horrible, gloating eyes he gazed down upon the writhing form of the old man, and his lips moved as in speaking, though no words were actually audible.

'He asks again for the name,' explained the other, as the clerk struggled with the intense hatred and loathing that threatened every moment to result in screams and action. His ankles and wrists pained him so that he could scarcely keep still, but a merciless power held him to the scene.

He saw the old man, with a fierce cry, raise his tortured head and spit up into the face at the panel, and then the shutter slid back again, and a moment later the increased glow beneath the body, accompanied by awful writhing, told of the application of further heat. There came the odour of burning flesh; the white beard curled and burned to a crisp; the body fell back limp upon the red-hot iron, and then shot up again in fresh agony; cry after cry, the most awful in the world, rang out with deadened sound between the four walls; and again the panel slid back creaking, and revealed the dreadful face of the torturer.

Again the name was asked for, and again it was refused; and this time, after the closing of the panel, a door opened, and the tall thin man with the evil face came slowly into the chamber. His features were savage with rage and disappointment, and in the dull red glow that fell upon them he looked like a very prince of devils. In his hand he held a pointed iron at white heat.

'Now the murder!' came from Thorpe in a whisper that sounded as if it was outside the building and far away.

Jones knew quite well what was coming, but was unable even to close his eyes. He felt all the fearful pains himself just as though he were actually the sufferer; but now, as he stared, he felt something more besides; and when the tall man deliberately approached the rack and plunged the heated iron first into one eye and then into the other, he heard the faint fizzing of it, and felt his own eyes burst in frightful pain from his head. At the same moment, unable longer to control himself, he uttered a wild shriek and dashed forward to seize the torturer and tear him to a thousand pieces.

Instantly, in a flash, the entire scene vanished; darkness rushed in to fill the room, and he felt himself lifted off his feet by some force like a great wind and borne swiftly away into space.

When he recovered his senses he was standing just outside the house and the figure of Thorpe was beside him in the gloom. The great doors were in the act of closing behind him, but before they shut he fancied he caught a glimpse of an immense veiled figure standing upon the threshold, with flaming eyes, and in his hand a bright weapon like a shining sword of fire.

'Come quickly now – all is over!' Thorpe whispered.

'And the dark man —?' gasped the clerk, as he moved swiftly by the other's side.

'In this present life is the Manager of the company.'

'And the victim?'

'Was yourself!'

'And the friend he – *I* refused to betray?'

'I was that friend,' answered Thorpe, his voice with every moment sounding more and more like the cry of the wind. 'You gave your life in agony to save mine.'

'And again, in this life, we have all three been together?'

'Yes. Such forces are not soon or easily exhausted, and justice is not satisfied till all have reaped what they sowed.'

Jones had an odd feeling that he was slipping away into some other state of consciousness. Thorpe began to seem unreal. Presently he would be unable to ask more questions. He felt utterly sick and faint with it all, and his strength was ebbing.

'Oh, quick!' he cried, 'now tell me more. Why did I see this? What must I do?'

The wind swept across the field on their right and entered the wood beyond with a great roar, and the air round him seemed filled with voices and the rushing of hurried movement.

'To the ends of justice,' answered the other, as though speaking out of the centre of the wind and from a distance, 'which sometimes is entrusted to the hands of those who suffered and were strong. One wrong cannot be put right by another wrong, but your life has been so worthy that the opportunity is given to —'

The voice grew fainter and fainter, already it was far overhead with the rushing wind.

'You may punish or —' Here Jones lost sight of Thorpe's figure altogether, for he seemed to have vanished and melted away into the wood behind him. His voice sounded far across the trees, very weak, and ever rising.

'Or if you can rise to the level of a great forgiveness —'

The voice became inaudible … The wind came crying out of the wood again.

❄

Jones shivered and stared about him. He shook himself violently and rubbed his eyes. The room was dark, the fire was out; he felt cold and stiff. He got up out of his armchair, still trembling, and lit the gas. Outside the wind was howling, and when he looked at his watch he saw that it was very late and he must go to bed.

He had not even changed his office coat; he must have fallen asleep in the chair as soon as he came in, and he had slept for several hours. Certainly he had eaten no dinner, for he felt ravenous.

3

Next day, and for several weeks thereafter, the business of the office went on as usual, and Jones did his work well and behaved outwardly with perfect propriety. No more visions troubled him, and his relations with the Manager became, if anything, somewhat smoother and easier.

True, the man *looked* a little different, because the clerk kept seeing him with his inner and outer eye promiscuously, so that one moment he was broad and red-faced, and the next he was tall, thin, and dark, enveloped, as it were, in a sort of black atmosphere tinged with red. While at times a confusion of the two sights took place, and Jones saw the two faces mingled in a composite countenance that was very horrible indeed to contemplate. But, beyond this occasional change in the outward appearance of the Manager, there was nothing that the secretary noticed as the result of his vision, and business went on more or less as before, and perhaps even with a little less friction.

But in the rooms under the roof in Bloomsbury it was different, for there it was perfectly clear to Jones that Thorpe had come to take up his abode with him. He never saw him, but he knew all the time he was there. Every night on returning from his work he was greeted by the well-known whisper, 'Be ready when I give the sign!' and often in the night he woke up suddenly out of deep sleep and was aware that Thorpe had that minute moved away from his bed and was standing waiting and watching somewhere in the darkness of the room. Often he followed him down the stairs, though the dim gas jet on the landings never revealed his outline; and sometimes he did not come into the room at all, but hovered outside the window, peering through the dirty panes, or sending his whisper into the chamber in the whistling of the wind.

For Thorpe had come to stay, and Jones knew that he would not get rid of him until he had fulfilled the ends of justice and accomplished the purpose for which he was waiting.

Meanwhile, as the days passed, he went through a tremendous struggle with himself, and came to the perfectly honest decision that the 'level of a great forgiveness' was impossible for him, and that he must therefore accept the alternative and use the secret knowledge placed in his hands – and execute justice. And once this decision was arrived at, he noticed that Thorpe no longer left him alone during the day as before, but now accompanied him to the office and stayed more or less at his side all through business hours as well. His whisper made itself heard in the streets and in the train, and even in the Manager's room where he worked; sometimes warning, sometimes urging, but never for a moment suggesting the abandonment of the main purpose, and more than once so plainly audible that the clerk felt certain others must have heard it as well as himself.

The obsession was complete. He felt he was always under Thorpe's eye day and night, and he knew he must acquit himself like a man when the moment came, or prove a failure in his own sight as well in the sight of the other.

And now that his mind was made up, nothing could

prevent the carrying out of the sentence. He bought a pistol, and spent his Saturday afternoons practising at a target in lonely places along the Essex shore, marking out in the sand the exact measurements of the Manager's room. Sundays he occupied in like fashion, putting up at an inn overnight for the purpose, spending the money that usually went into the savings bank on travelling expenses and cartridges. Everything was done very thoroughly, for there must be no possibility of failure; and at the end of several weeks he had become so expert with his six-shooter that at a distance of 25 feet, which was the greatest length of the Manager's room, he could pick the inside out of a halfpenny nine times out of a dozen, and leave a clean, unbroken rim.

There was not the slightest desire to delay. He had thought the matter over from every point of view his mind could reach, and his purpose was inflexible. Indeed, he felt proud to think that he had been chosen as the instrument of justice in the infliction of so well-deserved and so terrible a punishment. Vengeance may have had some part in his decision, but he could not help that, for he still felt at times the hot chains burning his wrists and ankles with fierce agony through to the bone. He remembered the hideous pain of his slowly roasting back, and the point when he thought death *must* intervene to end his suffering, but instead new powers of endurance had surged up in him, and awful further stretches of pain had opened up, and unconsciousness seemed farther off than ever. Then at last the hot irons in his eyes … It all came back to him, and caused him to break out in icy perspiration at the mere thought of it … the vile face at the panel … the expression of the dark face … His fingers worked. His blood boiled. It was utterly impossible to keep the idea of vengeance altogether out of his mind.

Several times he was temporarily baulked of his prey. Odd things happened to stop him when he was on the point of action. The first day, for instance, the Manager fainted from the heat. Another time when he had decided to do the deed, the Manager did not come down to the office at all. And a third time, when his hand was actually in his hip pocket, he suddenly heard Thorpe's horrid whisper telling him to wait, and turning, he saw that the head cashier had entered the room noiselessly without his noticing it. Thorpe evidently knew what he was about, and did not intend to let the clerk bungle the matter.

He fancied, moreover, that the head cashier was watching him. He was always meeting him in unexpected corners and places, and the cashier never seemed to have an adequate excuse for being there. His movements seemed suddenly of particular interest to others in the office as well, for clerks were always being sent to ask him unnecessary questions, and there was apparently a general design to keep him under a sort of surveillance, so that he was never much alone with the Manager in the private room where they worked. And once the cashier had even gone so far as to suggest that he could take his holiday earlier than usual if he liked, as the work had been very arduous of late and the heat exceedingly trying.

He noticed, too, that he was sometimes followed by a certain individual in the streets, a careless-looking sort of man, who never came face to face with him, or actually ran into him, but who was always in his train or omnibus, and whose eye he often caught observing him over the top of his newspaper, and who on one occasion was even waiting at the door of his lodgings when he came out to dine.

There were other indications too, of various sorts, that led him to think something was at work to defeat his purpose, and that he must act at once before these hostile forces could prevent.

And so the end came very swiftly, and was thoroughly approved by Thorpe.

It was towards the close of July, and one of the hottest days London had ever known, for the City was like an oven, and the particles of dust seemed to burn the throats of the unfortunate toilers in street and office. The portly Manager, who suffered cruelly owing to his size, came down perspiring and gasping with the heat. He carried a light-coloured umbrella to protect his head.

'He'll want something more than that, though!' Jones laughed quietly to himself when he saw him enter.

The pistol was safely in his hip pocket, every one of its six chambers loaded.

The Manager saw the smile on his face, and gave him a long steady look as he sat down to his desk in the corner. A few minutes later he touched the bell for the head cashier – a single ring – and then asked Jones to fetch some papers from another safe in the room upstairs.

A deep inner trembling seized the secretary as he noticed these precautions, for he saw that the hostile forces were at work against him, and yet he felt he could delay no longer and must act that very morning, interference or no interference. However, he went obediently up in the lift to the next floor, and while fumbling with the combination of the safe, known only to himself, the cashier, and the Manager, he again heard Thorpe's horrid whisper just behind him:

'You must do it to-day! You must do it to-day!'

He came down again with the papers, and found the Manager alone. The room was like a furnace, and a wave of dead heated air met him in the face as he went in. The moment he passed the doorway he realised that he had been the subject of conversation between the head cashier and his enemy. They had been discussing him. Perhaps an inkling of his secret had somehow got into their minds. They had been watching him for days past. They had become suspicious.

Clearly, he must act now, or let the opportunity slip by

perhaps for ever. He heard Thorpe's voice in his ear, but this time it was no mere whisper, but a plain human voice, speaking out loud.

'Now!' it said. 'Do it now!'

The room was empty. Only the Manager and himself were in it.

Jones turned from his desk where he had been standing, and locked the door leading into the main office. He saw the army of clerks scribbling in their shirt-sleeves, for the upper half of the door was of glass. He had perfect control of himself, and his heart was beating steadily.

The Manager, hearing the key turn in the lock, looked up sharply.

'What's that you're doing?' he asked quickly.

'Only locking the door, sir,' replied the secretary in a quite even voice.

'Why? Who told you to ––?'

'The voice of Justice, sir,' replied Jones, looking steadily into the hated face.

The Manager looked black for a moment, and stared angrily across the room at him. Then suddenly his expression changed as he stared, and he tried to smile. It was meant to be a kind smile evidently, but it only succeeded in being frightened.

'That *is* a good idea in this weather,' he said lightly, 'but it would be much better to lock it on the *outside*, wouldn't it, Mr Jones?'

'I think not, sir. You might escape me then. Now you can't.'

Jones took his pistol out and pointed it at the other's face. Down the barrel he saw the features of the tall dark man, evil and sinister. Then the outline trembled a little and the face of the Manager slipped back into its place. It was white as death, and shining with perspiration.

'You tortured me to death four hundred years ago,' said the

clerk in the same steady voice, 'and now the dispensers of justice have chosen me to punish you.'

The Manager's face turned to flame, and then back to chalk again. He made a quick movement towards the telephone bell, stretching out a hand to reach it, but at the same moment Jones pulled the trigger and the wrist was shattered, splashing the wall behind with blood.

'That's *one* place where the chains burnt,' he said quietly to himself. His hand was absolutely steady, and he felt that he was a hero.

The Manager was on his feet, with a scream of pain, supporting himself with his right hand on the desk in front of him, but Jones pressed the trigger again, and a bullet flew into the other wrist, so that the big man, deprived of support, fell forward with a crash on to the desk.

'You damned madman!' shrieked the Manager. 'Drop that pistol!'

'That's *another* place,' was all Jones said, still taking careful aim for another shot.

The big man, screaming and blundering, scrambled beneath the desk, making frantic efforts to hide, but the secretary took a step forward and fired two shots in quick succession into his projecting legs, hitting first one ankle and then the other, and smashing them horribly.

'Two more places where the chains burnt,' he said, going a little nearer.

The Manager, still shrieking, tried desperately to squeeze his bulk behind the shelter of the opening beneath the desk, but he was far too large, and his bald head protruded through on the other side. Jones caught him by the scruff of his great neck and dragged him yelping out on to the carpet. He was covered with blood, and flopped helplessly upon his broken wrists.

'Be quick now!' cried the voice of Thorpe.

There was a tremendous commotion and banging at the door, and Jones gripped his pistol tightly. Something seemed to crash through his brain, clearing it for a second, so that he thought he saw beside him a great veiled figure, with drawn sword and flaming eyes, and sternly approving attitude.

'Remember the eyes! Remember the eyes!' hissed Thorpe in the air above him.

Jones felt like a god, with a god's power. Vengeance disappeared from his mind. He was acting impersonally as an instrument in the hands of the Invisibles who dispense justice and balance accounts. He bent down and put the barrel close into the other's face, smiling a little as he saw the childish efforts of the arms to cover his head. Then he pulled the trigger, and a bullet went straight into the right eye, blackening the skin. Moving the pistol two inches the other way, he sent another bullet crashing into the left eye. Then he stood upright over his victim with a deep sigh of satisfaction.

The Manager wriggled convulsively for the space of a single second, and then lay still in death.

There was not a moment to lose, for the door was already broken in and violent hands were at his neck. Jones put the pistol to his temple and once more pressed the trigger with his finger.

But this time there was no report. Only a little dead click answered the pressure, for the secretary had forgotten that the pistol had only six chambers, and that he had used them all. He threw the useless weapon on to the floor, laughing a little out loud, and turned, without a struggle, to give himself up.

'I *had* to do it,' he said quietly, while they tied him. 'It was simply my duty! And now I am ready to face the consequences, and Thorpe will be proud of me. For justice has been done and the gods are satisfied.'

He made not the slightest resistance, and when the two policemen marched him off through the crowd of shuddering little clerks in the office, he again saw the veiled figure moving majestically in front of him, making slow sweeping circles with the flaming sword, to keep back the host of faces that were thronging in upon him from the Other Region.

The Tarn of Sacrifice (1921)

John Holt, a vague excitement in him, stood at the door of the little inn, listening to the landlord's directions as to the best way of reaching Scarsdale. He was on a walking tour through the Lake District, exploring the smaller dales that lie away from the beaten track and are accessible only on foot.

The landlord, a hard-featured north countryman, half innkeeper, half sheep farmer, pointed up the valley. His deep voice had a friendly burr in it.

'You go straight on till you reach the head,' he said, 'then take to the fell. Follow the "sheep-trod" past the Crag. Directly you're over the top you'll strike the road.'

'A road up there!' exclaimed his customer incredulously.

'Aye,' was the steady reply. 'The old Roman road. The same road,' he added, 'the savages came down when they burst through the Wall and burnt everything right up to Lancaster —'

'They were held – weren't they – at Lancaster?' asked the other, yet not knowing quite why he asked it.

'I don't rightly know,' came the answer slowly. 'Some say they were. But the old town has been that built over since, it's hard to tell.' He paused a moment. 'At Ambleside,' he went on presently, 'you can still see the marks of the burning, and at the little fort on the way to Ravenglass.'

Holt strained his eyes into the sunlit distance, for he would soon have to walk that road and he was anxious to be off. But the landlord was communicative and interesting. 'You can't miss it,' he told him. 'It runs straight as a spear along the fell top till it meets the Wall. You must hold to it for about eight miles. Then you'll come to the Standing Stone on the left of the track —'

'The Standing Stone, yes?' broke in the other a little eagerly.

'You'll see the Stone right enough. It was where the Romans came. Then bear to the left down another "trod" that comes into the road there. They say it was the war-trail of the folk that set up the Stone.'

'And what did they use the Stone for?' Holt inquired, more as though he asked it of himself than of his companion.

The old man paused to reflect. He spoke at length.

'I mind an old fellow who seemed to know about such things called it a Sighting Stone. He reckoned the sun shone over it at dawn on the longest day right on to the little holm in Blood Tarn. He said they held sacrifices in a stone circle there.' He stopped a moment to puff at his black pipe. 'Maybe he was right. I have seen stones lying about that may well be that.'

The man was pleased and willing to talk to so good a listener. Either he had not noticed the curious gesture the other made, or he read it as a sign of eagerness to start. The sun was warm, but a sharp wind from the bare hills went between them with a sighing sound. Holt buttoned his coat about him. 'An odd name for a mountain lake – Blood Tarn,' he remarked, watching the landlord's face expectantly.

'Aye, but a good one,' was the measured reply. 'When I was a boy the old folk had a tale that the savages flung three Roman captives from that crag into the water. There's a book been written about it; they say it was a sacrifice, but most likely they were tired of dragging them along, *I* say. Anyway, that's what the writer said. One, I mind, now you ask me, was a priest of some heathen temple that stood near the Wall, and the other two were his daughter and her lover.' He guffawed. At least he made a strange noise in his throat. Evidently, thought Holt, he was sceptical yet superstitious. 'It's just an old tale handed down, whatever the learned folk may say,' the old man added.

'A lonely place,' began Holt, aware that a fleeting touch of awe was added suddenly to his interest.

'Aye,' said the other, 'and a bad spot too. Every year the Crag takes its toll of sheep, and sometimes a man goes over in the mist. It's right beside the track and very slippery. Ninety foot of a drop before you hit the water. Best keep round the tarn and leave the Crag alone if there's any mist about. Fishing? Yes, there's some quite fair trout in the tarn, but it's not much fished. Happen one of the shepherd lads from Tyson's farm may give it a turn with an "otter",' he went on, 'once in a while, but he won't stay for the evening. He'll clear out before sunset.'

'Ah! Superstitious, I suppose?'

'It's a gloomy, chancy spot – and with the dusk falling,' agreed the innkeeper eventually. 'None of our folk care to be caught up there with night coming on. Most handy for a shepherd, too – but Tyson can't get a man to bide there.' He paused again, then added significantly: 'Strangers don't seem to mind it though. It's only our own folk —'

'Strangers!' repeated the other sharply, as though he had been waiting all along for this special bit of information. 'You don't mean to say there are people living up there?' A curious thrill ran over him.

'Aye,' replied the landlord, 'but they're daft folk – a man and his daughter. They come every spring. It's early in the year yet, but I mind Jim Backhouse, one of Tyson's men, talking about them last week.' He stopped to think. 'So they've come back,' he went on decidedly. 'They get milk from the farm.'

'And what on earth are they doing up there?' Holt asked.

He asked many other questions as well, but the answers were poor, the information not forthcoming. The landlord would talk for hours about the Crag, the tarn, the legends and the Romans, but concerning the two strangers he was uncommunicative. Either he knew little, or he did not want to discuss them; Holt felt it was probably the former. They were educated town-folk, he gathered with difficulty, rich apparently, and they spent their time wandering about the fell, or fishing. The man was often seen upon the Crag, his girl beside him, bare-legged, dressed as a peasant. 'Happen they come for their health, happen the father is a learned man studying the Wall' – exact information was not forthcoming.

The landlord 'minded his own business', and inhabitants were too few and far between for gossip. All Holt could extract amounted to this: the couple had been in a motor accident some years before, and as a result they came every spring to spend a month or two in absolute solitude, away from cities and the excitement of modern life. They troubled no one and no one troubled them.

'Perhaps I may see them as I go by the tarn,' remarked the walker finally, making ready to go. He gave up questioning in despair. The morning hours were passing.

'Happen you may,' was the reply, 'for your track goes past their door and leads straight down to Scarsdale. The other way over the Crag saves half a mile, but it's rough going along the scree.' He stopped dead. Then he added, in reply to Holt's good-bye: 'In my opinion it's not worth it,' yet what he meant exactly by 'it' was not quite clear.

❄

The walker shouldered his knapsack. Instinctively he gave the little hitch to settle it on his shoulders – much as he used to give to his pack in France. The pain that shot through him as he did so was another reminder of France. The bullet he had stopped on the Somme still made its presence felt at times … Yet he knew, as he walked off briskly, that he was one of the lucky ones. How many of his old pals would never walk again, condemned to hobble on crutches for the rest of their lives!

How many, again, would never even hobble! More terrible still, he remembered, were the blind ... The dead, it seemed to him, had been more fortunate ...

He swung up the narrowing valley at a good pace and was soon climbing the fell. It proved far steeper than it had appeared from the door of the inn, and he was glad enough to reach the top and fling himself down on the coarse springy turf to admire the view below.

The spring day was delicious. It stirred his blood. The world beneath looked young and stainless. Emotion rose through him in a wave of optimistic happiness. The bare hills were half hidden by a soft blue haze that made them look bigger, vaster, less earthly than they really were. He saw silver streaks in the valleys that he knew were distant streams and lakes. Birds soared between. The dazzling air seemed painted with exhilarating light and colour. The very clouds were floating gossamer that he could touch. There were bees and dragon-flies and fluttering thistle-down. Heat vibrated. His body, his physical sensations, so-called, retired into almost nothing. He felt himself, like his surroundings, made of air and sunlight. A delicious sense of resignation poured upon him. He, too, like his surroundings, was composed of air and sunshine, of insect wings, of soft, fluttering vibrations that the gorgeous spring day produced ... It seemed that he renounced the heavy dues of bodily life, and enjoyed the delights, momentarily at any rate, of a more ethereal consciousness.

Near at hand, the hills were covered with the faded gold of last year's bracken, which ran down in a brimming flood till it was lost in the fresh green of the familiar woods below. Far in the hazy distance swam the sea of ash and hazel. The silver birch sprinkled that lower world with fairy light.

Yes, it was all natural enough. He could see the road quite clearly now, only a hundred yards away from where he lay. How straight it ran along the top of the hill! The landlord's expression recurred to him: 'Straight as a spear.' Somehow, the phrase seemed to describe exactly the Romans and all their works … The Romans, yes, and all their works …

He became aware of a sudden sympathy with these long dead conquerors of the world. With them, he felt sure, there had been no useless, foolish talk. They had known no empty words, no bandying of foolish phrases. 'War to end war', and 'Regeneration of the race' – no hypocritical nonsense of that sort had troubled their minds and purposes. They had not attempted to cover up the horrible in words. With them had been no childish, vain pretence. They had gone straight to their ends.

Other thoughts, too, stole over him, as he sat gazing down upon the track of that ancient road; strange thoughts, not wholly welcome. New, yet old, emotions rose in a tide upon him. He began to wonder … Had he, after all, become brutalized by the War? He knew quite well that the little 'Christianity' he inherited had soon fallen from him like a garment in France. In his attitude to Life and Death he had become, frankly, pagan. He now realized, abruptly, another thing as well: in reality he had never been a 'Christian' at any time. Given to him with his mother's milk, he had never accepted, felt at home with Christian dogmas. To him they had always been an alien creed. Christianity met none of his requirements …

But what were his 'requirements'? He found it difficult to answer.

Something, at any rate, different and more primitive, he thought …

Even up here, alone on the mountain-top, it was hard to be absolutely frank with himself. With a kind of savage, honest determination, he bent himself to the task. It became suddenly important for him. He must know exactly where he stood. It seemed he had reached a turning point in his life.

The War, in the objective world, had been one such turning point; now he had reached another, in the subjective life, and it was more important than the first.

As he lay there in the pleasant sunshine, his thoughts went back to the fighting. A friend, he recalled, had divided people into those who enjoyed the War and those who didn't. He was obliged to admit that he had been one of the former – he had thoroughly enjoyed it. Brought up from a youth as an engineer, he had taken to a soldier's life as a duck takes to water. There had been plenty of misery, discomfort, wretchedness; but there had been compensations that, for him, outweighed them. The fierce excitement, the primitive, naked passions, the wild fury, the reckless indifference to pain and death, with the loss of the normal, cautious, pettifogging little daily self all these involved, had satisfied him. Even the actual killing …

He started. A slight shudder ran down his back as the cool wind from the open moorlands came sighing across the soft spring sunshine. Sitting up straight, he looked behind him a moment, as with an effort to turn away from something he disliked and dreaded because it was, he knew, too strong for him. But the same instant he turned round again. He faced the vile and dreadful thing in himself he had hitherto sought to deny, evade. Pretence fell away. He could not disguise from himself, that he had thoroughly enjoyed the killing; or, at any rate, had not been shocked by it as by an unnatural and ghastly duty. The shooting and bombing he performed with an effort always, but the rarer moments when he had been able to use the bayonet … the joy of feeling the steel go home …

He started again, hiding his face a moment in his hands, but he did not try to evade the hideous memories that surged. At times, he knew, he had gone quite mad with the lust of slaughter; he had gone on long after he should have stopped.

Once an officer had pulled him up sharply for it, but the next instant had been killed by a bullet. He thought he had gone on killing, but he did not know. It was all a red mist before his eyes and he could only remember the sticky feeling of the blood on his hands when he gripped his rifle …

And now, at this moment of painful honesty with himself, he realized that his creed, whatever it was, must cover all that; it must provide some sort of a philosophy for it; must neither apologize nor ignore it. The heaven that it promised must be a man's heaven. The Christian heaven made no appeal to him, he could not believe in it. The ritual must be simple and direct. He felt that in some dim way he understood why those old people had thrown their captives from the Crag. The sacrifice of an animal victim that could be eaten afterwards with due ceremonial did not shock him. Such methods seemed simple, natural, effective. Yet would it not have been better – the horrid thought rose unbidden in his inmost mind – better to have cut their throats with a flint knife … slowly?

Horror-stricken, he sprang to his feet. These terrible thoughts he could not recognize as his own. Had he slept a moment in the sunlight, dreaming them? Was it some hideous nightmare flash that touched him as he dozed a second? Something of fear and awe stole over him. He stared round for some minutes into the emptiness of the desolate landscape, then hurriedly ran down to the road, hoping to exorcize the strange sudden horror by vigorous movement. Yet when he reached the track he knew that he had not succeeded. The awful pictures were gone perhaps, but the mood remained. It was as though some new attitude began to take definite form and harden within him.

He walked on, trying to pretend to himself that he was some forgotten legionary marching up with his fellows to defend the Wall. Half unconsciously he fell into the steady tramping pace of his old regiment: the words of the ribald songs they had sung going to the front came pouring into his mind. Steadily and almost mechanically he swung along till he saw the Stone as a black speck on the left of the track, and the instant he saw it there rose in him the feeling that he stood upon the edge of an adventure that he feared yet longed for. He approached the great granite monolith with a curious thrill of anticipatory excitement, born he knew not whence.

But, of course, there was nothing. Common sense, still operating strongly, had warned him there would be, could be, nothing. In the waste the great Stone stood upright, solitary, forbidding, as it had stood for thousands of years. It dominated the landscape somewhat ominously. The sheep and cattle had used it as a rubbing-stone, and bits of hair and wool clung to its rough, weather-eaten edges; the feet of generations had worn a cup-shaped hollow at its base. The wind sighed round it plaintively. Its bulk glistened as it took the sun.

A short mile away the Blood Tarn was now plainly visible; he could see the little holm lying in a direct line with the Stone, while, overhanging the water as a dark shadow on one side, rose the cliff-like rock they called 'the Crag'. Of the house the landlord had mentioned, however, he could see no trace, as he relieved his shoulders of the knapsack and sat down to enjoy his lunch. The tarn, he reflected, was certainly a gloomy place; he could understand that the simple superstitious shepherds did not dare to live there, for even on this bright spring day it wore a dismal and forbidding look. With failing light, when the Crag sprawled its big lengthening shadow across the water, he could well imagine they would give it the widest possible berth. He strolled down to the shore after lunch, smoking his pipe lazily – then suddenly stood still. At the far end, hidden hitherto by a fold in the ground, he saw the little house, a faint column of blue smoke rising from the chimney, and at the same moment a woman came out of the low door and began to walk towards the tarn. She had seen him, she was moving evidently in his direction; a few minutes later she stopped and stood waiting on the path – waiting, he well knew, for him.

And his earlier mood, the mood he dreaded yet had forced himself to recognize, came back upon him with sudden redoubled power. As in some vivid dream that dominates and paralyses the will, or as in the first stages of an imposed hypnotic spell, all question, hesitation, refusal sank away. He felt a pleasurable resignation steal upon him with soft, numbing effect. Denial and criticism ceased to operate, and common sense died with them. He yielded his being automatically to the deeps of an adventure he did not understand. He began to walk towards the woman.

It was, he saw as he drew nearer, the figure of a young girl, nineteen or twenty years of age, who stood there motionless with her eyes fixed steadily on his own. She looked as wild and picturesque as the scene that framed her. Thick black hair hung loose over her back and shoulders; about her head was bound a green ribbon; her clothes consisted of a jersey and a very short skirt which showed her bare legs browned by exposure to the sun and wind. A pair of rough sandals covered her feet. Whether the face was beautiful or not he could not tell; he only knew that it attracted him immensely and with a strength of appeal that he at once felt curiously irresistible. She remained motionless against the boulder, staring fixedly at him till he was close before her. Then she spoke:

'I am glad that you have come at last,' she said in a clear, strong voice that yet was soft and even tender. 'We have been expecting you.'

'You have been expecting me!' he repeated, astonished beyond words, yet finding the language natural, right and true. A stream of sweet feeling invaded him, his heart beat faster, he felt happy and at home in some extraordinary way he could not understand yet did not question.

'Of course,' she answered, looking straight into his eyes with welcome unashamed. Her next words thrilled him to the core of his being. 'I have made the room ready for you.'

Quick upon her own, however, flashed back the landlord's words, while common sense made a last faint effort in his thought. He was the victim of some absurd mistake evidently. The lonely life, the forbidding surroundings, the associations of the desolate hills had affected her mind. He remembered the accident.

'I am afraid,' he offered, lamely enough, 'there is some mistake. I am not the friend you were expecting. I —' He stopped. A thin slight sound as of distant laughter seemed to echo behind the unconvincing words.

'There is no mistake,' the girl answered firmly, with a quiet smile, moving a step nearer to him, so that he caught the subtle perfume of her vigorous youth. 'I saw you clearly in the Mystery Stone. I recognized you at once.'

'The Mystery Stone,' he heard himself saying, bewilderment increasing, a sense of wild happiness growing with it.

Laughing, she took his hand in hers. 'Come,' she said, drawing him along with her, 'come home with me. My father will be waiting for us; he will tell you everything, and better far than I can.'

He went with her, feeling that he was made of sunlight and that he walked on air, for at her touch his own hand responded as with a sudden fierceness of pleasure that he failed utterly to understand, yet did not question for an instant. Wildly, absurdly, madly it flashed across his mind: 'This is the woman I shall marry – *my* woman. I am her man.'

They walked in silence for a little, for no words of any sort offered themselves to his mind, nor did the girl attempt to speak. The total absence of embarrassment between them occurred to him once or twice as curious, though the very idea of embarrassment then disappeared entirely. It all seemed natural and unforced, the sudden intercourse as familiar and effortless as though they had known one another always.

'The Mystery Stone,' he heard himself saying presently, as the idea rose again to the surface of his mind. 'I should like to know more about it. Tell me, dear.'

'I bought it with the other things,' she replied softly.

'What other things?'

She turned and looked up into his face with a slight expression of surprise; their shoulders touched as they swung along; her hair blew in the wind across his coat. 'The bronze collar,' she answered in the low voice that pleased him so, 'and this ornament that I wear in my hair.'

He glanced down to examine it. Instead of a ribbon, as he had first supposed, he saw that it was a circlet of bronze, covered with a beautiful green patina and evidently very old. In front, above the forehead, was a small disk bearing an inscription he could not decipher at the moment. He bent down and kissed her hair, the girl smiling with happy contentment, but offering no sign of resistance or annoyance.

'And,' she added suddenly, 'the dagger.'

Holt started visibly. This time there was a thrill in her voice that seemed to pierce down straight into his heart. He said nothing, however. The unexpectedness of the word she used, together with the note in her voice that moved him so strangely, had a disconcerting effect that kept him silent for a time. He did not ask about the dagger. Something prevented his curiosity finding expression in speech, though the word, with the marked accent she placed upon it, had struck into him like the shock of sudden steel itself, causing him an indecipherable emotion of both joy and pain. He asked instead, presently, another question, and a very commonplace one: he asked where she and her father had lived before they came to these lonely hills. And the form of his question – his voice shook a little as he said it – was, again, an effort of his normal self to maintain its already precarious balance.

The effect of his simple query, the girl's reply above all, increased in him the mingled sensations of sweetness and menace, of joy and dread, that half alarmed, half satisfied him. For a moment she wore a puzzled expression, as though making an effort to remember.

'Down by the sea,' she answered slowly, thoughtfully, her voice very low. 'Somewhere by a big harbour with great ships coming in and out. It was there we had the break – the shock – an accident that broke us, shattering the dream we share To-day.' Her face cleared a little. 'We were in a chariot,' she went on more easily and rapidly, 'and father – my father was injured, so that I went with him to a palace beyond the Wall till he grew well.'

'You were in a chariot?' Holt repeated. 'Surely not.'

'Did I say chariot?' the girl replied. 'How foolish of me!' She shook her hair back as though the gesture helped to clear her mind and memory. 'That belongs, of course, to the other dream. No, not a chariot; it was a car. But it had wheels like a chariot – the old war-chariots. You know.'

'Disk-wheels,' thought Holt to himself. He did not ask about the palace. He asked instead where she had bought the Mystery Stone, as she called it, and the other things. Her reply bemused and enticed him farther, for he could not unravel it. His whole inner attitude was shifting with uncanny rapidity and completeness. They walked together, he now realized, with linked arms, moving slowly in step, their bodies touching. He felt the blood run hot and almost savage in his veins. He was aware how amazingly precious she was to him, how deeply, absolutely necessary to his life and happiness. Her words went past him in the mountain wind like flying birds.

'My father was fishing,' she went on, 'and I was on my way to join him, when the old woman called me into her dwelling and showed me the things. She wished to give them to me, but I refused the present and paid for them in gold. I put the fillet on my head to see if it would fit, and took the Mystery Stone in my hand. Then, as I looked deep into the stone, this present dream died all away. It faded out. I saw the older dreams again – *our* dreams.'

'The older dreams!' interrupted Holt. 'Ours!' But instead of saying the words aloud, they issued from his lips in a quiet whisper, as though control of his voice had passed a little from him. The sweetness in him became more wonderful, unmanageable; his astonishment had vanished; he walked and talked with his old familiar happy Love, the woman he had sought so long and waited for, the woman who was his mate, as he was hers, she who alone could satisfy his inmost soul.

'The old dream,' she replied, 'the very old – the oldest of all perhaps – when we committed the terrible sacrilege. I saw the High Priest lying dead – whom my father slew – and the other whom *you* destroyed. I saw you prise out the jewel from the image of the god – with your short bloody spear. I saw, too, our flight to the galley through the hot, awful night beneath the stars – and our escape ...'

Her voice died away and she fell silent.

'Tell me more,' he whispered, drawing her closer against his side. 'What had *you* done?' His heart was racing now. Some fighting blood surged uppermost. He felt that he could kill, and the joy of violence and slaughter rose in him.

'Have you forgotten so completely?' she asked very low, as he pressed her more tightly still against his heart. And almost beneath her breath she whispered into his ear, which he bent to catch the little sound: 'I had broken my vows with you.'

'What else, my lovely one – my best beloved – what more did you see?' he whispered in return, yet wondering why the fierce pain and anger that he felt behind still lay hidden from betrayal.

'Dream after dream, and always we were punished. But the last time was the clearest, for it was here – here where we now walk together in the sunlight and the wind – it was here the savages hurled us from the rock.'

A shiver ran through him, making him tremble with an unaccountable touch of cold that communicated itself to her as well. Her arm went instantly about his shoulder, as he stooped and kissed her passionately. 'Fasten your coat about you,' she said tenderly, but with troubled breath, when he released her, 'for this wind is chill although the sun shines brightly. We were glad, you remember, when they stopped to kill us, for we were tired and our feet were cut to pieces by the long, rough journey from the Wall.' Then suddenly her voice grew louder again and the smile of happy confidence came back into her eyes. There was the deep earnestness of love in it, of love that cannot end or die. She looked up into his face. 'But soon now,' she said, 'we shall be free. For you have come, and it is nearly finished – this weary little present dream.'

'How,' he asked, 'shall we get free?' A red mist swam momentarily before his eyes.

'My father,' she replied at once, 'will tell you all. It is quite easy.'

'Your father, too, remembers?'

'The moment the collar touches him,' she said, 'he is a priest again. See! Here he comes forth already to meet us, and to bid you welcome.'

Holt looked up, startled. He had hardly noticed, so absorbed had he been in the words that half intoxicated him, the distance they had covered. The cottage was now close at hand, and a tall, powerfully built man, wearing a shepherd's rough clothing, stood a few feet in front of him. His stature, breadth of shoulder and thick black beard made up a striking figure. The dark eyes, with fire in them, gazed straight into his own, and a kindly smile played round the stern and vigorous mouth.

'Greeting, my son,' said a deep, booming voice, 'for I shall call you my son as I did of old. The bond of the spirit is stronger than that of the flesh, and with us three the tie is indeed of triple strength. You come, too, at an auspicious hour, for the omens are favourable and the time of our liberation is at hand.' He took the other's hand in a grip that might have killed an ox and yet was warm with gentle kindliness, while Holt, now caught wholly into the spirit of some deep reality he could not master yet accepted, saw that the wrist was small, the fingers shapely, the gesture itself one of dignity and refinement.

'Greeting, my father,' he replied, as naturally as though he said more modern words.

'Come in with me, I pray,' pursued the other, leading the way, 'and let me show you the poor accommodation we have provided, yet the best that we can offer.'

He stooped to pass the threshold, and as Holt stooped likewise the girl took his hand and he knew that his bewitchment was complete. Entering the low doorway, he passed through a kitchen, where only the roughest, scantiest furniture was visible, into another room that was completely bare. A heap of dried bracken had been spread on the floor in one corner to form a bed. Beside it lay two cheap, coloured blankets. There was nothing else.

'Our place is poor,' said the man, smiling courteously, but with that dignity and air of welcome which made the hovel seem a palace. 'Yet it may serve, perhaps, for the short time that you will need it. Our little dream here is wellnigh over, now that you have come. The long weary pilgrimage at last draws to a close.' The girl had left them alone a moment, and the man stepped closer to his guest. His face grew solemn, his voice deeper and more earnest suddenly, the light in his eyes seemed actually to flame with the enthusiasm of a great belief. 'Why have you tarried thus so long, and where?' he asked in a lowered tone that vibrated in the little space. 'We have sought you with prayer and fasting, and she has spent her nights for you in tears. You lost the way, it must be. The lesser dreams entangled your feet, I see.' A touch of sadness entered the voice, the eyes held pity in them. 'It is, alas, too easy, I well know,' he murmured. 'It is too easy.'

'I lost the way,' the other replied. It seemed suddenly that his heart was filled with fire. 'But now,' he cried aloud, 'now that I have found her, I will never, never let her go again. My feet are steady and my way is sure.'

'For ever and ever, my son,' boomed the happy, yet almost solemn answer, 'she is yours. Our freedom is at hand.'

He turned and crossed the little kitchen again, making a sign that his guest should follow him. They stood together by the door, looking out across the tarn in silence. The afternoon sunshine fell in a golden blaze across the bare hills that seemed to smoke with the glory of the fiery light. But the Crag loomed dark in shadow overhead, and the little lake lay deep and black beneath it.

'Acella, Acella!' called the man, the name breaking upon his companion as with a shock of sweet delicious fire that filled his entire being, as the girl came the same instant from behind the cottage. 'The Gods call me,' said her father. 'I go now to the hill. Protect our guest and comfort him in my absence.'

Without another word, he strode away up the hillside and

presently was visible standing on the summit of the Crag, his arms stretched out above his head to heaven, his great head thrown back, his bearded face turned upwards. An impressive, even a majestic figure he looked, as his bulk and stature rose in dark silhouette against the brilliant evening sky. Holt stood motionless, watching him for several minutes, his heart swelling in his breast, his pulses thumping before some great nameless pressure that rose from the depths of his being. That inner attitude which seemed a new and yet more satisfying attitude to life than he had known hitherto, had crystallized. Define it he could not, he only knew that he accepted it as natural. It satisfied him. The sight of that dignified, gaunt figure worshipping upon the hill-top enflamed him …

'I have brought the stone,' a voice interrupted his reflections, and turning, he saw the girl beside him. She held out for his inspection a dark square object that looked to him at first like a black stone lying against the brown skin of her hand. 'The Mystery Stone,' the girl added, as their faces bent down together to examine it. 'It is there I see the dreams I told you of.'

He took it from her and found that it was heavy, composed apparently of something like black quartz, with a brilliant polished surface that revealed clear depths within. Once, evidently, it had been set in a stand or frame, for the marks where it had been attached still showed, and it was obviously of great age. He felt confused, the mind in him troubled yet excited, as he gazed. The effect upon him was as though a wind rose suddenly and passed across his inmost subjective life, setting its entire contents in rushing motion.

'And here,' the girl said, 'is the dagger.'

He took from her the short bronze weapon, feeling at once instinctively its ragged edge, its keen point, sharp and effective still. The handle had long since rotted away, but the bronze tongue, and the holes where the rivets had been, remained, and, as he touched it, the confusion and trouble in his mind increased to a kind of turmoil, in which violence, linked to something tameless, wild and almost savage, was the dominating emotion. He turned to seize the girl and crush her to him in a passionate embrace, but she held away, throwing back her lovely head, her eyes shining, her lips parted, yet one hand stretched out to stop him.

'First look into it with me,' she said quietly. 'Let us see together.'

She sat down on the turf beside the cottage door, and Holt, obeying, took his place beside her. She remained very still for some minutes, covering the stone with both hands as though to warm it. Her lips moved. She seemed to be repeating some kind of invocation beneath her breath, though no actual words were audible. Presently her hands parted. They sat together gazing at the polished surface. They looked within.

'There comes a white mist in the heart of the stone,' the girl whispered. 'It will soon open. The pictures will then grow. Look!' she exclaimed after a brief pause, 'they are forming now.'

'I see only mist,' her companion murmured, gazing intently. 'Only mist I see.'

She took his hand and instantly the mist parted. He found himself peering into another landscape which opened before his eyes as though it were a photograph. Hills covered with heather stretched away on every side.

'Hills, I see,' he whispered. 'The ancient hills —'

'Watch closely,' she replied, holding his hand firmly.

At first the landscape was devoid of any sign of life; then suddenly it surged and swarmed with moving figures. Torrents of men poured over the hill-crests and down their heathery sides in columns. He could see them clearly – great hairy men, clad in skins, with thick shields on their left arms or slung over their backs, and short stabbing spears in their hands. Thousands upon thousands poured over in an endless stream. In the distance he could see other columns sweeping in a turning movement. A few of the men rode rough ponies and seemed to be directing the march, and these, he knew, were the chiefs …

The scene grew dimmer, faded, died away completely. Another took its place.

By the faint light he knew that it was dawn. The undulating country, less hilly than before, was still wild and uncultivated. A great wall, with towers at intervals, stretched away till it was lost in shadowy distance. On the nearest of these towers he saw a sentinel clad in armour, gazing out across the rolling country. The armour gleamed faintly in the pale glimmering light, as the man suddenly snatched up a bugle and blew upon it. From a brazier burning beside him he next seized a brand and fired a great heap of brushwood. The smoke rose in a dense column into the air almost immediately, and from all directions, with incredible rapidity, figures came pouring up to man the wall. Hurriedly they strung their bows, and laid spare arrows close beside them on the coping. The light grew brighter. The whole country was alive with savages; like the waves of the sea they came rolling in enormous numbers. For several minutes the wall held. Then, in an impetuous, fearful torrent, they poured over …

It faded, died away, was gone again, and a moment later yet another took its place.

But this time the landscape was familiar, and he recognized the tarn. He saw the savages upon the ledge that flanked the dominating Crag; they had three captives with them. He saw two men. The other was a woman. But the woman had fallen exhausted to the ground, and a chief on a rough pony rode back to see what had delayed the march. Glancing at the captives, he made a fierce gesture with his arm towards the water far below. Instantly the woman was jerked cruelly to her feet and forced onwards till the summit of the Crag was reached. A man snatched something from her hand. A second later she was hurled over the brink.

The two men were next dragged on to the dizzy spot where she had stood. Dead with fatigue, bleeding from numerous wounds, yet at this awful moment they straightened themselves, casting contemptuous glances at the fierce savages surrounding them. They were Romans and would die like Romans. Holt saw their faces clearly for the first time.

He sprang up with a cry of anguished fury.

'The second man!' he exclaimed. 'You saw the second man!'

The girl, releasing his hand, turned her eyes slowly up to his, so that he met the flame of her ancient and undying love shining like stars upon him out of the night of time.

'Ever since that moment,' she said in a low voice that trembled, 'I have been looking, waiting for you —'

He took her in his arms and smothered her words with kisses, holding her fiercely to him as though he would never let her go. 'I, too,' he said, his whole being burning with his love, 'I have been looking, waiting for you. Now I have found you. We have found each other ...!'

The dusk fell slowly, imperceptibly. As twilight slowly draped the gaunt hills, blotting out familiar details, so the strong dream, veil upon veil, drew closer over the soul of the wanderer, obliterating finally the last reminder of To-day. The little wind had dropped and the desolate moors lay silent, but for the hum of distant water falling to its valley bed. His life, too, and the life of the girl, he knew, were similarly falling, falling into some deep shadowed bed where rest would come at last. No details troubled him, he asked himself no questions. A profound sense of happy peace numbed every nerve and stilled his beating heart.

He felt no fear, no anxiety, no hint of alarm or uneasiness

vexed his singular contentment. He realized one thing only – that the girl lay in his arms, he held her fast, her breath mingled with his own. They had found each other. What else mattered?

From time to time, as the daylight faded and the sun went down behind the moors, she spoke. She uttered words he vaguely heard, listening, though with a certain curious effort, before he closed the thing she said with kisses. Even the fierceness of his blood was gone. The world lay still, life almost ceased to flow. Lapped in the deeps of his great love, he was redeemed, perhaps, of violence and savagery …

'Three dark birds,' she whispered, 'pass across the sky … they fall beyond the ridge. The omens are favourable. A hawk now follows them, cleaving the sky with pointed wings.'

'A hawk,' he murmured. 'The badge of my old Legion.'

'My father will perform the sacrifice,' he heard again, though it seemed a long interval had passed, and the man's figure was now invisible on the Crag amid the gathering darkness. 'Already he prepares the fire. Look, the sacred island is alight. He has the black cock ready for the knife.'

Holt roused himself with difficulty, lifting his face from the garden of her hair. A faint light, he saw, gleamed fitfully on the holm within the tarn. Her father, then, had descended from the Crag, and had lit the sacrificial fire upon the stones. But what did the doings of the father matter now to him?

'The dark bird,' he repeated dully, 'the black victim the Gods of the Underworld alone accept. It is good, Acella, it is good!' He was about to sink back again, taking her against his breast as before, when she resisted and sat up suddenly.

'It is time,' she said aloud. 'The hour has come. My father climbs, and we must join him on the summit. Come!'

She took his hand and raised him to his feet, and together they began the rough ascent towards the Crag. As they passed along the shore of the Tarn of Blood, he saw the fire reflected in the ink-black waters; he made out, too, though dimly, a rough circle of big stones, with a larger flag-stone lying in the centre. Three small fires of bracken and wood, placed in a triangle with its apex towards the Standing Stone on the distant hill, burned briskly, the crackling material sending out sparks that pierced the columns of thick smoke. And in this smoke, peering, shifting, appearing and disappearing, it seemed he saw great faces moving. The flickering light and twirling smoke made clear sight difficult. His bliss, his lethargy were very deep. They left the tarn below them and hand in hand began to climb the final slope.

Whether the physical effort of climbing disturbed the deep pressure of the mood that numbed his senses, or whether the cold draught of wind they met upon the ridge restored some vital detail of To-day, Holt does not know. Something, at any rate, in him wavered suddenly, as though a centre of gravity had shifted slightly. There was a perceptible alteration in the balance of thought and feeling that had held invariable now for many hours. It seemed to him that something heavy lifted, or rather, began to lift – a weight, a shadow, something oppressive that obstructed light. A ray of light, as it were, struggled through the thick darkness that enveloped him. To him, as he paused on the ridge to recover his breath, came this vague suggestion of faint light breaking across the blackness. It was objective.

'See,' said the girl in a low voice, 'the moon is rising. It lights the sacred island. The blood-red waters turn to silver.'

He saw, indeed, that a huge three-quarter moon now drove with almost visible movement above the distant line of hills; the little tarn gleamed as with silvery armour; the glow of the sacrificial fires showed red across it. He looked down with a shudder into the sheer depth that opened at his feet, then turned to look at his companion. He started and shrank back. Her face, lit by the moon and by the fire, shone pale as death; her black hair framed it with a terrible suggestiveness; the eyes, though brilliant as ever, had a film upon them. She stood in an attitude of both ecstasy and resignation, and one outstretched arm pointed towards the summit where her father stood.

Her lips parted, a marvellous smile broke over her features, her voice was suddenly unfamiliar: 'He wears the collar,' she uttered. 'Come. Our time is here at last, and we are ready. See, he waits for us!'

There rose for the first time struggle and opposition in him; he resisted the pressure of her hand that had seized his own and drew him forcibly along. Whence came the resistance and the opposition he could not tell, but though he followed her, he was aware that the refusal in him strengthened. The weight of darkness that oppressed him shifted a little more, an inner light increased. The same moment they reached the summit and stood beside – the priest. There was a curious sound of fluttering. The figure, he saw, was naked, save for a rough blanket tied loosely about the waist.

'The hour has come at last,' cried his deep booming voice that woke echoes from the dark hills about them. 'We are alone now with our Gods.' And he broke then into a monotonous rhythmic chanting that rose and fell upon the wind, yet in a tongue that sounded strange; his erect figure swayed slightly with its cadences; his black beard swept his naked chest; and his face, turned skywards, shone in the mingled light of moon above and fire below, yet with an added light as well that burned within him rather than without. He was a weird, magnificent figure, a priest of ancient rites invoking his deathless deities upon the unchanging hills.

But upon Holt, too, as he stared in awed amazement, an inner light had broken suddenly. It came as with a dazzling blaze that at first paralysed thought and action. His mind cleared, but too abruptly for movement, either of tongue or hand, to be possible. Then, abruptly, the inner darkness rolled away completely. The light in the wild eyes of the great chanting, swaying figure, he now knew was the light of mania.

The faint fluttering sound increased, and the voice of the girl was oddly mingled with it. The priest had ceased his invocation. Holt, aware that he stood alone, saw the girl go past him carrying a big black bird that struggled with vainly beating wings.

'Behold the sacrifice,' she said, as she knelt before her father and held up the victim. 'May the Gods accept it as presently They shall accept us too!'

The great figure stooped and took the offering, and with one blow of the knife he held, its head was severed from its body. The blood spattered on the white face of the kneeling girl. Holt was aware for the first time that she, too, was now unclothed; but for a loose blanket, her white body gleamed against the dark heather in the moonlight. At the same moment she rose to her feet, stood upright, turned towards him so that he saw the dark hair streaming across her naked shoulders, and, with a face of ecstasy, yet ever that strange film upon her eyes, her voice came to him on the wind:

'Farewell, yet not farewell! We shall meet, all three, in the underworld. The Gods accept us!'

Turning her face away, she stepped towards the ominous figure behind, and bared her ivory neck and breast to the knife. The eyes of the maniac were upon her own; she was as helpless and obedient as a lamb before his spell.

Then Holt's horrible paralysis, if only just in time, was lifted. The priest had raised his arm, the bronze knife with its ragged edge gleamed in the air, with the other hand he had already gathered up the thick dark hair, so that the neck lay bare and open to the final blow. But it was two other details, Holt thinks, that set his muscles suddenly free, enabling him to act with the swift judgment which, being wholly unexpected, disconcerted both maniac and victim and frustrated the awful culmination. The dark spots of blood upon the face he loved, and the sudden final fluttering of the dead bird's wings upon the ground – these two things, life actually touching death, released the held-back springs.

He leaped forward. He received the blow upon his left arm and hand. It was his right fist that sent the High Priest to earth with a blow that, luckily, felled him in the direction away from the dreadful brink, and it was his right arm and hand, he became aware some time afterwards only, that were chiefly of use in carrying the fainting girl and her unconscious father back to the shelter of the cottage, and to the best help and comfort he could provide …

It was several years afterwards, in a very different setting, that he found himself spelling out slowly to a little boy the lettering cut into a circlet of bronze the child found on his study table. To the child he told a fairy tale, then dismissed him to play with his mother in the garden. But, when alone, he rubbed away the verdigris with great care, for the circlet was thin and frail with age, as he examined again the little picture of a tripod from which smoke issued, incised neatly in the metal. Below it, almost as sharp as when the Roman craftsman cut it first, was the name Acella. He touched the letters tenderly with his left hand, from which two fingers were missing, then placed it in a drawer of his desk and turned the key.

'That curious name,' said a low voice behind his chair. His wife had come in and was looking over his shoulder. 'You love it, and I dread it.' She sat on the desk beside him, her eyes troubled. 'It was the name father used to call me in his illness.'

Her husband looked at her with passionate tenderness, but said no word.

'And this,' she went on, taking the broken hand in both her own, 'is the price you paid to me for his life. I often wonder what strange good deity brought you upon the lonely moor that night, and just in the very nick of time. You remember …?'

'The deity who helps true lovers, of course,' he said with a smile, evading the question. The deeper memory, he knew, had closed absolutely in her since the moment of the attempted double crime. He kissed her, murmuring to himself as he did so, but too low for her to hear, 'Acella! *My* Acella …!'

Imagination

The Genesis of Ideas (1937)

'Writing – oh, writing's just a function like any other natural operation. Writing's functional.' The sentence still rings on in my mind, though I first heard it twenty-five years ago. It was rather a challenge to a young scribbler, especially as the speaker was a very prominent London doctor, the editor of *Brains*. It was, at any rate, what Elgar – his eyes twinkling at me sideways while composing music for my children's play – called 'a talking point': something to discuss and argue about.

I recall the summer afternoon on a Dorsetshire lawn and the group beneath the flowering limes, and the general conversation, for it was about writing men and the methodical way some of them turn out so many words a morning, much as they take their bath or do their 'daily dozen'. And the doctor's thesis, as we chatted over the tea cups and watched the butterflies, was something like this: that the average man receives only a very few impressions per minute, whereas the sensitive, high-strung type called 'artist', receives them in enormously higher ratio. Impressions pour in upon him in a rapid flood – from light, colour, sound, form, and all the rest. He becomes packed with them, overfed, supercharged. And he must do something about all this food. He must get rid of it somehow, otherwise he may become mentally poisoned by it. If, luckily, he has some talent for expression, out the impressions pour. 'Writing's functional.'

The rest of the conversation has gone the way of most other conversations, but one point remains – viz: that these impressions recorded and registered need not reappear immediately. They may lie fallow for days, months, years. Only they are not, of course, forgotten, and at a moment favourable to their emergence they pop out again, to enrich a sentence or decorate a theme. Some external detail of the day contributes the right evocative touch, there's a click in some cupboard's latch – and memory gives up her dead.

The genesis of a story in a writer's mind is 'a talking point' that has psychological interest. Once started, a story runs along well or ill; it's the actual starting point that claims attention. Everything, everybody, I read somewhere in an article by H G Wells, is the germ of a possible story. It's the easiest thing in the world, with no mystery about it, to pick a theme. Watch any man with real attention – in a train, a hotel, a dentist's room – and begin to wonder about him: how he lives, earns money, loves, where he's going, whence he's come – and he will begin to grow on you. Other characters arrive … the man lives and feels and does things. A story is born before you know where you are. The secret here lies in those two words 'with attention', for attention, of course, sets the imagination working.

I have myself watched, with 'some attention', at any rate, this genesis of a story, preferably, let us agree, of a short story rather than a novel calling for a biggish canvas. I must not dogmatize, but it seems to me that it starts with an emotion, a strong, deep emotion that seeks, naturally, to express itself. It may be caused, let us say, by beauty of nature, rapture of music, wonder, horror of the supernatural, but, whatever the cause, the emotion, boiling and bursting for expression, seeks an outlet. If, at the moment, it finds none, what happens to it? It is not forgotten because it is unforgettable. It may pass, but it does not die. It sinks slowly out of sight. It goes down into that enormous storehouse of things unused, unexpressed – the subconscious. And there it lies until some chance click of the cupboard latch releases it. Only the Subconscious invariably *dramatizes*. That lost emotion reappears in dramatic form. The writer gets rid of it by dramatizing it. A story.

I mentioned having attempted to watch this process in myself. An incident, if it is not too egotistical, occurs to me in Egypt, where I often spent the winter. My mind was completely absorbed at the time in a long book, but I was open, naturally, to the numerous impressions of that vivid and haunting land. The desert, for instance, and, above all, its waterlessness. Death from thirst was an idea no observant traveller could help thinking about sometimes; but it had not touched me personally, and no thought of a story about it had entered my mind. Nonetheless, I had more than once visualised its horror imaginatively – and one morning I woke with a sentence running in my head: 'You will drown but you will not know you drown.'

It was a curious sentence, and a curious feeling accompanied it – the conviction, namely, that it was the climax to some dream which had escaped on waking, leaving only this sentence behind. That there had been a dream I felt positive, but not being expert in my friend Dunne's method of dream-recovery ('Experiment in Time'), I left it alone, and went instead, straight to my writing table. 'I will just sit down,' I said to myself, 'and begin a commonplace little story, any little story, and see what happens. That curious sentence may come up in the climax and justify itself.' I chose the desert as *mise en scène*, since my window looked out upon it; and I realised, of course, that the only way to drown without knowing you were drowning would be to be unconscious when you went under water. And my commonplace little story ran along smoothly enough, gathered momentum, and found its natural, logical climax in precisely that sentence, although I had no idea until the few final paragraphs how the sentence could justify itself. The story appeared in a London paper and later in a book, but whether a good or a poor story is not the point; the point that interests me is my feeling that the entire story first lay complete in my subconscious. It was a subconscious dramatization of my emotion about thirst in a waterless desert. It came up – upside down – in sleep. But its genesis lay in that emotion of weeks before; the subconscious had dramatized it for me. If the process can be described as functional, my friend, the doctor, may be right.

What to me seemed an even more striking instance of powerful emotion dramatizing itself in story form had occurred some years earlier, after a journey I made through the Caucasus. The stupendous grandeur of those almost legendary mountains made a profound impression upon a young and sensitive mind. What a climax, after the Isles of Greece, Smyrna, Athens, the Golden Horn, to land at Batoum, the Colchis of the Argonauts and Golden Fleece, and pass on, via Tiflis, into Shelley's 'lovely vale in the Indian Caucasus' where his Prometheus became unbound! The flood of emotions was deep and strong, and the slight inaccuracy of 'Indian' made no difference. Briefly – after an extended tour, I came home supercharged, yet, apart from a few travel sketches, found I had nothing to write. Bewildered and confused with so much wonder and 'awful loveliness', the mind seemed literally speechless. It was months later, the seething mass having settled down a bit, that I sat down to do a fantastic tale of sorts about one of those remote and secret Caucasian Valleys where the Exiled Gods of Greece were still visible. The idea in my mind was rather vague, though the tale ran smoothly enough, it seemed, when – suddenly, up rose something much bigger, breaking through my tale of old Greek Gods. I let it come, for indeed it soon became irresistible, taking complete possession of me. Literally, it came pouring through me. I tore up the Greek Gods and, yielding to this new obsession, out came what I always like best of all my books – 'The Centaur'. Nor is there any doubt in my mind that this, my favourite book, an interpretation of the Soul of the Caucasus in semi-story form, is an expression of the emotions experienced there which had lain fallow all these months before rising to the surface – dramatized by the subconscious.

I have specialized myself in horror and mystery tales with a so-called 'supernatural' background. All my early books explored this suggestive region, and I often suspect that the 'horror' part of them represented my gruesome experiences of crime and evil, accumulated when I was a newspaper reporter in New York. I was in my early twenties, unusually impressionable, but I did not begin to write till the age of thirty-six. The harvest of five years' newspaper reporting was ready for the plucking; I owe some of those sheaves to the City Editors of the *Evening Sun* and *New York Times*. The 'supernatural' part I owe to no one but myself, for even in earliest childhood it brought me a strange thrill. As a boy I longed to see a ghost, and whenever I could hear of a haunted house with a fairly reliable story behind it, I went to pass a night in it. I never saw anything, but if luck or hysteria had come my way, I should doubtless, to borrow from Shelley's 'Hymn to Intellectual Beauty', have 'shrieked and clasped my hands in ecstasy'. With growing years, however, this childish desire to see a ghost passed into something better: I wanted to understand what faculty *enabled* one to see a ghost, or, rather, to be aware of any 'other-worldly' manifestation at all. My interest lay then in the extension of human faculty, and in the possibility that the mind has powers which only manifest themselves occasionally. And this interest is stronger in me today than ever. It leads into an enormous and very tricky field, of course. The researches of modern psychology, studies of multiple personality, new conceptions of time and space, and the serious possibility that normal consciousness may experience strange extensions, give to the whole question now a semi-scientific flavour.

The true 'other-worldly' story, however, must never be scientific; its appeal must be to that core of superstition which lies in every mother's son of us. We are still close enough to primitive days to fear the dark, and a successful tale in this *genre* must reach that darkness in us to get across. Reason, of course, must abdicate. And I think the writer of such a tale must himself feel something of superstitious fear and 'other-worldly' dread. To sit down and write a ghost story, one must first *feel* ghostly. Told reasonably and logically, it may be a good and clever tale, but the essential thrill characteristic of the real ghost story will be lacking. In my own humble case, the stories, such as 'The Willows', 'The Wendigo', the 'John Silence' tales, that frightened the reader, frightened me still more as I was writing them. Shuddering oneself, the right words come. It is obvious, too, that with the passing of the years, those delicious 'other-worldly thrills' and shivers of primitive emotion that so easily stirred superstitious wonder in youth, became overlaid with the scientific thought and reading of a scientific age. The ghostly stories are no longer *felt* as they once were.

The Ghost Story itself is a curious form in any case, for it seems almost an Anglo-Saxon, possibly Celtic, thing. The Latins will have none of it. The Northerns prefer legends, myths, traditions, sagas. During ten years in the United States I rarely came across a ghost story proper. In England, Scotland, Ireland, on the other hand, a ghost story is almost as much a subject of ordinary conversation as the weather. This is, again, what Elgar called a 'talking point'. Yet when I am asked here in London to 'tell one of your ghost stories' on our BBC, I always prefer to tell a 'queer' story, in which the 'other-worldly' or supernatural plays a very minor part, rather than a ghost-story proper. Wireless, ether waves, machinery, scientific atmosphere generally, seem to me to produce in listeners an attitude hardly favourable to the emergence of that superstitious core that should be reached.

Among writers of such tales, the authentic touch, too, has always seemed to me a very rare and delicate matter, for it is a touch not due to skill, precisely. Henry James achieved it without a false note in 'The Two Magics', though we are told that he himself thought little of that masterpiece in horror. Lefanu excelled, almost without exception. Mrs Oliphant, to go further back, and the American authoress (whose name escapes me) of 'The Wind in the Rose Bush,' were both masters, or mistresses, of its elusive magic. FitzJames O'Brien, in his 'Diamond Lens', I felt, just missed it, if only just. Arthur Machen, E F Benson, achieving other wonders, possess it not.

By Water (1914)

The night before young Larsen left to take up his new appointment in Egypt he went to the clairvoyante. He neither believed nor disbelieved. He felt no interest, for he already knew his past and did not wish to know his future. 'Just to please me, Jim,' the girl pleaded. 'The woman is wonderful. Before I had been five minutes with her she told me your initials, so there *must* be something in it.' 'She read your thought,' he smiled indulgently. 'Even I can do that!' But the girl was in earnest. He yielded; and that night at his farewell dinner he came to give his report of the interview.

The result was meagre and unconvincing: money was coming to him, he was soon to make a voyage, and – he would never marry. 'So you see how silly it all is,' he laughed, for they were to be married when his first promotion came. He gave the details, however, making a little story of it in the way he knew she loved.

'But was that all, Jim?' The girl asked it, looking rather hard into his face. 'Aren't you hiding something from me?' He hesitated a moment, then burst out laughing at her clever discernment. 'There *was* a little more,' he confessed, 'but you take it all so seriously; I —'

He had to tell it then, of course. The woman had told him a lot of gibberish about friendly and unfriendly elements. 'She said water was unfriendly to me; I was to be careful of water, or else I should come to harm by it. Fresh water only,' he hastened to add, seeing that the idea of shipwreck was in her mind.

'Drowning?' came the question quickly.

'Yes,' he admitted with reluctance, but still laughing; 'she did say drowning, though drowning in no ordinary way.'

The girl's face showed uneasiness a moment. 'What does

that mean – drowning in no ordinary way?' There was a catch in her breath.

But that he could not tell her, because he did not know himself. He gave, therefore, the woman's exact words: 'You will drown, but will not know you drown.'

It was unwise of him. He wished afterwards he had invented a happier report, or had kept this detail back. 'I'm safe in Egypt, anyhow,' he laughed. 'I shall be a clever man if I can find enough water in the desert to do me harm!' And all the way from Trieste to Alexandria he remembered the promise she had extracted – that he would never once go on the Nile unless duty made it imperative for him to do so. He kept that promise like the literal, faithful soul he was. His love was equal to the somewhat quixotic sacrifice it occasionally involved. Fresh water in Egypt there was practically none other, and in any case the natron works where his duty lay had their headquarters some distance out into the desert. The river, with its banks of welcome, refreshing verdure, was not even visible.

Months passed quickly, and the time for leave came within measurable distance. In the long interval luck had played the cards kindly for him, vacancies had occurred, early promotion seemed likely, and his letters were full of plans to bring her out to share a little house of their own. His health, however, had not improved; the dryness did not suit him; even in this short period his blood had thinned, his nervous system deteriorated, and, contrary to the doctor's prophecy, the waterless air had told upon his sleep. A damp climate liked him best. And once the sun had touched him with its fiery finger.

His letters made no mention of this. He described the life to her, the work, the sport, the pleasant people, and his chances of increased pay and early marriage. And a week before he sailed he rode out upon a final act of duty to inspect the latest diggings his Company were making. His course lay some twenty miles into the desert behind El-Chobak towards the limestone hills of Guebel Haidi, and he went alone, carrying lunch and tea, for it was the weekly holiday of Friday, and the men were not at work.

The accident was ordinary enough. On his way back in the heat of early afternoon his pony stumbled against a boulder on the treacherous desert film, threw him heavily, broke the girth, bolted before he could seize the reins again, and left him stranded some ten or twelve miles from home. There was a pain in his knee that made walking difficult, a buzzing in his head that troubled sight and made the landscape swim, while, worse than either, his provisions, fastened to the saddle, had vanished with the frightened pony into those blazing leagues of sand. He was alone in the Desert, beneath the pitiless afternoon sun, twelve miles of utterly exhausting country between him and safety.

Under normal conditions he could have covered the distance in four hours, reaching home by dark; but his knee pained him so that a mile an hour proved the best he could possibly do. He reflected a few minutes. The wisest course was to sit down and wait till the pony told its obvious story to the stable, and help should come. And this was what he did, for the scorching heat and glare were dangerous; they were terrible; he was shaken and bewildered by his fall, hungry and weak into the bargain; and an hour's painful scrambling over the baked and burning little gorges must have speedily caused complete prostration. He sat down and rubbed his aching knee. It was quite a little adventure. Yet, though he knew the Desert might not be lightly trifled with, he felt at the moment nothing more than this – and the amusing description of it he would give in his letter, or – intoxicating thought – by word of mouth. In the heat of the sun he began to feel drowsy. He was exhausted. A soft torpor crept over him. He dozed. He fell asleep.

It was a long, a dreamless sleep … for when he woke at length the sun had just gone down, the dusk lay awfully upon the enormous desert, and the air was chilly. The cold had waked him. Quickly, as though on purpose, the red glow faded from the sky; the first stars shone; it was dark; the heavens were deep violet. He looked round and realised that his sense of direction had gone entirely. Great hunger was in him. The cold already was bitter as the wind rose, but the pain in his knee having eased, he got up and walked a little – and in a moment lost sight of the spot where he had been lying. The shadowy desert swallowed it. 'Ah,' he realised, 'this is not an English field or moor. I'm in the Desert!' The safe thing to do was to remain exactly where he was; only thus could the rescuers find him; once he wandered he was done for. It was strange the search-party had not yet arrived. To keep warm, however, he was compelled to move, so he made a little pile of stones to mark the place, and walked round and round it in a circle of some dozen yards' diameter. He limped badly, and the hunger gnawed dreadfully; but, after all, the adventure was not so terrible. The amusing side of it kept uppermost still. Though fragile in body, his spirit was not unduly timid or imaginative; he *could* last out the night, or, if the worst came to the worst, the next day as well. But when he watched the little group of stones, he saw that there were dozens of them, scores, hundreds, thousands of these little groups of stones. The desert's face, of course, is thickly strewn with them. The original one was lost in the first five minutes. So he sat down again. But the biting cold, and the wind that licked his very skin beneath the light clothing, soon forced him up again. It was ominous; and the night huge and shelterless. The shaft of green zodiacal light that hung so strangely in the western sky for hours had faded away; the stars were out in their bright thousands; no guide was anywhere; the wind moaned and puffed among the sandy mounds; the vast sheet of desert stretched mockingly upon the world; he heard the jackals cry …

And with the jackals' cry came suddenly the unwelcome realisation that no play was in this adventure any more, but that a bleak reality stared at him through the surrounding darkness. He faced it – at bay. He was genuinely lost. Thought blocked in him. 'I must be calm and think,' he said aloud. His voice woke no echo; it was small and dead; something gigantic ate it instantly. He got up and walked again. Why did no one come? Hours had passed. The pony had long ago found its stable, or – had it run madly in another direction altogether? He worked out possibilities, tightening his belt. The cold was searching; he never had been, never could be warm again; the hot sunshine of a few hours ago seemed the merest dream. Unfamiliar with hardship, he knew not what to do, but he took his coat and shirt off, vigorously rubbed his skin where the dried perspiration of the afternoon still caused clammy shivers, swung his arms furiously like a London cabman, and quickly dressed again. Though the wind upon his bare back was biting, he felt warmer a little. He lay down exhausted, sheltered by an over-hanging limestone crag, and took snatches of fitful dog's-sleep, while the wind drove overhead and the dry sand pricked his skin. One face continually was near him; one pair of tender eyes; two dear hands smoothed him; he smelt the perfume of light brown hair. It was all natural enough. His whole thought, in his misery, ran to her in England – England where there was soft fresh grass, big sheltering trees, hemlock and honeysuckle in the hedges – while the hard black Desert guarded him, and consciousness dipped away at little intervals under this dry and pitiless Egyptian sky …

It was perhaps five in the morning when a voice spoke and he started up with a sudden jerk – the voice of that clairvoyante woman. The sentence fled away into the darkness, but one word remained: *Water!* At first he wondered, but at once explanation came. Cause and effect were obvious. The clue was physical. His body needed water, and so the thought came up into his mind. He was thirsty.

This was the moment when fear first really touched him. Hunger was manageable, more or less – for a day or two, certainly. But thirst! Thirst and the Desert were an evil pair that, by cumulative suggestion gathering since childhood days, brought terror in. Once in the mind it could not be dislodged. In spite of his best efforts, the ghastly thing grew passionately – because his thirst grew too. He had smoked much; had eaten spiced things at lunch; had breathed in alkali with the dry, scorched air. He searched for a cool flint pebble to put into his burning mouth, but found only angular scraps of dusty limestone. There were no pebbles here. The cold helped a little to counteract, but already he knew in himself subconsciously the dread of something that was coming. What was it? He tried to hide the thought and bury it out of sight. The utter futility of his tiny strength against the power of the universe appalled him. And then he knew. The merciless sun was on the way, already rising. Its return was like the presage of execution …

It came. With true horror he watched the marvellous swift dawn break over the sandy sea. The eastern sky glowed hurriedly as from crimson fires. Ridges, not noticeable in the starlight, turned black in endless series, like flat-topped billows of a frozen ocean. Wide streaks of blue and yellow followed, as the sky dropped sheets of mauve light upon the wind-eaten cliffs and showed their under sides. They did not advance; they waited till the sun was up – and then they moved; they rose and sank; they shifted as the sunshine lifted them and the shadows crept away. But in an hour there would be no shadows any more. There would be no shade.

The little groups of stones began to dance. It was horrible. The unbroken, huge expanse lay round him, warming up, twelve hours of blazing hell to come. Already the monstrous Desert glared, each bit familiar, since each bit was a repetition of the bit before, behind, on either side. It laughed at guidance and direction. He rose and walked; for miles he walked, though how many, north, south, or west, he knew not. The frantic thing was in him now, the fury of the Desert; he took its pace, its endless, tireless stride, the stride of the burning, murderous Desert that is waterless. He felt it alive – a blindly heaving desire in it to reduce him to its conditionless, awful dryness. He felt – yet knowing this was feverish and *not* to be believed – that his own small life lay on its mighty surface, a mere dot in space, a mere heap of little stones. His emotions, his fears, his hopes, his ambition, his love – mere bundled group of little unimportant stones that danced with apparent activity for a moment, then were merged in the undifferentiated surface underneath. He was included in a purpose greater than his own.

The will made a plucky effort then. 'A night and a day,' he laughed, while his lips cracked smartingly with the stretching of the skin, 'what is it? Many a chap has lasted days and days ...!' Yes, only he was not of that rare company. He was ordinary, unaccustomed to privation, weak, untrained of spirit, unacquainted with stern resistance. He knew not how to spare himself. The Desert struck him where it pleased – all over. It played with him. His tongue was swollen; the parched throat could not swallow. He sank ... An hour he lay there, just wit enough in him to choose the top of a mound where he could be most easily seen. He lay two hours, three, four hours ... The heat blazed down upon him like a furnace ... The sky, when he opened his eyes once, was empty ... then a speck became visible in the blue expanse; and presently another speck. They came from nowhere. They hovered very high, almost out of sight. They appeared, they disappeared, they – reappeared. Nearer and nearer they swung down, in sweeping stealthy circles ... little dancing groups of them, miles away but ever drawing closer – the vultures ...

He had strained his ears so long for sounds of feet and voices that it seemed he could no longer hear at all. Hearing had ceased within him. Then came the water-dreams, with their agonising torture. He heard *that* ... heard it running in silvery streams and rivulets across green English meadows. It rippled with silvery music. He heard it splash. He dipped hands and feet and head in it – in deep, clear pools of generous depth. He drank; with his skin he drank, not with mouth and throat alone. Ice clinked in effervescent, sparkling water against a glass. He swam and plunged. Water gushed freely over back and shoulders, gallons and gallons of it, bathfuls and to spare, a flood of gushing, crystal, cool, life-giving liquid ... And then he stood in a beech wood and felt the streaming deluge of delicious summer rain upon his face; heard it drip luxuriantly upon a million thirsty leaves. The wet trunks shone, the damp moss spread its perfume, ferns waved heavily in the moist atmosphere. He was soaked to the skin in it. A mountain torrent, fresh from fields of snow, dashed foaming past, and the spray fell in a shower upon his cheeks and hair. He dived – head foremost ... Ah, he was up to the neck ... and *she* was with him; they were under water together; he saw her eyes gleaming into his own beneath the copious flood.

The voice, however, was not hers ... 'You will drown, yet you will not know you drown ...!' His swollen tongue called out a name. But no sound was audible. He closed his eyes. There came sweet unconsciousness ...

A sound in that instant *was* audible, though. It was a voice – voices – and the thud of animal hoofs upon the sand. The specks had vanished from the sky as mysteriously as they came. And, as though in answer to the sound, he made a movement – but an automatic, an unconscious movement. He did not know he moved. And the body, uncontrolled, lost its precarious balance. He rolled; but he did not know he rolled. Slowly, over the edge of the sloping mound of sand, he turned sideways. Like a log of wood he slid gradually, turning over and over, nothing to stop him – to the bottom. A few feet only, and not even steep; just steep enough to keep rolling slowly. There was a – splash. But he did not know there was a splash.

They found him in a pool of water – one of these rare pools the Desert Bedouin mark preciously for their own. He had lain within three yards of it for hours. He was drowned … but he did not know he drowned …

Imagination (1910)

Having dined upon a beefsteak and a pint of bitter, Jones went home to work. The trouble with Jones – his first name William – was that he possessed creative imagination: that luggage upon which excess charges have to be paid all through life – to the critic, the stupid, the orthodox, the slower minds without the 'flash'. He was alone in his brother's flat. It was after nine o'clock. He was half-way into a story, and had – stuck! Sad to relate, the machinery that carries on the details of an original inspiration had blocked. And to invent he knew not how. Unless the imagination 'produced' he would not allow his brain to devise mere episodes – dull and lifeless substitutes. Jones, poor fool, was also artist.

And the reason he had 'stuck' was not surprising, for his story was of a kind that might well tax the imagination of any sane man. He was writing at the moment about a being who had survived his age – a study of one of those rare and primitive souls who walk the earth to-day in a man's twentieth-century body, while yet the spirit belongs to the Golden Age of the world's history. You may come across them sometimes, rare, ingenuous, delightful beings, the primal dews still upon their eyelids, the rush and glow of earth's pristine fires pulsing in their veins, careless of gain, indifferent to success, lost, homeless, exiled – *dépaysés* ... The idea had seized him. He had met such folk. He burned to describe their exile, the pathos of their loneliness, their yearnings and their wanderings – rejected by a world they had outlived. And for his type, thus representing some power of unexpended mythological values strayed back into modern life to find itself denied and ridiculed – he had chosen a Centaur! For he wished it to symbolise what he believed was to be the next stage in human evolution: Intuition no longer neglected, but developed equally with Reason. His Centaur was to stand for instinct (the animal body close to Nature) combined with, yet not dominated by, the upright stature moving towards deity. The conception was true and pregnant.

And – he had stuck. The detail that blocked him was the man's *appearance*. How would such a being look? In what details would he betray that, though outwardly a man, he was inwardly this survival of the Golden Age, escaped from some fair Eden, splendid, immense, simple, and beneficent, yet – a Centaur?

Perhaps it was just as well he had 'stuck', for his brother would shortly be in, and his brother was a successful business man with the money-sense and commercial instincts strongly developed. He dealt in rice and sugar. With his brother in the flat no Centaur could possibly survive for a single moment. 'It'll come to me when I'm not thinking about it,' he sighed, knowing well the waywardness of his particular genius. He threw the reins upon the subconscious self and moved into an arm-chair to read in the evening paper the things the public loved – that public who refused to buy his books, pleading they were 'queer'. He waded down the list of immoralities, murders and assaults with a dreamy eye, and had just reached the witness's description of finding the bloody head in the faithless wife's bedroom, when there came a hurried, pelting knock at the door, and William Jones, glad of the relief, went to open it. There, facing him, stood the bore from the flat below. Horrors!

It was not, however, a visit after all. 'Jones,' he faltered, 'there's an odd sort of chap here asking for you or your brother. Rang my bell by mistake.'

Jones murmured some reply or other, and as the bore vanished with a hurry unusual to him, there passed into the flat a queer shape, born surely of the night and stars and desolate places. He seemed in some undefinable way bent, humpbacked, very large. With him came a touch of open spaces, winds, forests, long clean hills and dew-drenched fields.

'Come in, please ...' said Jones, instantly aware that the man was not for his brother. 'You have something to – er —' he was going to use the word 'ask', then changed it instinctively – '*say* to me, haven't you?'

The man was ragged, poor, outcast. Clearly it was a begging episode; and yet he trembled violently, while in his veins ran fire. The caller refused a seat, but moved over to the curtains by the window, drawing them slightly aside so that he could see out. And the window was high above old smoky London – open. It felt cold. Jones bent down, always keeping his caller in view, and lit the gas-stove. 'You wish to see me,' he said, rising again to an upright position. Then he added more hurriedly, stepping back a little towards the rack where the walking-sticks were, 'Please let me know what I can do for you!'

Bearded, unkempt, with massive shoulders and huge neck, the caller stood a moment and stared. 'Your name and address,' he said at length, 'were given to me' – he hesitated a moment, then added – 'you know by whom.' His voice was deep and windy and echoing. It made the stretched cords of the upright piano ring against the wall. 'He told me to call,' the man concluded.

'Ah yes; of course,' Jones stammered, forgetting for the moment who or where he was. Let me see – where are you' – the word did not want to come out – 'staying?' The caller made an awful and curious movement; it seemed so much bigger than his body. 'In what way – er – can I be of assistance?' Jones hardly knew what he said. The other volunteered so little. He was frightened. Then, before the man could answer, he caught a dreadful glimpse, as of something behind the outline. It moved. Was it shadow that thus extended his form? Was it the glare of that ugly gas-stove that played tricks with the folds of the curtain, driving bodily outline forth into mere vacancy? For the figure of his strange caller seemed to carry with it the idea of projections, extensions, growths, in themselves not monstrous, fine and comely, rather – yet awful.

The man left the window and moved towards him. It was a movement both swift and enormous. It was instantaneous.

'Who are you – *really*?' asked Jones, his breath catching, while he went pluckily out to meet him, irresistibly drawn. 'And what is it you *really* want of me?' He went very close to the shrouded form, caught the keen air from the open window behind, sniffed a wind that was not London's stale and weary wind, then stopped abruptly, frozen with terror and delight. The man facing him was splendid and terrific, exhaling something that overwhelmed.

'What can I … do … for … you?' whispered Jones, shaking like a leaf. A delight of racing clouds was in him.

The answer came in a singular roaring voice that yet sounded far away, as though among mountains. Wind might have brought it down.

'There is nothing you can do for me! But, by Chiron, there is something I can do for you!'

'And that is?' asked Jones faintly, feeling something sweep against his feet and legs like the current of a river in flood.

The man eyed him appallingly a moment.

'Let you see me!' he roared, while his voice set the piano singing again, and his outline seemed to swim over the chairs and tables like a fluid mass. 'Show myself to you!'

The figure stretched out what looked like arms, reared gigantically aloft towards the ceiling, and swept towards him. Jones saw the great visage close to his own. He smelt the odour of caves, river-beds, hillsides – space. In another second he would have been lost ––

His brother made a great rattling as he opened the door. The atmosphere of rice and sugar and office desks came in with him.

'Why, Billy, old man, you look as if you'd seen a ghost. You're white!'

William Jones mopped his forehead. 'I've been working rather hard,' he answered. 'Feel tired. Fact is – I got stuck in a story for a bit.'

'Too bad. Got it straightened out at last, I hope?'

'Yes, thanks. *It came to me* – in the end.'

The other looked at him. 'Good,' he said shortly. 'Rum thing, imagination, isn't it?' And then he began talking about his day's business – in tons and tons of food.

Notes on the text

KATE MACDONALD

'Mid the Haunts of the Moose (1900)

Indian: the former term used by white people for the First Nations in Canada.

'Hebrew of the Woods': anti-Semitic expressions were commonly used without consideration in this period. Using the image of the large-nosed Jew was a routine slur.

vegetarian: vegetarian diets were considered to be eccentric and unhealthy for humans in this period, and also inherently pacifist.

Bruin: from the Middle English for 'brown', a folkname for a bear, first recorded in the seventeenth century.

buck-fever: the trembling of the hands from excitement when the animal is within the hunter's sights.

disport herself matutinally: she would bathe or wash herself in the lake in the mornings in privacy.

indifferent lasting powers: their stamina for the long days on foot is reputed to not be high.

Skeleton Lake (1906)

hunting bloomers: a rare variation on women's 'dress reform' clothing from this period, which is more usually associated with a daring costume for cycling. Women would not wear trousers in public, albeit as part of a uniform, until the First World War.

wax cylinders: the original sound recording device.

The Wolves of God (1921)

Kettletoft: a settlement on the south coast of Sanday, a large island in the north-east of the Orkneys, north of mainland Scotland.

treeless: the Orkney islands have very few trees, as they can only grow where the salt air and sea winds will not wither them.

opportunities: to make money and gain promotion.

heaving uplands: Sanday, and indeed most of the Orkney islands, is very flat, with no upland areas.

ain't you: the men are not speaking in an Orkney dialect.

factor: Scots term for a land or estate manager.

evening flight: of duck or other wildfowl landing on the lake, or loch, for the night. The only lochs in the Orkneys are on the mainland, and there are none on Sanday.

fowling pieces: duck-shooting guns.

creature wants: a variation of 'creature comforts', meaning the necessities of life: warmth, food and drink.

the Swarf: the southernmost tip of Sanday.

Wendigo: an evil spirit from First Nations folklore, which Blackwood wrote about in 'The Wendigo' (1908).

The Winter Alps (1910)

funiculaires: counterbalanced railway carriages drawn up a steep slope by a pair of cables.

saisissant: French, striking, startling or arresting.

battlements that on their front bear stars: from 'Book 2: The Solitary' of William Wordsworth's poem *The Excursion* (1814); the correct text is 'towers begirt / With battlements that on their restless fronts / Bore stars'.

The Glamour of the Snow (1911)

Valais Alps: a western range of the Alps in Switzerland and Italy.

'who understood': a satirical description of women who claim to be particularly understanding or sensitive to others, inviting confidences.

flappers: a slang term in this period for adolescent girls and young women.

shibboleths: deriving from Judges 12, 406, a test of foreignness, but used here in the sense of customs and habits held by particular groups.

punctilious: very correct on matters of etiquette, in this case on not addressing a woman to whom he had not yet been introduced.

alone at midnight: he worries that the girl's reputation might be compromised if they had been seen alone together at night.

luged: sledging alone or with one companion.

bal costumé: a fancy dress dance.

green morocco desk: a small travelling wooden box bound in decorative leather, with a sloping lid, used to contain papers and also to write upon.

telemark: a skiing technique and also a type of boot fastening on the ski that leaves the heels free, for better manoeuvrability.

Un monsieur qui fait du ski à cette heure! Il est Anglais, donc ...: French, 'That man is going skiing at this time of night! But, he's English, so ...', suggesting that the English will do mad things.

'synagogue': the sense suggests that this is an obscure French name for an assembly of evil spirits, an anti-Semitic analogue from the term for a Jewish congregation.

The Sacrifice (1913)

Remington: an early make of typewriter.

"s ist bald ein Uhr, Herr! Aufstehen!": German, It's almost one o'clock sir! Get up!

couloirs: fissures or vertical corridors through difficult rock crevices.

On Reincarnation (1930)

Did I not sing ... Carthage Bay: lines from the play *Paolo and Francesca* (1900) by the British playwright Stephen Phillips.

Devachan: from Theosophical teachings, the temporary place of gratified desires where souls go after death, and from there they are reborn into life again.

E D Walker: American journalist who wrote *Reincarnation* (1888).

Mrs Besant: a British socialist and Theosophist, who worked for social reform and progressive religion in the late nineteenth century in Britain and later in colonial India.

M'Taggart: *Some Dogmas of Religion* by John McTaggart was published in 1906.

Soul of a People: Fielding Hall's *Soul of a People* (1889) is based on his experiences in Burma (Myanmar) and Buddhism.

Did the majority: if the majority.

Human Personality and its Survival of Bodily Death: *Human Personality and its Survival of Bodily Death* by Frederick Myers was published in 1903.

Dr Osty: Dr Eugene Osty was a French physician and psychic researcher, also a member of the Society for Psychical Research. He was the author of several books on psychic subjects.

Gurthis: no books by an author of this name are recorded.

Planet Mars: *From India to the Planet Mars* by Théodore Flournoy (1900) is a classic of early psychology, which extended the understanding of the unconscious.

The Insanity of Jones (1907)

Theosophical Society: one of the aims of this nineteenth-century international society was to investigate unexplained laws of nature and latent mental or psychical powers in humans.

defalcation: the theft or appropriation of money by the person responsible for its security.

The Tarn of Sacrifice (1921)

tarn: north country dialect word for a pool of water in remote places.

the Wall: Hadrian's Wall, the old Roman border wall marking the most northerly point of Roman administrative and military rule during their occupation of southern Britain.

mind: Scots, to remember.

War to end war: a phrase that arose during the First World War.

Regeneration of the race: in 1911 two influential books were published entitled with variations on this phrase, by the British sexologist Havelock Ellis and Caleb W Saleeby, an English obstetrician who advocated eugenics, though by 1921 he had moved away from that ideology.

very short skirt: relative to the fashions of 1921; the skirt was probably still below knee-length.

The Genesis of Ideas (1937)

Elgar: Sir Edward Elgar, great British composer of the early twentieth century.

daily dozen: a set of exercises devised for daily use by Walter Camp, a sports journalist and American football coach.

Experiment in Time: *An Experiment With Time* by J W Dunne was published in 1927, and had an immediate impact on writers and thinkers interested in precognition and time.

'lovely vale in the Indian Caucasus': from Percy Bysshe Shelley's verse drama *Prometheus Unbound* (1820).

'Hymn to Intellectual Beauty': poem published in 1817.

Lefanu: Sheridan Lefanu, nineteenth-century Irish writer of much-lauded Gothic, horror and ghost stories.

Mrs Oliphant: Margaret Oliphant was a nineteenth-century author of delicately structured ghost stories.

'The Wind in the Rose Bush': this collection was written by Mary E Wilkins Freeman and published in 1903.

FitzJames O'Brien: formerly named Michael, he was an Irish poet and a soldier in the American Civil War.

By Water (1914)

natron works: natron, used extensively in Ancient Egypt to preserve bodies for mummification, is a naturally occurring salt dug from the soil beside some saline lakes.

Imagination (1910)

dépaysés: French, those who are out of place.

From the Abyss

Weird Fiction, 1907–1945

by D K Broster

D K Broster was one of the great British historical novelists of the twentieth century, but her Weird fiction has long been forgotten. She wrote some of the most impressive supernatural short stories to be published between the wars. Melissa Edmundson, editor of Handheld's *Women's Weird*, has curated a selection of Broster's best and most terrifying work. Stories in *From the Abyss* include these tales of particular archaeological and architectural interest:

- 'The Window', in which a deserted chateau exacts revenge when one particular window is opened.
- 'The Pavement', in which the protectress of a Roman mosaic cannot bear to let it go.
- 'Clairvoyance', in which the spirit of a vengeful Japanese swordmaster enters an adolescent girl.
- 'The Pestering', in which a cursed hidden treasure draws its victim across centuries to find it.
- 'The Taste of Pomegranates' draws two young women into the palaeolithic past.

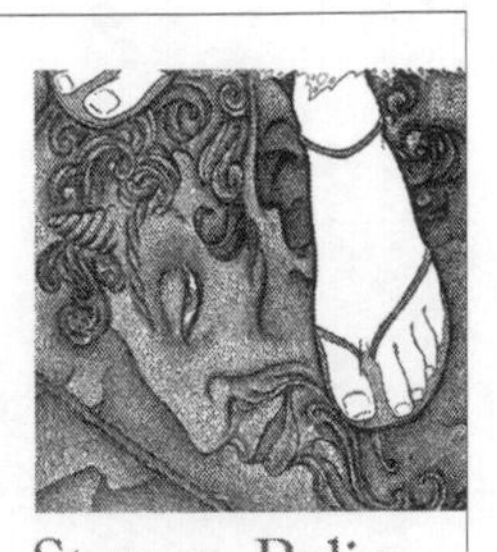

Strange Relics

Stories of Archaeology and the Supernatural, 1895–1954

Edited by Amara Thornton and Katy Soar

A new anthology of twelve classic short stories combining the supernatural and archaeology. Never before have so many relics from the past caused such delicious and intriguing shivers down the spine. From a Neolithic rite to Egyptian religion to Roman remains to medieval masonry to some uncanny ceramic tiles in a perfectly ordinary American sun lounge, the relics in these stories are, frankly, horrible.

Stories include:

- 'The Ape', by E F Benson
- 'Roman Remains', by Algernon Blackwood
- 'Ho! The Merry Masons', by John Buchan
- 'Through the Veil', by Arthur Conan Doyle
- 'View From A Hill', M R James
- 'Curse of the Stillborn', by Margery Lawrence
- 'Whitewash', by Rose Macaulay,
- 'The Shining Pyramid', by Arthur Machen
- 'Cracks of Time', by Dorothy Quick
- 'The Cure', by Eleanor Scott

The Outcast and The Rite

Stories of Landscape and Fear, 1925–38

by Helen de Guerry Simpson

The long forgotten Australian author Helen de Guerry Simpson (1897–1940) was a prize-winning historical novelist, and wrote uncanny terror like a scalpel applied lightly to the nerves. She published many supernatural short stories before her untimely death in 1940 in London. This new edition selects the best of her unsettling writing. Featured stories about historic structures with intentions of their own include:

- 'As Much More Land', in which an Oxford undergraduate challenges a haunted bedroom to scare him.
- 'Teigne', in which a house with a curse is stripped of all its fittings.
- 'Disturbing Experience of an Elderly Lady', in which a new-made widow buys the house she has always longed for.

The Introduction is by Melissa Edmundson, senior lecturer at Clemson University, South Carolina, a leading scholar of women's Weird fiction and supernatural writing from the early twentieth century.

British Weird

Selected Short Fiction, 1893–1937

edited by James Machin

'Classic stories, but also less familiar ones' – *Washington Post*

British Weird is a new anthology of classic Weird short fiction by British writers, first published between the 1890s and the 1930s. This collection – curated by James Machin, author of Palgrave Gothic's *Weird Fiction in Britain, 1880–1939* – assembles stories to thrill, entertain, and chill. Stories that embrace the malignant qualities of structures and artefacts:

- 'The Willows' by Algernon Blackwood, in which the river strands two canoeists in a night of alien terror.
- 'Man-Size in Marble' by Edith Nesbit (1893), in which statuary walks.
- 'Randalls Round' by Eleanor Scott (1927), in which a mound should not be disturbed.
- 'N' by Arthur Machen (1934), in which a particular window gives London an entirely a new aspect.
- 'Mappa Mundi' by Mary Butts (1937), in which the streets of Paris have an alternative existence.
- Includes 'Ghosties and Ghoulies', Mary Butts' ground-breaking essay from 1933 on the supernatural in modern fiction.

Machin's introduction describes the background for these excellent stories in the Weird tradition, and identifies their use of peculiarly British preoccupations in supernatural short fiction.